An Indian in Cowboy Country

An Asian Indian discovers his personal and professional potential in the heart of Texas.

An Indian in Cowboy Country is more than a fictional tale of an India-born engineer who overcomes cultural differences to succeed in America. It shares the challenges anyone might experience in life and in business and looks at important lessons learned along the way.

Satish Sharma, an engineering graduate from the prestigious Indian Institute of Technology, is an immigrant who comes to America seeking a better life.

From Bombay, India, where he was born and raised, to Houston, Texas, where he is called "an Indian in cowboy country," Sharma feels out of place. He faces personal, professional, and romantic challenges on both shores, but he eventually flourishes in the United States—the land of universal inclusion.

To Nicole Rajant

Best Wishes

Pradeep Jamal

117 B 63 '08

AN INDIAN IN COWBOY COUNTRY

———————— ❧ ————————

AN INDIAN IN COWBOY COUNTRY

Stories from an Immigrant's Life

Pradeep Anand

iUniverse, Inc.
New York Lincoln Shanghai

An Indian in Cowboy Country
Stories from an Immigrant's Life

iUniverse books may be ordered through booksellers or by contacting:

iUniverse
2021 Pine Lake Road, Suite 100
Lincoln, NE 68512
www.iuniverse.com
1-800-Authors (1-800-288-4677)

This is a work of fiction. All of the characters, names, incidents, organizations, and dialogue in this novel are either the products of the author's imagination or are used fictitiously.

ISBN-13: 978-0-595-40790-3 (pbk)
ISBN-13: 978-0-595-67834-1 (cloth)
ISBN-13: 978-0-595-85155-3 (ebk)
ISBN-10: 0-595-40790-0 (pbk)
ISBN-10: 0-595-67834-3 (cloth)
ISBN-10: 0-595-85155-X (ebk)

Printed in the United States of America

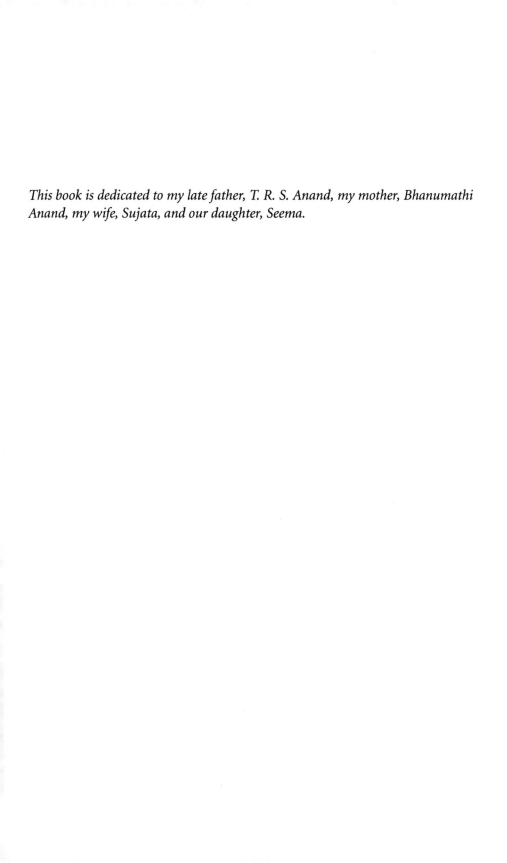

This book is dedicated to my late father, T. R. S. Anand, my mother, Bhanumathi Anand, my wife, Sujata, and our daughter, Seema.

Foreword

Every one of us believes that we have an experience to share, a unique story to tell. Not many of us, though, have Pradeep Anand's talent to do so. His protagonist, Satish Sharma, could be you or me, or anybody who has spent time in Mumbai or at an Indian Institute of Technology (IIT), or any professional who went to the United States with dreams of doing something different and making it big.

I spent a good part of my life in small towns in India, where Mumbai was the place you wanted to visit at least once in your life. When I was on the verge of leaving high school, going to IIT was the defining aspiration for the Indian middle class—it was the magic wand that opened doors to the world.

For all of us, acceptance to IIT exposed a panorama of experiences and emotions: a completely new education system, a big city, and a campus life with diverse cultures, and, most important, diversity of opinion. IIT was the place where we came of age, and learned street-smart ways to succeed. Despite rigorous academic demands, we were drawn to hostel and campus activities, our Mood Indigo cultural festival, potboiler movies and serious cinema, and endless debates and arguments over the meaning of life.

Just one generation ago, for many graduates, opportunities and life after IIT meant moving West, usually to the United States, to a new set of rules in life. To these adventurers, crossing the seven seas also meant an awkward balancing act between old and new worlds, a reality even today for any globally distributed workforce.

An Indian in Cowboy Country is a must read. Pradeep has done an amazing job, with great simplicity, in chronicling, through stories about Satish Sharma, an Asian Indian's journey in an alien society, simultaneously maintaining one's moorings and moral center.

To me, Pradeep Anand is a true renaissance man. At IIT Bombay, he was poet, author, editor, singer, leader, humanist, gracious host, and caring friend.

To this day, when I listen to Neil Young's album *Harvest* on my iPod, I recall Pradeep singing "Old Man," but with it come memories of his many facets, especially his stories and writings that never failed to entertain me. I am glad to see that after decades of silence, he has rediscovered his muse, to move and entertain his readers again in his own unique, gentle way.

Way to go, PA!

Nandan Nilekani
CEO, Infosys Technologies Limited

Acknowledgments

There are no words in the human language that can express the depth of my gratitude for my parents. Besides being the best mother and father any child can have, they were also my first English teachers.

My mother taught me to appreciate the beauty of the language, and my introverted father, an avid reader, stocked our home with Indian, European, and American books and magazines that I read with my sisters and brother.

My storytelling is greatly influenced by my maternal grandfather, P. Sundaresan Iyer, and maternal grandmother, S. Kokila Iyer, who spent much of their golden years showering us with love and affection and telling us stories from Indian mythology, Tamil folklore, and family history.

God bless all my teachers. I was always a distracted student who could daydream, in an instant. I thank my gurus for their patience and dedication, especially those at Don Bosco High School (Matunga, Bombay) and the Indian Institute of Technology (IIT), Bombay. I contributed immensely to their desire to retire early.

While my grandparents, parents, and teachers created the foundation, this book would not have been possible without the most enthusiastic support from my wife, Sujata, who was my first reader and fan. My daughter, Seema, constantly encouraged me through the publication process by promising to read the first published copy. My siblings Uma, Pushpa, and Ramesh, and their spouses Sankaran, Suryamurty, and Zarina, respectively, provided steady support.

My sincere gratitude goes to many friends around the world. Kirat Patel (India), Indu Eerikal (Singapore), and Ram Gopalan (USA), persistently urged me for decades to write my first book. Kasim Mookhtiar (India) invoked divine reasons to encourage me. He said, "You have a God-given talent to write. It's your responsibility to share it with the world." Ajit Paralkar (USA) nudged me along this journey with patient, insightful critique and guidance.

I am also grateful to my numerous friends for their support, especially those in the Greater Houston area (my *Phamily*) and those belonging to the global IIT alumni fraternity.

Finally, my heartfelt gratitude goes out to the people of Houston, Texas, and Bombay, India. I left the city of Mumbai when it was called Bombay and the older colonial name persists in my vocabulary, except when I speak Marathi. I love the city of my birth where I spent the first half of my life. I miss its intense people and distinctive vibrancy.

I also love my current home, the city of Houston, Texas, and its people, especially those in the oil & gas industry. They are the warmest and friendliest I have ever met. Their genuine acceptance of people from around the globe makes this city an excellent, ethnic crucible for experiencing and assimilating global cultures.

Pradeep Anand
June 2005

Rites of Passage

Sixteen-year-old Satish Sharma had had an idyllic childhood in Bombay in the optimistic, idealistic afterglow that followed India's independence from the British. Then his Eden attracted a snake.

Bombay was a bright, shining example of how the diversity of India, with its linguistic, religious, economic, and caste divisions, could be united into a cohesive country. It was the most American of Indian cities: free enterprise reigned, cinema thrived, and opportunities to better one's life flourished. Its busy harbor (India's largest), its hundreds of textile mills and ancillary industries, and its financial institutions provided employment to millions of people.

Its economic engine attracted many more from the rest of the mostly agrarian country, which seemed to be constantly plagued by the twin ravages of droughts and floods that sent never-ending impoverished hordes to the metropolis known as the "Gateway of India."

Almost everyone in Bombay was from elsewhere. Despite the diversity, this population was a cohesive one, bonded together by the city's unique amalgamated culture that sharply contrasted the rest of the country where a local culture, language, or religion loomed over and dominated its citizens.

Before World War I, Satish's grandfather, an educated immigrant with a high school certificate, moved to Bombay from Tamil Nadu, a southern Indian state. Over the tumultuous years that ended in India's freedom, he and his family lost most of their Tamil characteristics and merged into the mainstream local mores of the city.

For sixteen years, Satish lived peacefully with his parents, grandparents, and little sister among neighbors who shared common middle-class values in this densely populated, buoyant paradise, where life was safe, simple, and satisfying, as a childhood should be.

Then one day it changed.

It had taken Satish and his schoolmates from his all-boys Catholic school several weeks to convince their conservative parents that they were mature enough to see an A-rated movie that, legally, only those eighteen and older were permitted to see. After much cajoling and begging, they were permitted to see a Western movie, *The Last Train from Gun Hill*, starring Kirk Douglas and Anthony Quinn.

He had bargained hard with his parents. He offered a recently released James Bond movie as an alternative to the Western. His parents, seeing that he was committed to seeing his first adults-only movie with or without their permission, quickly consented to the lesser evil. His friends' parents, upon hearing that Satish's parents had capitulated, also fell in line.

Satish was a big fan of Westerns, and had seen every U-rated (for universal viewing) Western movie to hit Bombay since 1956. Like Willie Nelson, his heroes were always cowboys. For years, the neighborhood kids and he played games pretending to be cowboys, wearing their plastic monsoon hats with their edges smoothly curved up, like their Hollywood Western heroes.

Besides cowboy movies, he and his friends were also avid Western comic book readers, exchanging and sharing tattered, dog-eared books with each other. Their insatiable appetites were fed by neighborhood circulating libraries that provided monthly rental subscriptions to two comic books a day.

On a Thursday, a weekly school holiday, eleven gawky teenage boys embarked on an anxious afternoon adventure. Normally, they wore shorts and short-sleeved shirts, but for that special day, they elected to wear trousers long-sleeved shirts to conceal their hairless, virgin arms and legs.

All had traces of moustaches and most were about five feet nine inches tall. They were all unusually tall for their age, but there was still this uncertainty that at least one of them would be ejected from the theater for being underage.

Theater management sold tickets to anyone who came up to the ticket window, but if they were ejected for being underage, their tickets would be confiscated and they would lose the price of these nonrefundable tickets—a tiny fortune for each of them.

They received allowances for public transportation to school but they walked instead, and kept the change to fund this monthly sojourn to a South Bombay movie theater. The specter of losing a month's worth of thrifty effort did not deter them from making an "all for one and one for all" pact—if one of them was ejected, they would all troop out of the theater.

The youthful congregation, in uncomfortable clothes for the humid weather, convened at Dadar (Central Railway) station and dug deep into their pockets. They pulled out their savings and counted to see if they had enough to afford both railway and movie tickets.

They discovered that if they bought railway tickets, they would have to buy the cheapest movie tickets. This meant sitting in the first row, watching giant, elongated, disproportionate images on the screen.

Since it was their first A-rated movie, they decided to travel ticketless. The risk of being caught by a railway ticket checker (TC), paying a fine, and returning home was worth the reward of being able to see their first adults-only movie comfortably.

They broke up into smaller groups of twos and threes so they could sneak into the station without being noticed by the uniformed TC at the station's entrance. They regrouped on the platform and apprehensively waited for a fast train. It made only one stop between Dadar and Victoria Terminus, their destination, which significantly reduced the probability of a TC boarding their compartment.

In sixteen short years, they had mastered the art of boarding and dismounting from a Bombay commuter train. The instant a local train stopped at a station, a mass of people were turbulently ejected from a compartment, like water gushing from a hosepipe. Another mass boarded the train within the twenty seconds or so that a train stopped at a station.

At major stations such as Dadar, where the volumes were larger, the wait times were a bit longer, but barely adequate to execute the exchange of embarking and disembarking passengers.

The secret to entering a compartment was to position oneself strategically at the corner of a door, squeezing in through the edges while the disembarking passengers rushed out through the door's central area. There was some jostling, even manhandling, of novices who tried to enter the train head-on, in direct opposition to the exiting mass.

Similarly, when disembarking, they positioned themselves in the center of the exit and jumped out of a slowing train. The trick was to jump in a parallel direction to the motion rather than perpendicular to it or against it, a lesson they all learned in hard, bruising ways.

As a southbound fast train entered Dadar station, they split into four groups and positioned themselves at the edges of two open doors of the same compartment. With practiced finesse, they boarded the train, and scrutinized their surroundings for a uniformed TC. Luckily, there was none.

Twenty minutes later, they jumped off the train onto a platform at Victoria Terminus station that was packed with evening rush-hour commuters. Again the group splintered and individually slinked past a distracted TC, who was busy giving directions to someone in this most crowded railway station in India.

New Empire Theater was a five-minute walk away. As they came closer to it, they could feel and smell wafts of cool air-conditioning, a rarity in their lives in this warm, humid city.

The designated "oldest-looking"—that is, the one with the thickest moustache—went to the ticket window, and in his deepest voice asked for and bought eleven tickets. The boys did not gape at the movie photographs that were on display in the foyer; instead, they chose to get past their last barrier, the usher, who did not give them a second look as they breezed through.

They rushed into the theater hall, excited that they were now going to experience a teenager's rite of passage and see an A-rated movie. They wasted no time to get to their seats, only to watch a series of tiresome advertisement slides, stale short films, and a tediously long Indian News Review that captured the highlights of the past week in black and white. Then there was an unnecessary intermission.

They shared a bag of spicy popcorn, adapted for the Indian palate, and came back to their seats hurriedly, even before the lights began to dim. A few minutes later, an ornate red curtain rose leisurely, and the Indian censor board's familiar, indecipherable certificate, typed on a manual typewriter with missing letters, began flickering. Their eyes were focused on the large, emblazoned letter A.

Some of them noticed that the certificate also had a triangle on it. This indicated that the censors had sliced and cut out objectionable portions of the film that could upset the delicate moral balance of the adults of India. The triangle did not bother them, and they settled in their cushioned seats to watch the mighty battle between two best friends, Kirk Douglas and Anthony Quinn, set in a small town called Gun Hill. Not an eye blinked as the censor's certificate departed noisily, giving way to the Paramount Films logo.

The censor's amateurish film snipping was evident immediately. Loud and abrupt discontinuities in the soundtrack and action marked the beginning of the film. The initial tragedy of the movie, where Kirk Douglas's Native American Indian spouse is molested and killed, was crudely spliced. They asked each other in whispers, "What happened?" As the plot unfolded, they realized that

Marshall Morgan's wife had been murdered, and that one of the killers was the son of the man who had once saved his life.

The movie had its moments, but none as poignant as the final showdown when a friend was killed. A saddened Marshall Morgan, an emissary of blind justice, left Gun Hill alone on that last train.

Moments later, they stood at attention as the Indian national anthem began to play. Then eleven hungry teenagers were out on the warm and muggy street, talking to each other about the dramatic conclusion of their first adults-only movie, disappointed that there was nothing to it. They wondered aloud why the movie had received an A certificate. It was not particularly violent; even the final shootout was lacking in blood and gore.

Soon, the teenagers' focus shifted to satisfying their hunger pangs. The spare change they had between them was not adequate to feed them all, even at the cheapest Irani restaurant in this upscale neighborhood. They then noticed that at a restaurant next door to the movie theater they could help themselves to a large bowlful of dry *bhel* (spicy, puffed rice) and take as much as they could carry, compliments of the house.

All eleven of them split up with practiced ease and went into the restaurant. They wandered around for some time, pretending to look for their seated friends. Then, on their way out, pretending to be paying patrons, they scooped up puffed rice and stuffed some in their trouser pockets. They left the restaurant, and reconvened a few hundred yards away.

As they were eating this light snack and gloating over their plunder, five of the eleven compatriots announced, almost in unison, that they had been told to come home right after the movie.

The remaining six—Jimmy (Jamshed), Zia (Ziauddin), Cedric, Sandesh, Vijay, and Satish—understood their friends' need to comply with parental dictates. But since they did not have similar constraints, they decided to go to Sandesh's home to listen to a recent Beatles album on his imported Grundig stereo console.

Sandesh's older sister had sworn to kill him if he touched this album, but that did not deter them from their mission to listen to the Fab Four on a state-of-the-art stereophonic system. Moreover, his mother always had plenty of food to spare.

The five curfew-bound friends decided to go home by the lax Central Railway line. They emptied their pockets and gave their change to the six who had to travel by the stricter Western Railway system to the western half of Dadar. Personal experience had taught them that the odds of being caught for ticketless travel were substantially high on that line. Western Railway TCs seemed to be more vigilant and could somehow detect ticketless passengers with ease.

The six walked past the colonial Bombay Gymkhana, cutting across Cross Maidan. Maneuvering between cricket and soccer games, they reached Churchgate station, where they bought tickets and collectively boarded a fast train.

Sandesh's home was in the center of Dadar BB, the common name for this western half of Dadar. Jimmy and Satish lived on the eastern side of Tilak Bridge, in Dadar TT, which had two large neighborhoods: Parsi Colony and Hindu Colony. Gujarati-speaking Zoroastrians like Jimmy, who were originally from Persia and had come to India to escape religious persecution, dominated Parsi Colony. Hindu Colony's residents were mostly Marathi-speaking Hindus, with a smattering of people like Satish who spoke better Marathi, the local language, than their mother tongue.

Cedric was a Roman Catholic and lived in the Portuguese Church area, a Christian neighborhood a few minutes away from Sandesh's home. Zia's home was just north of Dadar BB, in Mahim, which had a large concentration of Muslims and Catholics. Vijay lived in Matunga, north of Dadar TT, an enclave where a majority of South Indian immigrants to the city lived; most spoke very little Marathi.

As their train approached Dadar BB station, they sensed that something was wrong. The platform was unusually crowded and, when they tried to disembark from the train, the incoming throng was uncommonly forceful and rough in its entry.

The vigor of the crowd pushed Zia, the skinniest among them, back into the compartment, while the rest pushed through and got off the train, shaken and disheveled.

Their shirts were out of their pants, their creased trousers ruffled, and their hair tousled and windswept. They did little to groom themselves. Their attention was drawn to the smoke and soot that filled the air. Jimmy dismissed these at first, attributing them to a steam engine that may have passed by, but Sandesh cautioned them—the smoke smelled of burned rubber.

Guardedly but briskly they left the station, noticing that there were no TCs around. Jimmy nervously joked that they had wasted their scarce money on train tickets.

Usually, the side street outside the station was a bustling market with loud hawkers and peddlers selling a variety of wares: clothes, handkerchiefs, slippers, sandals, flowers, vegetables, spices, country medicines, and fast food. These hawkers yelled to attract the attention of disembarking passengers. Street vendors occupied not only the spacious sidewalks but also parts of the road; there was little room for cars to pass without honking.

As they stepped out of the railway station, they did not hear the familiar, deafening cacophony. They heard nothing. There was neither a hawker nor a car in sight. The streets were empty. But in the distance, a mass of panic-stricken people was rushing toward the station and them.

They avoided the clamoring crowd by sticking to the edges of the street. When the crowd had passed them by, they began to walk vigorously in the direction of Sandesh's home, unconsciously breaking into a run, brushing past oncoming stragglers.

Sandesh's home was just five hundred yards away. Fifty yards from the station, they would make a left turn and run about three hundred yards on the adjoining street. Then they would turn right and rush another hundred and fifty yards to reach the safety of his home.

As they dashed through and made the first turn, they saw a mob at the other end of the street, throwing stones and flaming bundles of cloth at stores. Between the mob and them, three cars were burning. In the distance, a familiar red double-decker BEST bus stood naked, charred to its metallic frame.

They realized that they were cut off from Sandesh's home, and there were no other safe havens around them. They had no choice except to go back to the station and take the first train out of Dadar.

Just as they reached the station, hordes poured out of it and started running helter-skelter. A train had pulled in with a burning compartment, and all train services had been terminated. Railway police had taken over and were indiscriminately beating people and forcing them out of the station. Satish and his friends were trapped; they had missed the last train out of Dadar.

Just then, Cedric recalled that a family friend owned a car repair shop nearby. They could seek refuge there. There were no dissenters or second-guessers among them. Instantly, they ran breathlessly to the garage that stood at the dead end of a small lane.

They stopped at the tall iron gate, gazing up at the tiny spears and barbed wire that stood guard at the top. Undeterred, Cedric climbed up the gate. With a few minor bruises, he reached its crest. As soon as his head breached the crown of the gate, they could hear people yelling from within the garage, asking him to go away.

Cedric reached into his shirt and showed them the large, silver crucifix he wore around his neck. He yelled in Konkani, his mother tongue, that he needed help. The gate opened quickly, and they were led onto this large property strewn with dilapidated and decrepit cars.

Oscar, the fifty-year-old owner of the place, recognized Cedric. He admonished him and his friends for being out on such a dangerous evening.

He told them that there had been a political rally at the nearby Shivaji Park. The crowd had been brought to a frenzy by hate speeches that labeled South Indians as the cause of unemployment among Maharashtrians, people native to Bombay. After the meeting ended, crowds went around looting and burning shops, especially the South Indian owned restaurants that dotted the city. They also beat up any recognizable South Indian along the way.

Oscar, upon learning that Vijay and Satish were southerners, quickly escorted them to a tin-roofed, single-story, ramshackle building at the remote end of his lot. It was Oscar's office, and in the light of the solitary low-wattage bulb that illuminated the room, they could see a few filing cabinets and a desk with a manual typewriter. The stench of stale motor oil and gasoline was intense.

Oscar found two small stools for them to sit on, and, taking them behind the cabinets, asked the boys to sit still and be silent. As he left the building, he reached for a nearby lug wrench and smashed the lone bulb, instantly plunging the office into darkness. As their eyes adjusted to the night, they could see some light pouring in from the windows and around the edges of the shut door.

They sat for hours in the shadows, quietly listening. They heard waves of mobs passing through the area, some hurling stones at the solid steel gate and into the compound, hitting the cars. But nobody at Oscar's garage made a sound.

There was a deathly stillness between instances of mob fury, and they could hear sounds of gunfire, rare in the Bombay air. They sounded different from the gunshots in the movie they had just seen.

Vijay began to tremble with fear. Satish calmed him down, whispering to him that the crowds would be gone in a few hours. Vijay argued in low whispers that the worst was upon them. If a mob got to him, they would kill him because he was perceptibly a South Indian. He also spoke like one.

As time slipped by, the frequency of the mob waves diminished. Finally, around eleven o'clock, after about four hours of seclusion, normalcy seemed to have returned. Soon a few familiar sounds of the city began to fill the air; they could hear trains, trucks, and buses running in the distance.

Residents of the multistory buildings that overlooked the garage began switching on the lights in their homes. The dark office grew perceptibly brighter, but the two teenagers stayed put, waiting for Oscar. He came in a few minutes later and told then that they could go home.

Sandesh, Cedric, Jimmy, Vijay, and Satish thanked him and stepped out of the steel-gated compound, only to realize that they were now in a dark, dead-end canyon with a steel gate at their backs and tall cliffs of multi-story buildings on both sides. This inconspicuous lane, with destroyed streetlights, was strewn with large stones and small rocks.

The five of them split into two groups. Traveling on opposite sidewalks, each group began walking cautiously to the well-lit intersection, about two hundred yards away. They were focused on their goal at the end of the street, but they also watched the buildings through the corners of their eyes.

As they approached the intersection, a mob appeared without warning, blocking their path to the safety of the main street. There were about thirty young men in the horde, some with field-hockey sticks.

The five friends could not turn and run back to Oscar's garage—it was too far away. If they decided to run for the gate, which was closed up tight anyway, the pack could have easily overtaken them and would have beaten them to a pulp.

It was a lesson they had learned on this city's streets: never run from a Bombay mob; the pack would assume that you were guilty, administer swift street justice, and beat you mercilessly before police could come to your rescue.

Sandesh and Cedric stepped forward cautiously to confront the group. They spoke in Marathi to the gang, told them who they were, and asked them politely to let them through. Satish also stepped forward and spoke in Marathi to these people, who had no resemblance to his cultured, well-educated, middle-class neighbors from Hindu Colony.

The leader of this rabble heard their Marathi and signaled to the crowd to break up and let them through. After a few anxious moments of being shoved around and jostled as they went through the mass, Sandesh, Cedric, and Satish were in the light of the main street when they realized that Jimmy and Vijay had not followed them out. They went back to fetch them.

Jimmy, the ever-polite mama's boy, had inadvertently said "thank you" in English as he went through the throng, and the leader yelled for him to stop.

Jimmy did, and told him that he was a Parsi and not a South Indian. He passed through, leaving Vijay in the midst of an antagonistic and violent crowd.

Someone asked him in Marathi, "What's your name?" and Vijay answered truthfully, in textbook Marathi, but with a distinct and easily identifiable southern accent.

Instantaneously, fists flew. He was pounded and pummeled. Even after he fell to the street, unconscious, this frenzied, possessed gang kicked him in his stomach, back, and head. His four friends watched helplessly as his dark, viscous blood oozed slowly onto the black pavement, looking unlike anything they had seen in the movies.

They barely heard the shrill police whistle in the distance, but the mob did. It dispersed quickly, leaving behind the hate-filled leader who, before running away from the scene, raised his leg high and, with a grunt, gave Vijay one final kick in his eye.

When the cops arrived, an inspector ordered a police truck to the scene, and all five of them were taken to a nearby hospital, where Vijay was admitted. Sandesh and Cedric decided to stay back with Vijay; Jimmy and Satish decided that they would go to Vijay's home and inform his parents.

Vijay's parents did not have a phone, and there was no public transportation on the streets that night. They ran from the hospital and across Tilak Bridge to their homes to inform their parents that they were safe. Jimmy's mother refused to let him back on the streets again, while Satish's parents reluctantly permitted him to step out again.

He ran that night like he never had before, down the well-lit main road to Matunga, to Vijay's home, and breathlessly gave the bad news to his parents.

While Vijay's parents and older brother readied themselves to go to the hospital, he found a stray, hesitant taxi driver who, upon hearing his story, agreed to the fare.

It was one o'clock in the morning when an exhausted Satish returned to the safety of his home.

The next morning when he read the newspaper, he realized that he had been in the middle of Bombay's first post-independence ethnic riot. The ferocious hostility was restricted to South Indians and their restaurants in Maharashtrian areas.

The paper skimmed over the brutality that he had witnessed. It didn't mention the gunshots he had distinctly heard or the burned bus and cars he had seen. The violence was attributed to a small number of "bad elements and miscreants who had taken advantage of the situation."

When he stepped out of his home to go to school, he saw that, overnight, the city had returned to normal.

At school, the ten remnants of the previous day's movie team gathered under the shade of a giant Banyan tree across from the concrete basketball court to chat, like every normal school day. Soon the school was abuzz with their adventures of the previous night, and all day they were heroes for having survived a riot.

After school, Cedric, Jimmy, and Satish went to Vijay's home to inquire about his health. His parents were at the hospital, and his older brother informed them that Vijay was fine, but he had lost an eye. That last kick had damaged his eye beyond repair, but he would not lose the eyeball. They intended to keep it in case future medical breakthroughs could restore his eyesight.

Vijay recovered over the next few weeks and was soon back in class with a patch over his bandaged right eye. A month later, he was back to his spirited self, making faces and joking about his gray, disfigured, blind eye. He had only one complaint: his depth perception was not the same.

Later that year, Satish and his friends graduated from school and went their different ways.

Twenty years later, when Satish was in the lobby of a plush hotel in Bombay, Vijay came up to him, abruptly took off his sunglasses, and stared at him with that unmistakable gray glob of a blind eye. Vijay asked him if he recognized him. Of course, Satish did.

They went to a nearby coffee shop, joking if they had enough spare change between them for a cup of cappuccino. They talked how their lives had progressed after their graduation, their careers, and their new homes away from Bombay. Inevitably, the conversation came to their schooldays.

They reminisced about their twelve years as classmates, such as the time their class won the intramural cricket championship, Pope Paul VI's visit to their school, and many others. They talked for hours, reveling in their happy school years. Satish dove deep into his memory banks and recalled the most obscure events, but deliberately avoided that violent night. Sensing his discomfort, Vijay nudged him and asked lightheartedly, "Hey, remember the day we saw our first adults-only movie?"

The Final Exam

Ferocious and furious screaming was a common release of pre-exam tension at Satish's engineering school campus. The serene surroundings of the Indian Institute of Technology, Bombay, nestled in the hilly area between Powai and Vihar lakes, belied the cumulative stress that the students carried around on their slouched shoulders in their effort to fulfill Indian society's expectations of being the smartest engineering students in the country.

He and his mostly male fellow campus inmates (as they called themselves) led tortured lives, attempting to meet higher and higher academic standards thrust on them by exemplary fellow students and professors. When the pressure to perform reached a crescendo, especially late at night before an exam, an inmate went to his hostel (dormitory) window or balcony or to the terrace and let out a loud, painful scream into the night.

That anguished scream reverberated and resonated through the wings of the hostel, drawing sympathy from similarly stressed-out students, who in their turn screamed. Within minutes, a wave of agonized howls and yells, interspersed with the choicest multilingual cusswords, moved along from hostel wing to hostel wing, then from hostel to hostel, till every soul, flustered with his pursuit of high-quality engineering studies, had vented his frustration to the gentle but unmoved environs. Then silence and serenity descended on this campus of six hundred and sixty acres.

It was three AM on a hot April night. Satish sat at his desk, studying for his last exam on this campus. Clad in unbuttoned shorts and a T-shirt, he read his marked up textbook and his almost illegible notes, both illuminated by a limited cone of light emanating from the dim bulb of his table lamp. He had switched off the light bulb that dangled on a wire from the ceiling, but still the luminance in his room attracted mosquitoes and other insects from the campus' pastoral surroundings.

He had a table fan set at its highest speed and pointed at his bare legs to further ward off errant mosquitoes. Yet, involuntarily, he slapped various spots on his thighs and calves, hoping to dispatch an astonished vermin to its maker.

He was intensely focused on the complexities of electrolytic production of copper powder when the next wave of screams went through his hostel and his concentration snapped. He slammed his books shut, put his feet into his well-worn rubber flip flops, stood up, and buttoned his shorts. He grabbed an empty, cleaned-out glass ketchup bottle and stormed out of his room to get another refill of cold water from a water cooler in the hostel dining area.

He ran down two stories, three steps at a time, to the corridor. He walked past the dim fluorescent lights that had attracted a layer of assorted insects. He sniggered as he recalled a particular lamp's role in a Bollywood movie. Its hero, a student moonlighting as an electrical handyman, had pointed to a lamp and said that it was the culprit behind the power outage at the heroine's hostel. A loose connection was creating a surge, and the entire hostel had to be rewired.

The movie had been a big box office hit, but for Satish and his engineering mates, the "tube light" was the symbol of people's naiveté and gullibility in dealing with electrical products and services. Every time they passed the tube light, they repeated the dialogue from the movie in Hindi and chortled and guffawed, but tonight he could only break into a slight, sardonic smile as he went past it to the mess hall.

He acknowledged the sleepy uniformed security guard who sat on a steel chair at the entrance of the dining hall, and walked past him to the water cooler. As a faint dribble of slightly cold water slowly filled the bottle, he wondered how he was going to cover and cram so much material within the next five hours before the exam.

He was very sleepy and exhausted, and he wondered if he had enough energy to not only pull an all-nighter, but also be able to write an exhaustive three-hour exam early in the day. He decided that he would study for another hour, get about three hours of sleep, and write his exam after a refreshing shower and a full breakfast in the morning.

He had a swig of refrigerated water, splashed some on his face and his weary eyes, refilled the bottle to the brim, and rushed out with renewed determination. He noticed that the guard had fallen asleep, joined in this endeavor by two sleeping pariah dogs that subsisted on crumbs from the hostel cafeteria. Their emaciated bodies were testaments to the quality of the food at his hostel.

For the next hour, he studied his notes, hallucinating that he was assimilating at an astounding rate. At about four AM, on schedule, he shut his books, switched off the table lamp, and set his mechanical alarm clock for seven AM. He hoisted his table fan onto his chair and set it to oscillate from his head to his toe.

He got into bed. As he turned and curled up, he involuntarily listened to the usual sounds of a late April night: a steady drone of crickets and grasshoppers and a lone dog, perhaps a wolf, howling in the distance. At four AM, the campus was in a deep sleep. Just as he was about to sink into oblivion he heard an unusual sound, a muted scream that came from the terrace above his room.

Satish awoke with a start, listened carefully, and realized that it was the sound of someone crying ferociously and uncontrollably, but attempting to quiet himself. He jumped out of bed, instinctively slipped his feet into his flip flops, and ran to the bathroom, which had a dangerous metal ladder to the terrace—one slip and he would plummet down three floors to an unforgiving concrete base. Brushing aside his usual sense of caution, he heaved himself to the ladder and climbed up to the terrace.

As his eyes emerged over the terrace's edge, he saw someone sitting on the floor, crouched in a fetal position. His head was buried in his lap, and he was sobbing vigorously.

Despite his best effort to approach the crouching figure stealthily, his footsteps made crunching sounds as his feet crushed the gravel that covered the tarred surface of the terrace. The crouching figure turned to the approaching silhouette and yelled, "Who is it?" He sprang up, rushed to the edge, and stood there, as if poised to jump off.

"Stop. It's me, Satish," he replied urgently, his voice sufficiently loud to reach the intended recipient but not loud enough to wake students sleeping a few feet below them. The figure turned away from the low ledge, came to the middle of the terrace, and sat down. Satish rushed up and saw a familiar form, dully illuminated by a nearby streetlight.

"Kutty? What are you doing here? What happened?" he asked. Kutty lived four rooms away from his; they were buddies.

Kutty put his face into his crossed arms and began to bawl unashamedly. Satish sat down next to his friend, put a consoling arm on his shoulder, and asked him in a soothing voice, "What's wrong?"

Kutty's feeble voice came from within the uncontrollable sobs. "I am going to fail my final exam."

Kutty's formal name was Thomas Koshy. An only child, he was raised according to the Syrian Orthodox Christian faith in a small seaside town in

Kerala. His father, a tailor by profession, had died two months earlier. Kutty had been inconsolable since his death, and had to be regularly monitored by his friends, including Satish.

"I am going to fail tomorrow's exam," Kutty said as he reached out to his friend's outstretched hand to raise himself. "I was thinking about throwing myself off the terrace when you came."

Satish's six-foot athletic frame easily pulled up Kutty's diminutive, light body, and, when he heard of Kutty's intentions, his large hands gripped his friend's tightly. Appealing to Kutty's common sense, he asked, "That would have been stupid, wouldn't it? Who would have taken care of your mother after you were gone?"

In different circumstances, Kutty was the quintessential rational debater. Satish's assertive, rhetorical questions sparked his tendency to respond and deliberate. Kutty talked about how suicide was not quite a "stupid choice," quoting Nietzsche and Sartre, as he was kept away from the edge of the terrace, led to the ladder and carefully down to the bathroom and safer grounds.

As the two of them walked to the dining room for some cold water, Kutty continued his monologue about how nihilism and existentialism had the right answers to life's questions. He ranted, "Engineering studies were the most constricting education that could ever be imposed on us at this creative stage of our lives, when our minds needed to be expanded and exposed by the greatest thoughts in humankind."

When Satish saw the sleeping security guard, he shook him awake and told him to fetch Johnny, a mess servant, adding in Marathi, "Tell Johnny that I asked him to come to the mess hall quickly. Tell him it is urgent." The dazed guard ran into the interior of the hostel while the two of them made a beeline to the water cooler.

Both splashed some cold water on their faces. They walked to the mess tables and sat on the worn, right-angled metal chairs.

Satish sat across from Kutty, whose face, with its luminous white teeth, began to brighten as he continued to expostulate about what was wrong with the education system in India, particularly at IIT. He ranted about how the IIT system had a top-class student selection process and a terrific curriculum, but his teachers had been misguided dictators who rewarded students for regurgitating what was taught and said in class but crucified original thought.

Satish disagreed about the quality of professors, but rather than debating, he listened intently. When Kutty's intensity began to wane, he egged and prodded him on with a question rather than a contradiction, which would have veered the monologue to a dialogue. He wanted to get Kutty's mind away from his recent thought of hurling himself off the terrace. He also wanted Kutty to keep talking until Johnny, the senior "mess servant" (cafeteria waiter) and a Keralite like Kutty, could make a quick cup of tea to refresh them.

IITians, especially Kutty, were prone to talk endlessly as long as they could sip at a continuous supply of *chai* (Indian tea with milk).

He continued about how his life had been wasted because of "my stupid scholarship." After graduation he intended to go back to Mavelikara, "go back to my roots, wear a comfortable *lungi* (traditional garment worn around the waist) and a *kurta* (loose shirt), and contemplate on my navel."

Just as Satish sensed the confident, verging on arrogant, Kutty emerging, Johnny came to the table and asked if all was well. Before he could reply, Kutty grinned broadly and apologetically and told him in Malayalam, "Johnny, we just wanted some of your best, fresh morning tea. We have to stay awake till our exams are over."

A puzzled Johnny, barely awake, rubbed his eyes and looked at Satish, who said, "I am sorry to wake you up, Johnny, but we need a whole jug of tea, urgently." When Kutty excused himself, and went to the nearby restroom, Satish hurriedly went to Johnny in the kitchen, swore him to secrecy, and told him that Kutty was about to kill himself. He asked Johnny to keep the tea flowing and to interrupt them occasionally to make sure that all was well.

Johnny first brought out two cups and a jug of tea and served them. As they sipped their fresh tea, Johnny returned to the kitchen and came back with two plates of freshly made scrambled eggs, generous with tomatoes and onions, accompanied by hot, crisp, unburned toast—not the limp, soggy toast that was served during regular breakfast hours.

Johnny then went back to the kitchen and brought back two tall glasses of milk, saying, "You need milk for strength during your last exam." With that, he went to a remote end of the large hall and sat down, watching over the soon-to-be-graduates as they gorged down their last decent breakfast on this campus.

When they had finished eating, Johnny quickly cleared the table, hoping that the early birds, who were beginning to file into the mess hall, did not expect to be served breakfast, too. They would have to wait for regular breakfast hours. Satish realized Johnny's predicament, and suggested to his friend that they take a walk around the campus one last time. Kutty agreed.

A hidden cuckoo loudly proclaimed that morning had broken. The air was sultry and still. Silently the two friends stepped out of the hostel. They pushed the latched but unlocked, front gate open and walked up the eucalyptus-lined road to the campus' main building.

They passed the Gymkhana with its adjoining track, soccer, and hockey fields, and volleyball and basketball courts—venues of intense inter-hostel and inter-IIT rivalries. They recalled how Kutty, in his passionate desire to upset a close rival during a crucial tennis match, had mooned him, with stunning results. As they regaled in their sports exploits, the two proceeded uphill and stopped. The road was blocked by a small herd of cattle.

"Ah! The original residents of our campus," Kutty said. "I am going to miss them, especially accidentally stepping into their bullshit!"

"These are wild cows," Kutty continued. "They were here before the campus was built. Remember the time we tried to get rid of them, calling them a danger to students?"

Kutty recalled the time when they had received a call from the estate office saying that the local municipal corporation was going to help catch the campus cows, and transport and release them more than fifty miles away. The office needed student volunteers, over a weekend, to help round up the cows. They were among the dozen volunteers who participated in the cattle roundup.

It was the hardest and the most dangerous work they had done in their lives. Assisting the experienced municipal cow catchers, avoiding swatting tails and sharp horn tips, they prodded, pushed, and cajoled about thirty calves and cows first, and then some very uncooperative bulls, up metal inclines and into trucks. After ten exhausting hours of being cowboys, the worn-out students grew very emotional as they waved good-bye to the captive cows.

After the bovine witnesses to their cumulative lives on the campus had been banished for several days, the Indian cowboys could not erase the mournful moos and sad eyes from their memories. One late Sunday morning, they awoke to an excited shout, "The cows are back! The cows are back!" It had taken the herd and its homing instincts two weeks to find its way back home.

That early morning Satish and Kutty were unafraid, as they approached the squatted herd and patted some cows affectionately and reverentially. The cows, in response, mooed to them softly.

Kutty said, "They are saying goodbye," as he picked up his pace to catch Satish, who was already heading for the convocation hall.

Satish asked Kutty to sit on a raised concrete culvert near the "convo." He then sat next to him and asked, "Tell me, were you really going to throw yourself off the building?"

"I was thinking about it," Kutty replied. "But I don't have the guts to end my life."

"You were bawling your head off, Kutty. You know you are a bloody manic-depressive, don't you? You need to see a doctor!" Satish said.

"Thank you, Dr. Satish, for that diagnosis. Next patient, please," intoned Kutty in mockery as he jumped off the culvert and began walking down the road.

Satish followed him and said, "Listen. From now on, you are on your own. You will not have us around to help you with your mood swings."

"I know and that's what worries me. Do you really think that I am nervous about the last exam? It's a piece of cake! I am really concerned about what happens after the exam.

"This place has been my home, my paradise for five years, and I am going to lose it tomorrow. You people have been my family, my brothers, my protectors, and we are going to be thrown out tomorrow. This is the end."

Satish calmed his anxious, dramatic friend and shared with him that he, too, was concerned about life after IIT. He was not certain if he would stay in India or go to America. His parents wanted him to go abroad, but his guide, Professor Arjun, was insisting that he should take a job in India.

The mercurial Kutty had not applied for any job, and had received no job offers. He could not afford the application fees to apply to American universities; hence, he was not going to America either.

"What are you going to do after tomorrow?" asked a concerned Satish.

"Nothing."

"Nothing?"

"Not really nothing. I have a few ideas that I have been thinking about for all these years. I want to go home to Mavelikara, sit down, write a few papers, and submit them to a few journals."

"Technical papers?" asked an amused Satish. Kutty hated writing anything, especially technical papers.

"Yes, technical papers. I wanted to write so many but I did not have the time because of the stupid assignments, exams, and tests. Now that I am free from this place, I will sit on a beach, sip coconut water, scratch my belly, listen to the waves, and write."

"And who is going to support you while you write?"

"I have many rich uncles. All I have to do is convince one to support me and tell him that I will dedicate my papers to him. Maybe one of them has a large ego and a larger wallet, and will give me some money for my *bidis*, paper, pens, food, *lungi*, and *kurta* while I live in my mother's home. It's going to be simple living, high thinking for one year. Get all this rubbish out of my head and start a new life, both physically and mentally, and then go forth and conquer the world."

"I need a break, Satish," Kutty said, as if apologizing. "These five years were hard on me, and I am tired. Not one thing went my way except my academics, and that was such a waste. I could have learned what they taught me here by reading textbooks in Mavelikara."

Kutty was the brightest person that Satish had met, even by IIT standards. His constant bitching about the low standards on the campus always irritated him, but he kept quiet.

They walked on to the secluded "Ladies' Hostel" where the campus's thirty-two women students stayed, isolated from the two thousand male students who dominated the place. Satish wondered if his silent friend was lapsing into a depression when he turned to him and said, "Hey! Wasn't Urmilla the prettiest one of all in the ladies' hostel?"

"They were all pretty in their own way," Satish replied.

"*Array Vaa!* What a diplomat!" Kutty said. "Sure, I liked all of them, but Urmilla was the best. I even wrote a song for her once."

"What? Really? How come you never shared it with us?"

"Because you idiots would make fun of it and ridicule me. Where is Urmilla and where am I? She is so tall and fair, and I am short and dark. We are like Mutt and Jeff!"

Satish said, "Hey, I have an idea. Why don't you sing your song to her now?"

"What? Now? It's six in the morning!"

"What's more romantic than being woken up by a song? Go ahead. Serenade her. I know where she stays. I'll take you to her window."

"How do you know that?" Kutty asked suspiciously.

"Because I have been inside the ladies' hostel, on their hostel day. I was a special guest!"

"What? How come you never told us?"

"Because," Satish said, mimicking Kutty's Malayali accent and intonation, "You idiots would make fun of me and ridicule me. But that's not the point. Do you want to leave IIT without ever having poured your heart out to Urmilla? Sing your song!" Satish commanded.

And there, in the quiet of an early April morning, on the final day of the final exams of their final year, a beautiful alto voice arose and sang, "Ooormeeelaa, you are breaking my heart, you're shaking my confidence daily!" It was Kutty's version of Simon and Garfunkel's "Cecilia."

As he continued his soulful rendition, lights came on in the rooms of the ladies' hostel and curtains were drawn, every woman seeking the source of this soulful melody.

Satish, a familiar face on this campus, stood in the background near a tree, miming and signaling, "No, it's not me singing." He pointed at the Malayali who had lost his accent and sounded like a Jewish kid from New York City.

Finally, when Urmilla came to her window and parted her curtains, Kutty got down on his knees—it made him look shorter, but he did not care—and sang the song all over again. When he finished, he stood up and took a gracious bow. All the women in the window applauded loudly, and some yelled, "More! More!"

Kutty's eyes were only on Urmilla. He could see that she was pleased with his song. The flying kiss that she playfully threw in his direction brought a huge, radiant smile to his face. His glee was obvious to all. When he heard the encore requests, he reverted to his Malayali accent and said, "I know only one song. That's all!"

Just then, a hostel security guard, roused from his sleep by the commotion, spied the two men and ran toward them, brandishing a long stick. He was ready to inflict harm on these miscreants, who seemed to have invaded the privacy or the modesty of the women he was sworn to protect.

Upon seeing the aggressive posture of the security guard, the two friends instinctively ran away down the road to the main gate of the campus. They rushed through some overgrown oleander bushes and stopped only after they had reached the edge of Powai Lake, out of sight of the ladies' hostel and the excited guard. Both doubled over, panting for breath.

"Ow!" Kutty exclaimed. "The safety pin in my sandals broke and cut my skin!" Safety pins had fastened broken straps on his flip flops, and the flight had pushed the limits of one, exposing a sharp tip that tore into his flesh.

"Here, let me fix it," Satish said, taking the broken footwear.

As Kutty examined his bleeding foot, his friend retrieved the twisted safety pin and attempted to straighten it.

"This hurts, man," he said with a grimace.

"Do you want to go to the hospital?" Satish asked, though he knew what the response would be.

"You crazy? This is only a scratch—nothing that some turmeric powder won't fix. I'm okay. I can walk barefoot." He followed Satish with one good sandal in his hand.

As Kutty limped along and focused on the damage to his bloody foot, Satish gazed at the lake, which had receded to almost half its size in the summer heat. Powai Lake was still, blue, and beautiful that morning.

Satish was contemplative while his friend talked about Kerala, his home state, and its unappreciated natural splendor, ayurvedic clinics, and holy places.

"Any time you want to see beauty, come and stay with me at Mavelikara. You have not seen the best beauty in nature until you've seen Kerala. Its beauty will cleanse your mind. Then you get a good massage at an ayurvedic clinic that will cleanse your body. Later, you can go to Sabarimalai and cleanse your soul."

"Did you ever go to the Padmavati temple here on campus, Kutty?" Satish asked the Syrian Christian.

"Sure. I have been there. I've prayed to every god to get me out of this god-forsaken place," he laughed. "I promised to get every coconut in Kerala and break them at the temple if Padmavati would set me free from the clutches of this campus."

"In another five hours we will be free, Kutty," he assured him.

The diminutive Keralite remained silent and pensive for a few moments and then asked, "Free from what, Satish? I know the shackles that chained me and frustrated me here. What are your shackles? What are you free from?"

Satish did not reply. He had no answers to these questions.

Kutty continued, "Your life has been relatively simple. You follow the medi-ocre, middle-of-the-road, risk-free *Tam Bram* (Tamil Brahmin) formula of academic excellence, avoiding controversy. I can predict your life from now on. After IIT you will go abroad, get your master's, find a job, get your green card, come home, have an arranged marriage to some Tam Bram IAS officer's or corporate executive's daughter, and pine for her till she gets her green card and comes over.

"Then you will have two kids, a boy and girl, who will follow in your foot-steps of academic excellence while you become like your father or your father-in-law, working your butt off at some engineering company. In your spare time, you will attend Carnatic music concerts for cultural release, and go to the temple wearing *vibhuti* (sacred ash) on auspicious days for a spiritual connec-tion to God, as if he is only in temples.

"You think that there are no demons or devils in your life, Satish. That's because you have not looked for them and confronted them. I have, and that's the reason why I am so screwed up."

Satish wanted to react and respond, argue that Kutty was mistaken, but somewhere in his stinging invective was a kernel of truth. In fact, it was close to the whole truth.

"Go on, Kutty. I am listening," he said.

"Satish, I know what physical poverty is. I have lived it all my life, going around with a begging bowl to survive. But a different kind of poverty has wrapped its arms around you, my friend. It is the poverty of ignorance. And you are not alone in it.

"More than three hundred of us will graduate tomorrow, and we will all be acclaimed for our academic excellence. But look around at all of us—we have all been on this merry-go-round. Time after time, year after year, generation after generation, we return to the same spot. And we are all so ignorant and full of ourselves that we don't even recognize the place we've been before. The ride has so intoxicated us that our intellects are dulled. We rely on our instincts and we stay on to ride the same old merry circle. For all our academic brilliance, we are all pretty stupid."

Kutty looked around at the unspoiled woods they were walking through and noticed that his friend was pensive, his head bent over, looking at the ground as he took small, measured steps. Kutty was right. He was a conformist. If indeed he was on a merry-go-round, this was the time to pause and ponder.

"So, what should I do?" Satish asked.

"Ask yourself that question. Our graduation is the end of another revolution, another cycle. Do you want to stay on or jump off? Just give it some thought. The answer will surprise you."

Despite urging Satish to think for himself, Kutty went on to talk about having a clean slate and a blank sheet of paper, animatedly drawing flow charts and decision trees in the air, helping his friend consider various options and alternatives to leading the dream Tam Bram life.

"Be different, Satish. You'll never be sorry," Kutty said. He quickly added with a bright smile, "Let me put it another way: You are different; stay that way!"

Satish patted his little friend on his back and said, "Thanks. I'll think about it."

Barely avoiding keeling over from Satish's enthusiastic smack, a cocky Kutty retorted, "Don't thank me. You can thank your stars that that you had the good sense to pick me as a friend."

"I thought it was the other way around!" responded Satish, and until they reached the rear entrance of their hostel, the two friends verbally sparred.

Tired but not exhausted, they trudged up to their rooms, showered, and dressed in blue jeans and T-shirts. They picked up a few ballpoint pens, slipped into their rubber sandals, and called out for their wing-mates. They had their last breakfast together and headed for the main building to write their final exams.

After his sabbatical, Kutty went to Stanford University for a doctoral degree in computer science. Later, he became a successful high-tech entrepreneur. He now lives in a palatial house in the hills overlooking San Jose, California, with his wife, Urmilla, and their delightful daughter, Cecilia.

The Pilgrimage

On an uncomfortably hot summer night at one AM, Satish was alone on an empty railway platform in Triveni, near Allahabad, waiting for a train to take him back to New Delhi. For over two weeks, he had been on the road, visiting customers in Uttar Pradesh, a northern Indian state. He was exhausted and wanted to go home.

Except the stationmaster, there was no one else at the station. Satish dropped his suitcase on the platform and sat on it, waiting for his train to pull in. He had an hour to kill, so he began a conversation with the stationmaster. Despite the late hour and the hot weather, the stationmaster was dressed in a navy blue jacket, a clean white shirt tucked into white pants, a loosely knotted tie, and a dark blue hat with brass letters. He assured him that he would not have a long wait—trains were running on time ever since a state of emergency had been declared by the Indian government.

Satish was a conscientious objector to the emergency, which had suspended all individual rights in this democratic country. He had seen the violent hand of the emergency, and believed that the trains running on time, an often-repeated benefit of the emergency, was an unacceptable consolation for losing his fundamental rights.

Despite losing his political freedom, he had opted to stay and work in India, instead of going to America for graduate studies. Kutty's timely intervention calling for some introspection had halted him from joining the graduating flock that was bound for the United States.

Moreover, during his last days on campus, he was asked by his guide and mentor, Professor Arjun, if he would reconsider going to the U.S. and instead spend some time in India working toward his country's growth. If he did decide to stay, the teacher promised to recommend him to the best firms in the country. He would have a good job within weeks.

He respected Professor Arjun and found it difficult to refuse his guru's wishes. It was the minimum *guru-dakshina* (respectful repayment to teacher after completion of education) that he could offer his teacher.

When he told his parents and sister that he would not be going to the University of Houston for graduate studies, a gloom of disappointment descended on the family. It was rare for someone to be admitted with a fellowship to an American university, and even rarer for someone to turn it down. His sister, Lata, was immensely pleased to hear that he would still be around; she needed his help with her school curriculum.

Professor Arjun kept his promise. Though it was late in the recruiting season, Satish interviewed with many companies in quick succession. After a month of interviews and many job offers, he joined a multinational engineering company. It was a dream Tam Bram job that somewhat compensated his parents' disappointment with him for declining the American fellowship.

The firm trained him for a month on its products and services, then seconded him to various regional offices. Regional managers always complained that they were short on resources to "make the numbers," and he was loaned to fill these gaps.

In reality, the assignments were tests for Satish. Senior managers at the firm had heard about his extensive campus activities and his organizational and leadership skills. Recognizing the dearth of these in the firm, they had already put him on an informal fast track. If he performed well on this last trip to the worst-performing region of the country, he was assured of being promoted to a regional manager within months.

To Satish, his regional assignments had been a pilgrimage of sorts.

His first mission was at the western regional office, which needed help in turning around its business with an engineering firm in Nashik, two hundred kilometers north of Bombay. While normal work hours occupied his professional objectives, he spent the rest of his time along the banks of the Godavari River and farther north, where the river was called Panchavati.

According to Hindu mythology, Shri Ram, one of Lord Vishnu's incarnations, who was banished to a forest for fourteen years from his kingdom, spent time on Panchavati's banks with his wife, Seeta, and his brother, Laxman.

Shri Ram bathed in nearby Ramkund, and Hindus believed that the mortal remains—the ashes of the dead—immersed in these waters were swiftly transported to the feet of divinity, yielding *moksha*, or the release from the unending cycle of birth, life, death, and rebirth.

He visited the white-marbled Gandhi Memorial, built at the spot where the pacifist's ashes were absorbed by the waters of the Godavari. He walked nearby to an unheralded, unmarked location and recalled how, five years earlier, he had immersed his grandmother's ashes in this river, and then bathed himself in the cold January waters of Ramkund. Not knowing an appropriate Sanskrit prayer for the occasion, he whispered the *Gayatri Mantra* thrice, followed by three *Om Shanti's* for his grandmother, and prayed that her spirit had peacefully merged with the infinite.

His professional tasks were not so simple. The first day, he spent hours explaining to engineers and shop floor representatives why his firm's products were far superior to any others in the market. After a quick lunch in the employee cafeteria, he went down to the shop floor to demonstrate his product, pounding on its advantages in time, cost, and quality.

As a boy from the cafeteria began distributing afternoon tea in translucent, stained glasses, he sat at a bench with the employees and asked them in Marathi, their local language, what they really thought of his product. Most were impressed, and he sensed that there was tacit acceptance that his product had a substantial technical edge. However, the final authority and decision lay with the purchasing officer. "You know how they are," one said with a wink.

Late the next morning, he visited the purchasing officer, accompanied by his firm's local agent and distributor, and sat through a long, boring monologue of why his firm's products were far too expensive compared to a competitor who claimed to have technically equivalent products. He sat silently through the diatribe, which was unnecessarily vulgar. Then, at a crucial moment in the discussions, he abruptly asked the customer permission to leave the office and the building.

"There is no point continuing this discussion," Satish said politely as he left the room. The shocked agent followed him out. As soon as they left the premises, the agent pummeled him and his firm with verbal abuse, charging that the firm was going to the dogs. He added that he would make sure that it was the last time Satish set foot in his territory.

But before they could reach their car, the purchasing officer came running after them, begging them to come back to his office for further discussions. Satish declined, but suggested that they meet in quieter circumstances later that evening over dinner at his hotel. The duo drove off, leaving the purchasing officer in a cloud of dust raised by bald tires gaining traction on the gravel parking lot.

On the way back to the hotel, he explained to the agent that if the man turned up at the hotel, the deal was as good as signed; if he did not come, it was not theirs to begin with, and they were just an alternative to bring pricing pressure on the ultimate winner.

"You are too young to know all this. Where did you learn this? Did they teach you this at IIT?" the agent asked.

"No," he replied.

That evening, the purchasing officer showed up at his hotel with the agent. After a few beers and dinner at a pricey restaurant, the deal was consummated in principle.

The next morning at about five o'clock, an excited agent showed up at the hotel and told a rudely awakened and still sleepy Satish that the purchasing agent had signed the contract. Pleased with this windfall, the agent now wanted to pay homage at Sai Baba's *samadhi* (shrine), at Shirdi. He said that he would be honored if he came along. Satish was excited for the agent, but was ecstatic about going to Shirdi.

When Satish was a child, he was attracted to Sai Baba, a revered saint in Maharashtra. His Maharashtrian neighbors were ardent devotees, and every Thursday they had a *pooja* (Hindu ritual) that he attended regularly.

His mother told him that when he was five or so, he brought home a picture of Sai Baba and convinced his parents to have it framed and placed in a prime spot among the family deities. Soon, every Thursday, this framed picture of Sai Baba began receiving his family's prayers, accompanied by dabs of ground sandalwood paste and *kumkum* (auspicious red powder) on his forehead, and fresh flowers at his feet. Slowly, his parents and sister became ardent devotees. However, a visit to Shirdi eluded them.

Every time they made plans to visit his *samadhi*, they were confronted with some emergency or another—an outbreak of chicken pox or typhoid, torrential rains, or a death in the family—and the trip would be postponed. After several futile attempts, the family gave up on planning trips to Shirdi, saying that it was a bad omen to do so. If Sai Baba wished it, they would make the trip without taking the initiative.

Satish was waiting for the moment when someone would request him to go along to Shirdi. When the agent requested him he quickly agreed, and within the hour, they were on their way to Shirdi.

Shirdi was about a hundred torturous kilometers away on the Ahmadnagar-Manmad Road, and it took them three hours to get there. Recent monsoon rains had turned portions of the road into craters, but the sturdy Ambassador car they rode in, the agent's dexterous maneuverings, the singular focus on reaching Shirdi, and the fact that Satish slept most of the way made the journey, in hindsight, smooth and effortless.

A refreshed Satish woke up as they drove into Shirdi. The agent made a bee-line for a parking spot on the road, close to the *samadhi*. Several urchins surrounded the car and urged them to let them clean the car's muddy exterior. The agent appointed one to the task of restoring his car to a cleaner condition. He picked another to accompany them to the market to buy some offerings to the saint: flowers, coconuts, and some sweets.

Soon the three of them were at the *samadhi*. They entrusted their footwear to a woman outside for a fee, and went in. As Satish entered the sanctum sanctorum, he was overcome with joy that Sai Baba had finally granted him his wish to come visit this shrine.

He stood in the skimpy line that inched forward toward the marble statue of the saint, who sat in his familiar cross-legged pose with his slight, enigmatic smile. It was similar to the one in the picture he had brought home so long ago. However, unlike the picture where Sai Baba was dressed in simple, well-worn clothes of a Maharashtrian peasant, here the statue was wrapped in colorful silk shawls embroidered with gold threads.

As he grew closer, he began chanting the *Gayatri Mantra*. When it was his turn to address Sai Baba, tears welled up in his eyes. He bowed his head and touched the saint's *padukas*, the simple wooden clogs at the feet of the statue.

In his mind, there was nothing but gratitude for the saint's blessings, and he muttered, "*Loka samastha sukhino bhavanthu*," a Sanskrit version of "let all people of the world be happy." It was the only prayer that moved him profoundly.

He did not realize that he had been at Sai Baba's feet for long until he felt a nudge from the presiding priest, who politely asked him to move on. He complied. A few quick steps and he was out of the *samadhi*. He went to look for his shoes. To his chagrin, the lady who was entrusted with them was missing.

A distressed Satish searched for her along the street, running up and down its length, but he could not find her until she called out to him. She had not moved, but somehow he had not recognized her when he came out of the temple. Then, when he looked around for his agent and his little companion, he realized that he had lost them in the confusion exiting the temple. He went to the car and told the cleaning crew to pass on a message to the agent that he was going for some tea and would be back in two hours. He then left, looking for that cup of *chai* that he sorely missed.

Strolling around the temple's perimeter, he noticed an unlikely sign atop a restaurant: Madras Brahmin Hindu Hotel. He went into the small, dingy restaurant, which had four antique-looking dissimilar wooden tables, each surrounded by four dissimilar chairs. He pulled one out and sat down, making adequate noise to attract the attention of the staff.

His eyes had not adjusted to his dim surroundings when the dull silhouette of the person he was most unlikely to meet in the heart of Maharashtra emerged from within the restaurant. It was a bare-chested, South Indian priest, wearing a *vayshti* (unstitched cloth draped around the waist and the legs), his body, arms, and forehead smeared with hand-striped *vibhuti* that added a unique fragrance to his presence.

As he approached Satish, he tied his glistening, well-oiled long hair into a bun at the back of his head. From a distance, he addressed him and welcomed him in Tamil, apologizing that he was doing his morning prayers when he heard him in the restaurant.

"What can I get you, sir?" asked the priest.

"South Indian filter coffee, sir," he replied, abruptly changing his mind about the need for a cup of tea.

"We have just made some *idlis* (steamed rice and lentil patties) and *saambaar* (spicy lentil soup in a tamarind base) that we have just offered as *naivedyum* (food offering) to Sai Baba in our morning prayers. Why don't you have some *prasadam* (consecrated food) first?" the priest asked.

"Sure," he said, pleased with the nature of the *prasadam*, custom-made to suit his Tamil palate.

The priest, who seemed to be almost sixty years old, turned around, parted the soiled cotton curtain that separated the seating area from the kitchen, and disappeared. He reemerged with a camphor-lit brass cup with a long handle. He went to all the pictures of the deities on the walls of the restaurant, saying Sanskrit prayers and waving the smoke from the flame with palm of his right hand in their direction.

He then brought the brass cup to Satish, who stood up. He brought his palms together, enclosing the flame from a barely safe distance, and then pulled the tips of his palms to his forehead. His eyes were closed in a quiet concentration that was disturbed by the aroma of fresh *idlis* and *saambaar* that were placed on the table.

He opened his eyes to see the priest's wife. Unlike Tamil women, who typically preferred to wear brightly colored saris from their home state, this woman wore a modest, traditional Maharashtrian nine-yard Indori *sari* (traditional garment worn by Indian women), with its telltale stripes on the *palloo* (end of sari draped over the shoulder). Satish's late grandmother had also favored these Indori cotton saris.

The sight of a similarly attired Tamil matron, the fragrance of camphor and incense, and the aroma from steaming *idlis* and *saambaar* made him feel as if he was in his own kitchen, rather than at a restaurant in the middle of rural Maharashtra.

The priest's wife urged him to eat before the food got cold. Before he could cut a slice of *idli*, she went back to the kitchen and brought him a small plate of freshly pureed coconut *chutney* (crushed coconut, peppers and spices) to accompany his breakfast. She then retreated to the background and watched the young man relish his food.

Beaming that her *idlis* and *saambaar* were consumed with such delight, she asked him if wanted more, or perhaps a *dosai* (shallow-fried 'pancake' made of a batter of lentils and rice), whose batter had curdled just enough to give it a tangy tinge. Tempting as she made it sound, he declined, saying that he had to get back to Nashik soon.

The priest came, sat across from him, and asked in Tamil where he was from.

"Bombay," he replied, hoping that his monosyllabic response would be adequate.

"No, where are you from originally?" insisted the priest, not satisfied with the answer.

"Originally, we are from North Arcot, but I grew up in Bombay." He struggled to find grammatically correct Tamil words to address an elder.

"So, you speak Marathi and English?" the priest asked in pristine Marathi.

"Yes, I am sorry. I cannot speak Tamil very well," he said with a sheepish smile, apologizing for his inability to communicate in his mother tongue.

"That's okay. I understand all of them," the priest replied, "but I hope you don't mind my speaking in Tamil. I don't get to use it much here. You can reply in English or Tamil or Marathi; whatever makes you comfortable."

He then continued, "My name is Krishnaswamy, and I used to be a priest at the Tirumalai *devasthanam* (temple). But one day ten years ago, I had a dream where Sai Baba came to me and asked me to come to Shirdi."

His wife joined him at his table, and Krishnaswamy introduced her. "This is my wife," he said in English, pronouncing the word as "waif." Satish smiled in her direction, nodded his head and politely acknowledged her, and turned back to the priest, who continued.

"My daughters were all married and it was only the two of us, so we closed our home and came to Bombay first. We stayed with a few relatives and saw the city. Then we took an ST (State Transport) bus and came here."

When he paused, his wife jumped right in. "What a wonderful city, Bombay. We even saw some film stars," added the obviously star-struck wife.

"Yes, we saw Dilip Kumar. He came to visit his friends in Matunga, who lived in the same building where we were staying with our relatives," continued the husband.

"Yes, he came in a big white Impala car, and he actually waved to me when he saw me on the balcony. He was so handsome," she added.

"But that night, I got another dream. Sai Baba again asked me to come see him and, the next day, we cut short our stay in Bombay and came here," Krishnaswamy said.

"We came here ten years ago and we have never been back to Tirumalai since," said the wife, rushing to end the potentially long-winded story that her husband was about to start.

The husband continued, "We came here and stayed at the local *dharamshala*. After we had *darshan* (viewing), we tried to go back but could not. The first time, the ST buses were on strike. When the strike was over, I fell sick. When I went to the doctor, I had no money. He told me that it was okay, I could cook at his home for a few days after I got well. This extended my stay even longer.

"After that, when we tried again, my wife had very high fever and almost died. With no money, the doctor treated her, and I continued to cook for his family. When she was deliriously ill and unconscious, I prayed to Sai Baba to help save her life.

"He came to me again in my dreams and said that I would always be protected by him, but then who was going to feed his visiting devotees? I replied in my dream that I would feed his devotees, and the next morning I woke up to a miracle. She was in the kitchen making coffee for me, walking around as if nothing had happened. I told her about the dream, and she immediately said that we need to fulfill the promise."

The quiet wife, who was mildly surprised at her husband's short rendition of their miraculous story, added, "And we have been here since then and never once thought of going back to Tirumalai. We asked our daughters to sell our house, and we opened this place with the money we received for our belongings. Every summer, our daughters and our grandchildren come here for vacation. It is hot here, but it is cooler and drier than Madras, where they stay. That photo over there is a picture of our grandchildren."

Before the wife could dive into her grandchildren's superlative achievements at school and home, the priest continued, "For ten years, we had steady business from South Indians visiting Shirdi, but recently my customers have been from all over India."

He then asked his customer, "So, have you been a Sai Baba bhakta for a long time?"

Satish recounted his story, and ended just as the wife came with a stack of *dosais* on a stainless steel plate.

"You should listen to his story," the husband told his wife, but before she could do so, he volunteered, "His story is exactly the opposite of ours. Sai Baba kept putting obstacles in his way—you know how he likes to do that—and stopped him and his family from coming here till this morning at five o'clock, when his agent asked him to accompany him to Shirdi. Will wonders never cease? This is all Sai Baba's grace, my son. Enjoy it. He will always be with you."

Yes, Satish knew he was blessed but his focus was on the delicious homemade *dosais* that were being replaced on his plate as soon as he consumed them. He relished the *dosais* silently, except for the slight slurping sound as he sucked the *saambaar* from the tips of his fingers into his mouth.

Seeing that the young man's mind and mouth were preoccupied with the food that lay in front of him, Krishnaswamy remained silent and waited till his customer had finished and washed his hands.

"Come, have a cup of coffee," said the wife as she placed on the table two traditional stainless steel cups. One tall cup with a lip contained the coffee; a broader one, also with a lip, contained sugar.

Satish said "Thank you," and poured the coffee from the tall cup, from a height, into the broader cup. He then poured the mixture back into the taller cup. He went back and forth, several times, and created the perfect cup of coffee with a fragrant froth.

While he was preparing his coffee, Krishnaswamy sat across from him and asked, "What did you study?"

"Engineering," was the monosyllabic reply. He sipped the coffee carefully, without the hot stainless steel burning his lips. At first he got a taste of just the froth, but he was very impressed with the flavor.

Before he could compliment the drink, Krishnaswamy said, "Straight from the Nilgiris, my boy. We roasted and ground this coffee only last night, and made the decoction overnight in a special brass filter."

"Yes," added his wife. "Wherever he goes, he needs his brass *kooja* (pot) of boiled water from home, his Nilgiri coffee, and his Coimbatore butter."

"Yes, but enough about us. Where did you study engineering? VJTI or UDCT?" he asked.

"Neither," he replied. "I went to IIT in Bombay. I just graduated a few months ago."

"Aha!" exclaimed the priest. "Now I know why Sai Baba did not want you to come here! He wanted you to focus on your studies, and nothing else. That was the time to study and develop your principles. Now it is time to focus on building your career without sacrificing your principles."

"So why did he want me here now?" he asked, trying to piece the logic together.

The priest said, "Because, my boy, this is where your *vanvaas*—banishment to a forest—really begins. You see, the Ramayana is not just a mythological story about Rama, Seeta, Laxmana, Hanuman, and Raavana. It is about life."

He then paused and asked, "I am not boring you, am I?"

"No," he replied. "Go on, please. I want to hear about how this is my *vanvaas*."

"We are all born to discover and bring home our own divinity, our own purity, our own Seeta, who has been abducted by Raavana, whose darkness is cast on this universe in various forms. He casts his dark shadow on your senses, your mind, and your heart, constantly attracting you to the dark side.

"Your only weapons against him are Rama's army. Laxmana and Hanuman, who are the epitome of love and faith in him, and the various allies in his army that he had to win over, are your principles and values, which will be constantly challenged. These are what helped him regain Seeta in her purest, divine form.

"My son, till now, you have been in Rama's home, Ayodhya, protected by your teachers and your elders. Now, your *vanvaas* begins. You are in the forest alone, and as you go along in life, your faith and your principles will be challenged constantly.

"If you focus on the divine Seeta in you, your *vanvaas* will end soon. You, too, will pick up good allies along the way, and overcome the Raavana that is in all of us. Sai Baba brought you to his *samadhi* and to me because you needed divine blessings on this journey."

Just then, the agent walked in to the restaurant and said, "There you are. I have been looking all over for you. As soon as I saw this place, I knew you would be here."

Satish wanted to listen some more to the priest's discourse, but he knew that to reach Nashik safely before nightfall he had to leave soon.

"I have to go, sir," he said. He stood up and attempted to touch the priest's feet for his blessings.

The priest stopped his descent by gently grabbing his shoulders and told him, "You have my blessings. Remember that you are Rama on this life's journey, seeking Seeta."

He paid the priest for the food and coffee and left with the agent. They returned to their car, paid off the attending urchins, and set off for their tedious return trip to Nashik.

Soon the conversation came to the turnaround at the customer of the previous day. Satish was puzzled about how the agent had come to his hotel with the purchasing officer the previous evening.

"Well, after I dropped you at the hotel, I went back to the purchasing manager and told him that we wanted to spend some time with him that night. I asked him if he could bring a contract so that we could discuss it with him, and by late that night it was signed—all three copies," said the agent with obvious delight.

"But we did not discuss any contract over dinner, sir," said the bewildered recent graduate.

"No, we did not discuss it over dinner, but after we dropped you off at the hotel, we went to a top-class *tamasha* with many dancing girls singing raunchy *lavani* songs. The country liquor flowed like water. After a few hours of enjoying that *tamasha*, he signed the contract."

Satish was speechless while the gloating agent continued. "I have to thank you for this. If you had not made friends with the workers on the shop floor, then suddenly walked out, he would not have come running out after us and then come out for dinner. I knew that he just needed a little stimulus to sign the contract, and the *tamasha* did the trick! We are a good team. You do the technical talk, and I will take care of the rest. I am going to write a letter to your boss telling you are a good man."

Satish said nothing and sat silently. He closed his eyes, pretended to fall asleep, and thought about how he could possibly scrub off the *tamasha* dirt that had tainted his first victory.

Krishnaswamy was right. He had been banished. This was his *vanvaas*, and his Seeta state seemed very distant and unattainable.

As the year progressed, his pilgrimage continued. He visited several regional offices, aiding them in their quest for more business, and his professional reputation grew. At each one of the regional sites, he visited temples and, once, a church. He met several people like Krishnaswamy who shared philosophical and spiritual insights with him.

However, every professional victory was tainted and marred by unprincipled practices. Moreover, he witnessed several instances of growing violence against citizens in this police state of emergency that enveloped the country. Layers of grime were being added to distance him from his Seeta state.

His recent trip to Allahabad created another hollow professional victory that a dip in the holy Sangam, where the Ganges and the Jamuna rivers meet a third legendary river, the Saraswati, could not absolve.

As he sat in the lonely train station at Triveni, he realized that he was at a crossroad. His success assured him a substantial promotion. He would become the youngest regional manager at the firm.

But he could not ignore the yawning gap between the sleazy side of his professional life and his principles. He knew that the two could not coexist. He had to seek another path out of his forest.

A month later, on a monsoon morning in Bombay, Debra Cunnington was having a bad day when she came into the American consulate premises in her chauffeur-driven car. It was her first day back at work at the consulate after maternity leave. She was depressed and uncertain about leaving her newborn son with a local governess. Her first child was showing signs of a cold and cough, and Debra was filled with anxiety about how the child would survive his first day without her.

As her car paused for the consulate's huge iron gates to open, she saw hundreds of drenched men, women, and children in raincoats and under umbrellas, waiting in the rain for their visa interviews with her. Satish was one of these wet visa applicants.

The Interview

No one came to this hallowed hallway at Clark Oilfield Technologies without permission or an appointment. As Satish stood at its entrance, he was not quite sure how he felt. On one hand, he felt privileged to be one of a select few to enter this exclusive row of executive offices. On the other hand, he was anxious about his final interview with Pete Peterson, the president of a division of this conglomerate.

His peers, as well as his superiors, had assured him that this interview was a mere formality before being promoted to engineering manager. But he was apprehensive about his first formal encounter with this unpredictable, confrontational man, bear of a man.

To him, it was one last hurdle on his drawn-out path to a promotion, but that was furthest from his mind. He was more concerned about a higher priority—his green card interview the following month with the Immigration and Naturalization Service. He was excited at the idea of being an engineering manager because this promotion would strengthen his case during his impending green card interview.

An added benefit, he thought, was that the visibility of the position would accelerate his climb up the corporate ladder in the oil and gas industry. However, this progression was not the urgent need of the moment. His focus was on his green card, and on becoming a permanent resident of the United States. His life and his future depended on it.

"Que sera, sera," he hummed, recalling an unlikely popular song from his childhood in India. He walked down the hallway, dark mahogany panels reflecting little light from the pair of dull chandeliers that hung from the tall ceiling. Every alternate wooden panel had a portrait. The current CEO of the firm, Charlie Clark, sported a sunny, friendly smile, a bright red tie on a white shirt, and a sharp, dark blue suit. It was in sharp contrast to the founder's and his successors' portraits—grim, unsmiling gentlemen in formal but tired, crumpled garbs.

He walked past the glowering dead founders toward an office at the other end of this seemingly sinister hallway. He trod softly on the thick gray carpet, but he could hear his muffled footsteps as he approached a well-lit mahogany desk that almost hid Pete's diminutive executive assistant, Ms. Black.

As he approached her, he pushed back an imaginary lock of hair from his forehead. Using his fingers as an impromptu comb, he plowed through the back of his head to subdue any stragglers into neat formation. He stood briefly at Ms. Black's desk as she delicately ran her fingertips across a keyboard.

"Excuse me, Ms. Black," he said.

She looked up as if startled. Her glasses fell off her nose, but were saved by the safety string that held them around her neck. She knitted her eyebrows and waited for her aging eyes to adjust to her dim surroundings and the unrecognizable figure.

Ms. Black then saw a tall, slim Indian engineer with a toothy smile, dressed in a neat, white, short-sleeved shirt adorned with a colorful tie.

"I am here to see Mr. Petersen," he said.

"Yes, yes, he is expecting you. Please have a seat, Satish, and I will inform him that you are here," she said politely. She waved him to an ancient brown leather sofa in the huge, otherwise opulent front office.

When she went into Mr. Peterson's office, he sank deeply into the soft sofa. As he crossed his legs, he examined his pants to see if they were well creased. He saw that his black, laced shoes were properly shined. He noticed that his tie had a stain of red Tabasco sauce, but reconciled that it was not noticeable in the explosion of colors that adorned it.

He wondered what lay in store for him during this interview. He was not easily intimidated, and assurances that it was just a formality put him at ease, but he had a gnawing doubt about the outcome.

This long saga had begun several months earlier, when his name was first included in the list of candidates for the position. As weeks progressed and his formal interview with Pete kept being postponed because of some emergency or another, doubts crept into his mind.

"Why the delay? Are they considering other candidates?" he asked around.

There were rumors that Pete had recommended a slate of new candidates who were making their rounds in the firm, being interviewed for the same position. After they had interviewed with senior managers across the company, the conclusion was unanimous—Satish was better.

Yet, his final interview kept being postponed for weeks, till half an hour earlier, when he received an urgent message saying that Pete wanted to see him.

After studying at IIT Bombay and working in India for a year, Satish came to the University of Houston for his graduate studies in engineering. Upon completing his master's degree, his professor, Dr. Jones, referred him to a few Houston businesses, including Clark Oilfield Technologies, a firm that provided services to oil companies. The oil and gas industry was at the peak of its boom then. However, a year later oil prices dropped and the industry went into a tailspin, rapidly losing thousands of jobs.

His employer had fortunately decided to invest some of its newfound wealth from the boom in several leading-edge technologies. His talent was critical to one with the biggest promise.

In a short year, he had proven his technical prowess, and his name was included in a patent application that had been filed by his firm. A year later, he was the informal leader in a technical area. It was just a matter of time, he assumed, before he was promoted to manager. When his boss was transferred to the UK, his name came up as a possible successor. Tim O'Leary, the human resources vice president, was fond of Satish and had supported his candidature.

"Satish," he said, pronouncing his name with a "Sat" as in the past tense of sit, swiftly followed by the "ish" sound that was so common in the American vernacular. "Your name is on the list of candidates, but Pete wants us to do an external search, too." Tim sounded apologetic.

"That's okay. He'll soon find out that I am the best!" said a cocky Satish to Tim, who was more of mentor to him than a VP of HR.

"I am sure he will," said Tim. "But you know how he is."

"Yes, I do. He likes to bully and intimidate everyone with his size, his voice, his intellect, and the fact that he is married to the CEO's sister!" he said with a laugh.

Tim was a few decades older than he was and spoke with a distinct Boston Irish accent. In their numerous lunches together at the company cafeteria, Tim had shared with him stories of his career: different jobs he had held, and his struggle to become a respected professional in the corporate world.

Few people in the firm knew that he did not have a high school diploma. Fewer knew that Tim's career included being an auto repoman in New Jersey and a Bible salesman in Missouri!

Besides sharing good chemistry, they also shared a common opinion of their cafeteria's food. The only way to make it palatable was to add generous helpings of Tabasco sauce to spice up the bland fare. There was always a telltale bottle of Tabasco at their lunch table as they shared company politics, gossip, programs, policies, and, most important to Satish, impending layoffs.

"Don't worry, Satish. You will be the last person they will lay off. They'll fire my ass before yours. You make money for the company; I am just a cost center, and they can always find a cheaper HR director to take my place."

"Tim, there is no way that's going to happen," he reassured him. "You are Pete's eyes and ears. You are his Hoover, his CIA, KGB, and FBI rolled into one. And knowing you, I am sure you have pictures of Pete in compromising positions," he added with a grin.

"No, no. I don't have pictures," Tim said. "But I am getting there," he added with a big grin, which told Satish that his friend knew something that he was not quite ready to reveal.

Unlike his relationship with Tim, which was personal and amiable, the one with his VP of engineering, John Boudreaux, was strictly professional. While Tim was friendly, John was aloof and kept his distance. Every interaction Satish had with John was focused on business at hand and did not last a minute more than it had to.

There was no casual chitchat, no discussion about a recent football game. There was no small talk about the unpredictability of Houston's weather; for that matter, there was no exchange of season's greetings during the Christmas holiday.

John's team members were different. Every man was just the opposite, and they compensated for John's lack of warmth and personal touch. Satish often wondered how John had made it to such a senior position at the firm with such an obvious deficit. Tim later shared with him that John had been with a major oil company where he had developed this division's underlying technology.

When the oil company refused to fund its development, John left in a huff, making sure that he had the rights to his technologies. He approached several oilfield service companies, but only Clark gave him everything he asked for, including the right to lead the engineering group.

When Satish heard about John's background, his respect for his leader grew substantially. He unconsciously changed his attitude to one of awe.

Tim had said, "If there's one man who'll go to bat for you, it is John. What you're working on is John's technology, and his entire future depends on its success. And he thinks you are part of his core team. So give him a break, and you'll do fine."

He took Tim's advice to heart, but he had a difficult time going along with his VP's execution schemes. Just recently, he had dismissed some tool designs as being too "frail," only to discover later that they were John's original designs.

"The solutions had too many assumptions that will lead to low reliability and tool failures," he had complained loudly. He knew that the firm was under pressure to deliver a prototype tool fast, and deriving a more "elegant solution" meant more delays—more time to conduct more iterations of design, test and failure analyses. It would be a long time before manufacturing would get the new designs to build the prototype.

In a short year, Satish had learned that exploring and producing oil and gas was a dangerous business. One trivial mistake, and human lives and limbs were lost, and the environment and property could be destroyed. Safety was a mantra at Clark, which had a spotless record. It prided itself on its safety processes, and failure analyses were central to the firm's standard operating procedures.

Consequently, when he raised the specter of failure, red flags and alarms went off not only in his division but also at the corporate offices, reaching the ears of his CEO, Charlie Clark, at a quarterly review meeting.

"What do you mean the prototypes are going to be delayed by six months?" Charlie thundered at his brother-in-law.

Pete said, "We found a problem in the design. Our mean time between failure would have been unacceptable. No driller would use the tool for field testing."

"You think this delay, six months, is realistic?" asked a suspicious Charlie.

"We had to scrap all the parts we had manufactured so far, and we had to start from scratch. It's a complete redesign. If everything goes right from now on, we'll be six months late," replied Pete.

"Six months if we are lucky! What will I tell the board? Just last week I told them we were on schedule, and they finally approved another $200 million of capital for this year," said an exasperated CEO. "I am not going back in there to ask for more," Charlie said, towering over the seated Pete.

"No, no. I don't think we need more. We'll make do with what we have," Pete assured him.

Charlie glared at his brother-in-law and wondered what his sister saw in him. Quickly, he transformed to the sunny disposition depicted in the portrait in the hallway and said, "I want to talk to John and his team tomorrow, first thing. I want to know three things: what happened, what's our plan to fix it, and why do we think this plan will work."

"Okay, Charlie," Pete said as he gathered his scattered papers and made a beeline to Ms. Black's desk to arrange the meeting. It was already four PM. In about forty-five minutes, his engineering managers would be in their van-pools, headed home.

Satish came in the next morning and noticed an uncommon absence of all managers from their offices. En route to a cup of morning coffee, he stopped at his department secretary's cubicle.

Laura Stoller was a bright, attractive native Houstonian. At twenty-five, she was a senior secretary responsible for more than twenty engineers. She typed their memos and filed their documents, arranged their schedules, made travel plans and, above all, kept them organized. She found Satish to be refreshingly different from the other engineers. He was about her age and would talk to her like an equal. The others were sometimes condescending and always boring.

She was intrigued by this tall, good-looking Indian. She liked the stories he told her about India, its customs, its food, and his superior engineering college, but what she liked most about him was his insistence that she go back to school and get a college degree.

"Charlie wanted to see the team." Laura told him. "Urgently," she added in a mock, grim tone, imitating a male voice.

Seeing no reaction from him, she nodded and said, "Your ass is grass, Satish. They want to know why the field test is delayed. They'll need a scape-goat, and since you are at the bottom of the totem pole, you're it!"

"Why pick on me? I found problems that saved the company millions of dollars, and their safety record."

"Duh!" Laura said, grimacing at the Indian engineer's lack of insight. "You're the messenger. They shoot messengers here. Don't you know that your design and failure analysis screwed up two years of work? They had to start all over again. And if I know how these big boys act in these meetings, they are all pointing fingers," she said, and pointing at him, added, "and all the fingers are pointed at you, darlin.'"

"Get outa here," he responded with an air of bravado to his teasing secretary. He went to his cubicle, wondering if his green card application would be jeopardized in any way.

Elsewhere, in a conference room on the Clark campus, Charlie listened to John's team's latest plans to deliver the prototype tool in six months. He saw

Gantt chart after Gantt chart for all the activities, timelines for each one, and initials of people responsible for delivering results. Charlie noticed an unfamiliar set of initials on several activities that were on the critical path of this project.

"Who is SS?" he asked.

"That's Satish Sharma," John said. "He joined us more than a year ago. He did his master's at U of H with Dr. Jones."

Charlie was a U of H graduate too, and an active alumnus. He caught John's signal about Satish's credentials. He respected Dr. Jones.

"A Cougar, huh?" he acknowledged with a smile. "Good to see that we are not filling the place with Stanford graduates," he said, taking a dig at both Pete and John. "We need a little diversity here," he kidded.

A few weeks after this meeting there were layoffs, and Satish's boss was transferred to another division. His position was declared open, and its description displayed on notice boards throughout the company.

Months passed as the firm searched for a replacement. In the meantime, with the absence of a direct supervisor, Satish picked up the mantle and was soon representing his group at review meetings. His former boss's peers soon recognized the young man's talent and capabilities, and began to push for him.

"John, have we considered all internal candidates?" asked one at a weekly meeting.

"Yes we have, even in other divisions, but we found none," John replied.

"What about Satish?" another asked.

"Satish? Well, you know how Pete is. He'll never go for it. Besides, he is too young for the position," John said.

"He's been doing the work of a manager while we've been screwing around to find the perfect person," said another. "We may have the right candidate right here."

"Well, if y'all think that we have the best person, let me talk to Tim and see what I can do," John said to his team.

Laura gave Satish the news that his name had been thrown into the ring.

"Really? You're not just yanking my chain, are you, Laura?" he asked, unable to suppress his joy.

"You can go ask your lunch-buddy, Tim, or if you're real nice to me, I'll give you your interview schedule," she teased.

A few more weeks elapsed while he had formal interviews within the firm, and the response was unanimous—Satish was the best candidate to fill the position. However, Pete insisted that Tim had done an inadequate job of finding good external candidates and pushed him to get more people to interview.

Then one day, John, frustrated with the delay, took the uncharacteristic step of filling out a personnel change order form, promoting Satish to a manager. He signed it and sent it to Tim, who was astonished at John's courage. He knew Pete would be displeased with the move.

"Tim, we need a decision on this position if we are to meet our schedule," he told Tim. "Satish is the best man for the job. We have to stop pussyfooting and move on it."

"John, I agree with you," responded Tim. "I have been saying that for months!"

John was direct. "Tim, I want you to sign the PCO and send it to Pete. I've had enough."

"Fine. I'll sign it and send it to Pete," Tim responded. "But let me make sure that Steve agrees with it, too. I'll take care of that." There was always strength in numbers, and it would be prudent to get the VP of operations' concurrence to Satish's promotion. After John, Steve Longorio was the next most powerful person among Pete's direct reports.

A few days later, Satish received a call from Ms. Black. "I know this is short notice, but Mr. Peterson would like to see you today at four o'clock. Are you busy?"

"I'll be there, Ms. Black," he replied. "Thank you for calling me."

As soon as he hung up the phone, he picked it up again and called Tim. "I've got to see you right away."

"Yeah, I know why. Come on over."

He still had about half an hour before his appointment with Pete. He spent it with Tim, trying to understand the latest developments and the unexpected call for an urgent meeting. Tim explained to him what had transpired, especially the series of events that had been triggered by John's recent actions. "You'd better have some healthy respect for John, young man. He's going out on a limb for you."

"So, what should I expect in this interview?" Satish asked.

Tim replied, "Oh, you know Pete. He'll try to ask you some technical questions to show that he understands that area. He'll try to mess with your head. Nothing unusual, nothing out of the ordinary. This is just a formality."

As Satish sat in the large, well-worn leather sofa, waiting for Ms. Black to emerge from Pete's office, Tim's words—nothing unusual, nothing out of the ordinary, just a formality—kept echoing. He looked around to see if there was a coffee bar or anything to moisten his dry throat. Finding none, he turned his attention to the magazines on the large oak table.

"Focus, Satish, focus," he said to himself. "Focus on keeping your job and getting your green card. Not on the promotion; that can come later."

"Mr. Peterson will see you now," announced Ms. Black from Pete's door.

"Thank you, Ms. Black," he said as he went into the room. She shut the door behind him.

Pete's office was the largest, most imposing one he had ever seen. Satish had heard about its features. It was laden with rich mahogany panels on the walls, a formal library with richly bound volumes, a huge, almost red cherry desk, leather Queen Anne chairs, and a leather sofa in a corner with a matching love seat.

The adjoining room had a huge dark mahogany conference table and white boards on the walls. Pete's oversized desk faced large windows that overlooked the woods of the campus.

"Good afternoon, Mr. Peterson," he said as he entered the room.

"Afternoon," Pete said, without looking up from the papers that he was reading. "Sit."

"Thank you," he said as he took the seat directly in front of Pete. He watched him as he read some documents, his eyebrows visibly knit in anxiety. Pete then shut the file, set it aside on the edge of the table, and leaned back in his swiveling chair. He looked him in the eye and said, "So, you're Satish."

"Yes, sir," he replied with an enthusiastic yet nervous smile.

Pete leaned forward at the table, pulled out a book from a drawer, leaned back again, and started writing in it, keeping the book on his lap. Then he stopped, looked up at his nervous employee, and said, "John tells me that you'll be a good engineering manager, and so does Tim. I've seen your performance reviews. They are excellent."

"Thank you, sir," he acknowledged.

Ignoring Satish's response, Pete continued, "Everyone seems to feel that you're a keeper. And I've seen some of the reports you've done. They are good; not extraordinary, just good."

"Thank you, sir," he said, assuming that there was a compliment in there somewhere.

Pete continued, "I have another meeting in ten minutes, so let's get to the point. We all know why we are here. John wants to promote you to a manager, but," he said, and paused, looking at him dead-pan, "I am not going to sign the PCO form to promote you."

Then he paused to write something in his book. Satish sat in stunned silence. He had not expected such an abrupt statement. He did not know how to react.

"Don't you want to know why I am not going to promote you?" asked Pete, again looking up.

"No, sir," he said. "I mean, yes sir. Are you not satisfied with my work?"

"Your work is fine. You are a good worker bee. We need more people like you, but you are not a manager," Pete said.

"Sounds good," he said and began to rise from his seat, satisfied that his job and his green card were secure.

"Don't you want to know why I don't think you'll be a good manager?" asked Pete, gesturing him to sit down.

"No sir," he said. "I am sure you have good reasons. Maybe I am not ready for it and I have to wait."

Pete leaned back to write in his notebook, then looked up and said, "No. I cannot promote you because the oil industry will never accept an Indian as a chief. You are an Indian in cowboy country, and this redneck industry will never accept you as one of them." He paused to gauge Satish's reaction.

"Look at Billy Stayton, president of our contract drilling division. Do you think he will ever take you seriously when you tell his engineers what to do, which you will have to?" asked Pete.

"People take me seriously, sir, because I do good work. When I make engineering sense, they don't look at the color of my skin," he replied calmly, rapidly regaining his composure.

"Satish, I am doing you a favor. Get your green card and get out of this industry. I am from Minnesota, and even I feel the prejudice. You are an Indian and you look different, and the prejudice will be ten times worse." Pete sounded genuinely concerned for Satish's welfare.

He continued, "I cannot jeopardize this division's progress by having an Indian in a managerial position. You have to sell your ideas and positions, and I cannot take the risk that you will be rejected because you are different. This will impede the acceptance of our products in the market, by other divisions, and, most important, by our customers."

Satish remained silent and watched him scribble again in his book. Without looking up, Pete told him, "That's all. You can leave now."

He did not know what to think as he left Pete's office. He walked past Ms. Black and the next group of visitors without acknowledging them, a very unusual act. He walked past the portraits and wandered out of the building toward the cafeteria. There he picked up some bread crumbs that were kept for people who wanted to feed the resident ducks at the campus lake.

Picking up a large packet of stale bread, he walked to the lake and sat on a bench under a tree, throwing breadcrumbs into the water for fish and fowl. It was a nice March spring day. The grass and trees were beginning to resurrect, and there was not a cloud in the sky.

Ducks waddled around him, and the water was a beautiful blue-gray with tiny ripples. A jet plane taking off from the nearby Houston airport shattered this pastoral ambiance, but calm soon reigned as the plane left the area, speeding to its destination.

Like that plane, a few sentences from Pete had shattered his aspirations. He was angry at Pete for having been so blunt, abrupt, and crass with him.

He threw more crumbs in the water and watched some fish come close to the surface pick them before the ducks could reach them. Perhaps he was like the fish, destined for small crumbs, while people like Pete were like the ducks that owned the pond and its vicinity. If a fish came remotely close to their territory, they simply ate them. Perhaps he had come too close.

He sat on the bench, throwing crumbs and thinking, till it was well past five o'clock. His colleagues would have left for the day. To avoid encountering anyone, especially Tim, he went directly to his car in the parking lot and left the campus.

As he sped south on Highway 59 to his home, a modest garage apartment, he saw Houston's legendary freeway traffic jam on the other side of the freeway, headed north. He wondered if he and his career had unknowingly merged into that long trail of stranded motorists. They went through this routine, day after day, as if they had no choice or free will, just fulfilling their preordained destiny.

Twenty minutes later, he took the Shepherd-Greenbriar exit and proceeded to his home in the vicinity of Rice University.

Though he had had a job for almost two years after graduation, he had continued to stay in his student apartment, built on top of an aging three-car garage. It was small, about seven hundred square feet but had four distinct walled areas: a living room, a kitchen, a bedroom, and a bathroom. The living room had an unfinished oak wall unit that contained a cable-ready TV and his stereo system.

Scattered around the room were a few director's chairs, a beanbag, and small end tables with lamps. He had bought all of them at a garage sale in the neighborhood for $25, a steal.

He plopped on the beanbag, removed his tie, and threw it on the nearby chair. He reached for the remote and turned on the TV, which was tuned to local news. He immediately switched it off. He sprang up, went to his tiny kitchen, and put a pot of water on the old gas stove to make some tea. Then, abruptly, he switched off the stove, put the mug back, grabbed his tie from the living room, and went to put it away in his bedroom closet.

This room was sparse. It had a mattress, a phone, a clock radio, and a lamp, all on the floor. When he moved to this apartment, he discovered after he had signed the lease that he could not take his box spring up the curved staircase. Rather than lose his deposit, he decided to do without a regular bed. He bought a futon mattress that he put on top of a regular mattress, and he was quite comfortable with the arrangement.

Nobody thought any less of him because of his Spartan surroundings, especially Priya, his girlfriend, who was a graduate student at Rice.

He placed his tie on a hanger in the closet and then went to the phone to call her. He needed to talk to her, but there was no answer. He hung up the phone and decided to call Tom.

"What should I do, Tom?" he asked his older, single friend, an international banker who had lived around the world, especially in Asia.

"Let's talk over dinner. I've found this great Thai restaurant in Montrose. You'll love it. The food's hot, hot, hot!" Tom said.

Satish drove a couple of quick miles to Jimmy's Thai House, where he saw his friend, the lone customer in this new restaurant that had bamboo strips on its walls from floor to ceiling. The tables and chairs looked as if they were picked up from a used restaurant furniture store—they were too worn out for a new place. Pictures of the Thai king and his queen adorned the area near the cash register.

"Hi, Tom," he said as he entered the restaurant. He made his way to his friend before a waiter could escort him.

"Hi, sit down. Have some of this Thai beer. It's terrific," Tom said, raising his beer mug and pouring a waiting bottle into his Indian friend's frosted mug.

"Yeah, I'll have one. I need it today."

"I've already ordered some Tiger Cries, Thai street food that you don't get at regular Thai restaurants. It's beef, rare beef. I hope a Brahmin like you won't mind it," Tom said, smiling and taking a sip of his beer.

"Only Indian cows are sacred, my friend," replied Satish, smiling and joining the repartee.

Tom Holcombe was a jovial and jocular Texan who belonged to a prominent family that owned ranches that had turned into oilfields. He grew up in Fort Worth, but rather than joining the family ranks in managing ranches and production fields, he became an accountant at an American bank with worldwide operations. He had worked for over twenty years, and had recently taken a sabbatical to rethink his life.

Satish and Priya had met him at a festival of Satyajit Ray films at Rice University. He, like them, saw every film in this festival. After the third film or so, they began to acknowledge each other in the lobby. After the fifth film, they had discussions on the master's work during a break, and after the last film, he invited the two of them to join him for dinner at a great Ethiopian restaurant that he'd just discovered.

He regaled them with his stories and experiences, especially in Asia and India. He had gone on a tiger hunt with a maharaja of a small principality in Uttar Pradesh. He had seen most of Northern India, from New Delhi all the way to the Himalayas, and some of the south to Kerala and Madras.

He had stayed for long stretches in Calcutta and loved the Bengalis' artistic touch, finesse, and passion. He had strayed into Bombay, Satish's hometown, but did not like it too much. "It's too American, not at all Indian in its character!"

"The best Christmas I've ever had was in Goa," he had once said, and went on to describe the beaches, churches, food and drink, and the party atmosphere of Panaji, its capital. "Goans are the only people in India who know how to have a good time. Must be the Portuguese influence; look at Brazil, another fun country. You Indians take life too seriously—too much focus on karma, destiny, and the meaning of life."

Both Satish and Priya enjoyed Tom's company and his travel stories. His spacious condominium in the swanky, old money River Oaks area was full of artifacts and souvenirs from every place in the world that he had visited.

His most prized piece lay in the middle of his living room—a twenty-foot tiger skin that he claimed he shot in India! Each souvenir had a story, a very human one, and contributed to his view that no society was lesser than another. Each had its own distinct strengths, foibles, and flaws; none was perfect.

Tom was livid when Satish told him about his conversation with Pete.

"How dare this Minnesotan think that Texans are racists?" he said, his face turning red with unusual displeasure. "How dare a man from an all-white state say this about Texas? I am a tenth generation Texan, and I can tell you that the only reason we've become a great state is by accepting people of all colors and religions."

He paused with disbelief as he took another sip of his beer.

"Even before people came over on the Mayflower, Spanish people, including a Muslim Moor, came to Texas and lived here. Even the French were here before the Northern Europeans set foot on North America. We had diversity before the word was invented! And to say that Texans or the oil industry will not accept an Indian manager, that's ridiculous. This man is prejudiced, a racist, and he is just projecting his bigotry on other people," he said with finality, as the Tiger Cries arrived at the table.

"Thank you," said Satish to the waiter. Turning to Tom he asked, "So what should I do? Fight, flight, or do nothing?"

"Flight is not the right answer," he said. "You cannot retreat from this idiot. Nor can you do nothing. You have to take him head-on."

"What?" he asked in astonishment. This was not a response he had expected from Tom.

"Yes, you have to fight, and you have to understand that this will turn ugly. It will be your word against his." He paused for a moment, and then his eyes lit up. "I know a good attorney who can beat the jeepers out of Pete and Clark for doing this to you," he said with a sly smile.

"Tom, you don't understand. They have sponsored me for a green card, and I am almost at the end of that process. If I take this to court, they'll fire me and I'll have to go back to India. On the next flight!"

"Satish, that choice is the lesser of the two evils. Working for a company that tolerates this behavior is the pits. You will suffer every day. You will hate getting up in the morning because you have to go to work there, and you will hate every minute that you are there. Your performance will suffer, and Pete will be proven right. After that they'll fire you, and worse, every Indian who applies for a job after your departure will carry the stigma of being from your country."

Satish was silent.

The waiter came back and asked if the duo was ready to order. It was a welcome break in the conversation. He sipped his beer and ordered Chicken Masaman Curry while Tom ordered Pad Thai.

"Talk to Jeff Cohen. He is my attorney. He'll guide you through this. We have to take out people like Pete. They are a cancer to our society, a blight, and should be removed," Tom said with his characteristic smile. He raised his mug. "Take him out, Satish."

"Okay, I'll talk to Jeff. But wouldn't asking for his advice lead to a lawsuit? It's like going to a surgeon for medical advice—invariably, the solution is surgery!" Satish said.

"You're right. Jeff would love to take on Clark—they have deep pockets. But you have to fight. You cannot take this lying down. That's how the Brits took over your country, one maharaja at a time rolling over, till they took over the entire country. You have to learn something from your own history," Tom said. "You lose freedom in small, retreating steps."

"You're right, Tom. I have to take a stand. I just don't know what it should be. Give me Jeff's number. I'll talk to him tomorrow, first thing in the morning." Tom scribbled a number on his business card and gave it to him.

The waiter placed their food on the table, saying, "Enjoy." He politely walked away without turning his back to his customers.

"Dig in, but watch out for those Thai peppers," Tom cautioned.

While savoring the aromas, Satish cautiously mixed a little chicken curry with a lot of rice and ate a forkful. Yes, it was hot and spicy, but delightfully different from any food he had ever eaten before. The sweet flavor of coconut milk was powerful and blended well with the spices; neither overcame the other. The chicken was done just right, and every bite oozed curried zest.

"How's your Pad Thai?" he asked Tom.

"I tell you, I have eaten at the best Thai places in Thailand, and this Pad Thai is one of the best. Of course, our Texas shrimp makes all the difference!" Tom said, as he closed his eyes and savored a crustacean with great delight.

The waiter came back and lightly placed a check on the table. Satish grabbed it and said, "This one's on me."

"I'll get the next one," Tom said graciously.

As the two of them were walking to their respective cars, Tom reiterated to his friend, "It's fight, not flight. Remember that. Even Gandhi fought, though differently." With that final word, he drove off in his car.

Satish walked into his apartment to find four telephone messages, all from Priya, essentially saying, "It's me. Where are you? I'm done with my project. Can I come over? Call me."

Just as he reset the machine, he heard the phone ring and picked it up.

"Hi, it's me. Where have you been?" asked Priya.

"I tried to call you a little after six, but you were not there. I had dinner with Tom," he said.

"I am done for the day. Can I come over?" she asked.

"Sure. Do you want me to pick you up?"

"No. I'll walk. It's a nice day and I need the exercise. I think I am putting on some weight."

"Sure you are," he said, with a laugh.

Priya weighed only ninety-five pounds. She was a little over five feet four inches tall, and could pass for a Houston high school student. She too was from India.

Her father was a brigadier in the Indian army and her family moved their home every three years or so. When she was fourteen, he sent her to a private school in Bangalore to give his daughter some constancy in companionship, curriculum, and teachers. Later, when she graduated, she went to a college in Bangalore, living in dorms on its campus. When she came to Rice, she slipped into the American campus life with ease.

He had already graduated when Priya came to Rice. He first saw her at a campus event celebrating India's Independence Day.

Every year, during the weekend closest to August 15, Indian students put on a cultural show that had songs and dances from different parts of India. It was the same fare, year after year: classical dances from Tamil Nadu, Kerala, Andhra Pradesh, Orissa, and Manipur, some *Kathak*, and folk dances from Gujarat, Maharashtra, Karnataka, Bengal, and the predictable finale, a raucous *Bhangra* from Punjab. Mingled with these dances were other dances based on songs from Bollywood films, and renditions of patriotic songs.

The evening's explosion of colors, movement, and music enthralled Houstonians, campus faculty, and students. It was as if Fourth of July fireworks were being done live on stage.

To Satish, this was all ho-hum. He had seen the best performers of all these art forms, and these were just well-intentioned amateurs. He only came to the event to meet his friends, some of them still students, and others like him who had recently entered the local workforce.

When he entered the auditorium, a harried organizer came to him and said, "Satish, I need your help. Can you take pictures of the show?"

He agreed, and a camera was thrust into his hands. He took a favored place in the front row of the auditorium and took pictures of the participants, watching the performances and waiting for appropriate moments when entire dance ensembles were on stage.

When the Karnataka folkdance began, he noticed that one performer was especially talented. He could not take his eyes off of her. She was light on her feet, and her body, movements, and expressions were in perfect consonance with the upbeat music and the sprightly, joyous mood of the harvest festival this dance depicted.

When he took pictures, he made sure that she was in the center of every shot. He realized too late that he had exhausted the roll of film during this dance. An embarrassed Satish went scurrying around, looking for someone to give him another roll of film, but he did not find one.

A week later, he was invited to the event's cast party that was held at a prominent Indian doctor's expansive home. He arrived fashionably late to discover that his photographic exploits of the previous week had drawn varied responses.

Many were disappointed that he did not take their pictures. Some were pleased that there was at least one terrific picture of their performance. However, the Karnataka troupe was most pleased that there were so many pictures of its performance.

The hostess came up to him and said, "I think I know why you took so many pictures of the harvest dance. Come, let me introduce you around." She took him by his hand and led him across the living room.

He was embarrassed at being led by the petite, elegant hostess. Every eye in the room was on him, and on this conspicuous action. She took him to the kitchen and, addressing a woman who had her back to them, said, "Priya, I've caught the culprit."

Everyone in the kitchen burst out laughing as Priya turned to see what this commotion was all about. She almost dropped her drink when she saw Satish standing with her hostess.

"Priya, this is Satish. He is the one who took all those pictures," the hostess said, unable to curb her wide smile.

"Pleased to meet you," Priya said, trying to maintain her demeanor.

"Pleased to meet you, too," he said, with the silly smile of the smitten.

"Priya goes to Rice," volunteered the hostess. "So does Satish," she added as a quick afterthought.

"I've graduated, Aunty. I am working now," he said, graciously not correcting her about his being a U of H graduate.

"Oh, that's nice," said the hostess. "Anyway, you two go talk. You must have a lot in common. Priya, why don't you get some punch for Satish? It's so hot outside."

"Yes, Aunty," she said politely in a voice that he could barely hear. She went to the other end of the kitchen.

The hostess turned to him and said, "Don't let her soft voice and delicate looks fool you. She is tough and smart. You two will be good for each other."

"Thank you, Aunty. I don't know what to say," he said.

"Don't say anything. Just invite me to your wedding," she said as she walked away to greet other guests.

"Thank you, Priya," he said as he took a cup of punch from her. He could not tell if she had heard what her hostess had said.

For about a year after that meeting, they courted each other between his work and her university course loads. For the past six months, they had been inseparable.

Just as Satish finished cleaning his apartment for Priya's arrival, he heard the doorbell. He rushed to open the door.

"Hi," she said, kissing him lightly on his lips.

"How was your day?" she asked as they walked upstairs.

He said nothing as he followed her. She went into the living room, quickly turned around and hugged him tight. "I missed you, Satish."

"I missed you too," he replied softly as he let out a sigh in response to her reassuring hug.

"Want some tea? I'll make some," she volunteered.

"Sure," he said.

"What's wrong? Something happened? At work?"

"Yes, Priya," he said. As she put the kettle on, he began recounting the day's events and his chat with Tom over dinner.

She took two mugs of tea to the living room and placed them on one of the end tables. He pulled a beanbag and sat on it. She sat cross-legged across from him, and said, "Don't worry, everything will be all right."

"I know everything will be fine. They need me more than they can imagine. Their prototype was so badly designed, if they had gone for field-testing with it, they would have had a failure in minutes, and they would have been the laughingstock of the industry. But now, with the old design dead, they need me to design the new prototype."

"So, what are you going to do?" she asked gently.

"I don't know. One thing I do know is that I have to show my displeasure and disgust with Pete's behavior."

"Do you really have to show your displeasure?"

"Yes, Priya, I have to. I am tempted to hurt him. The choice is whether I hurt him directly, through a head-on confrontation, or should I simply leave the company and join some other firm?"

"Is there no other choice?"

"Yes, there is another alternative. Do nothing. Roll over and play dead."

She said, "First, just get your green card. Then do what you want to do. Just don't do anything rash and leave a bad taste behind."

He smiled, looked at her in her eyes, and said, "Are you, the daughter of an army man, telling me not to fight?"

"No, I am not telling you not to fight, sweetheart. You have to fight the right battle, at the right time, on your terms, not someone else's," she said with a pleasantness that was in sharp contrast to the idea. "Dad always said that you should pick your battles, and make the enemy react to you; not the other way around," she added with a wicked laugh.

The next morning, the first thing Satish heard was, "Wake up and have some tea." In front of him stood a neatly groomed Priya, all set to take on another day of graduate studies.

"I have to go," she said. "I have made some tea. It's in the kitchen. I have a seminar to attend in half an hour."

"May I drop you?"

"No, it's okay. By the time you get ready, I'll be in class."

As she walked away, she said, "Remember what I told you. First, get your green card. Do nothing till you are ready to fight the battle on your terms. Bye, sweetheart; I'll see you in the evening. Wait for me for dinner."

"Bye, Priya," he said from the bed as she shut the front door. He heard soft footsteps going down the wooden stairs. He rolled over and pulled the sheets over his eyes to get another fifteen minutes of sweet sleep.

Two hours later, he woke up with a start.

It was a little before noon when he arrived at his office cubicle. Almost everyone had left for lunch, and he made it to his cubicle without running into anyone. There was a stack of pink message slips on his desk.

All of them had two boxes checked, "return call" and "urgent." Most of them were from Tim; one was from John.

He called Tim first.

"Where the hell have you been?" asked Tim, his voice taut and tense.

"I overslept, Tim," he said casually. "I had a rough day yesterday."

"I hope you've not done anything stupid, Satish," said an agitated Tim.

"Like what? I just overslept. It could happen to anybody!"

"Come on over. I need to talk with you right now," commanded Tim. "Better still, let's go for lunch to the Chinese place. Separate cars." He hung up.

Satish rushed out of his cubicle. He sensed that he was the source of Tim's agitated state. He ran into Laura on the way out. Rushing past her, he said, "I am going for lunch."

"But where have you been? Tim wants to see right away, and so does John."

"Bye, see you in an hour," he said. He left Laura puzzled by his rare show of anxious haste.

Satish reached the restaurant and got a table, and a flustered Tim soon joined him.

"I hope you have not done anything stupid," Tim said as he walked over to the table.

Satish looked up, smiled, and asked, "Why do you say that?"

Tim took his seat, put his hands on the table, leaned forward, and said softly and apologetically, "Listen, my friend. What happened yesterday should not have happened."

"What do you mean? What happened?" he asked, still puzzled by the solemnity in Tim's voice.

"Your interview with Pete. It should not have happened."

"What? How do you know what happened? I did not talk to anyone about it," he said, his mind racing with suspicion. Was Tim taping conversations in Pete's room?

"Pete's a stupid man. He took notes of everything he said to you," Tim whispered. "What do you think he scribbles in his notebooks? The pompous ass thinks he is going to publish his memoirs, and he writes notes all the time."

"And you read them?" he asked.

"The moron came to me in my office with the notes to tell me why he was not going to promote you."

"Really?"

"Yes. He not only told me, but he showed me his notes."

"So?"

Tim leaned forward even further and whispered, "So? You dumb ass, this is discrimination of the highest order. You have the company by the balls."

Satish pulled back in his seat, smiled, and asked after a pause, "So?"

"Do you want me to spell it out? Clark will have to pull out its checkbook, sign it, and give you blank check. You write the number!"

"Right. So, you want to buy me out for the crap I went through yesterday?"

Tim said nothing.

"Tim, I don't want your money. It's tainted."

"Also, I don't think I can work for any company that has people like Pete as a leader. You will have my resignation when I return to my office."

"What?"

"Yes, Tim, you heard me right. I want nothing to do with Clark."

"What about your green card? You are so close to getting it!"

"It does not matter, Tim. I won't feel good getting my green card from Clark. Everything about it suddenly stinks. I want to be as far away from it as possible."

"Satish, don't be rash. Why don't you take the day off and think about it? If you still feel the same way tomorrow, we'll accept your resignation."

"Can't do that, Tim."

"Why not?"

"I have had enough time to think about it. You have to understand this about me, Tim. This is not a job. Engineering is my passion; solving challenging problems is my passion. I enjoy it, and I have to enjoy it. I don't do it for the money or the green card. Those are just consequences, not the motivation.

"The reason I am good at what I do is because I pour heart into my work. I don't stop working when I leave the office. I don't carry a heavy briefcase home, because I carry my unsolved work in my head. And even when my thinking mind is asleep, my subconscious mind, my working mind, continues to work on the problem, and sooner or later I have an approach, if not an answer."

Tim was silent.

"Tim," he continued. "Yesterday on my way home I saw miles and miles of cars on Highway 59. Hopeless, hapless people trapped in their cars, their jobs, and their lives with no choice, no free will. I don't want to be one of them, one of Thoreau's throng, men living in quiet desperation. If I stay at Clark, I will become one of them, compromising everyday, playing games, going down that slippery slope, till I too am stuck in that traffic on my way home to a wife and two kids in the burbs."

He paused, waiting to see if Tim had something to say. When Tim said nothing, he continued.

"Tim, I can see what's happening around here. You, John, and Charlie know Pete and his tendencies and do nothing about it. You are not innocent bystanders, though you may think you are. You are co-conspirators who, by saying and doing nothing, give Pete your approval to act the way he does.

"He is like a kid who steals candy at first. When the people around him condone it, he goes on to bigger things. The next thing you know he is on the evening news, having committed some ghastly crime. And you all are like the neighbors who say when he is arrested, "Oh! He was such a sweet kid!"

"What Pete did yesterday was not an accident, and I guarantee it was not the first time this has happened. You and Charlie have seen it happen in the past and have said and done nothing.

"I am no hero, and I am not going to do something rash. I'm not going to charge the hill and take it in a battle. That's not my style. But I am going to throw a lone stone at the fickle glass house you all have built around Pete, and shatter it.

"You will have my resignation this afternoon, Tim. Screw the green card. It's not worth it," he said.

Tim silently ate his Mongolian Beef, while his friend finished his Kung Pao Chicken, looking down the entire time. Tim broke the silence and said, "Satish, I can't stop you from what you want to do, but do me a favor and give me the resignation letter. Don't go to John."

"Okay, Tim. I'll do that."

"One more favor. Don't dictate your resignation letter to Laura. Come to my office and let Liz type it up for you."

"Okay, Tim," he said as he reached for his wallet.

"No, no. It's on me. This is a business lunch," Tim said with a smile. "I'll see you at my office in a few minutes."

Satish left Tim behind to pay the check and drove back along surface streets, rather than the freeway, to ponder what he had just said. He had no clue how he was going to "throw that lone stone at the fickle glass house" at Clark. The drive reaffirmed his decision.

When he arrived at Tim's office, Liz, his pleasant secretary told him, "Tim had to rush to a meeting with Charlie. He asked me to take down your letter and type it for your signature. So what is it, Satish?"

"To Tim O'Leary, VP, Human Resources. It is with deep regret that I submit my resignation from Clark Oilfield Technologies. I have enjoyed my work and tenure at Clark and I wish the firm and its wonderful people the very best in their endeavors. Sincerely, Satish Sharma."

Liz took it in shorthand and said, "Why don't you wait in Tim's office and I'll have it ready in few minutes." He had hardly sat down and examined Tim's desk when Liz walked in.

"Here you are, hon. Hope you are doing the right thing," said this silver-haired lady who reminded him of Edith in *All in the Family.*

"I'll be okay, Liz," he said as he signed his resignation letter.

As she took the signed letter she said, "One more thing. Tim said that you need to take the day off and call him in the morning before coming to work."

Then she smiled sweetly and said, "I think you need to leave now, and don't talk to anyone about this. It's our little secret." She was so like Edith.

"Okay, Liz," he said, and left for home. It was just about two o'clock. He could easily catch a good movie at Greenway Plaza, close to his home.

While he munched on a large bag of popcorn and watched Tom Conti and Kelly McGinnis in *Reuben, Reuben,* Tim sat stone-faced in Charlie's office.

"We cannot afford to lose this kid, Charlie," Tim said as he finished recounting the events of the last twenty-four hours.

"Yeah, I know. The prototype will be delayed for another year," replied Charlie. "But that's not why I don't want to lose him. He had the *cojones* to stand up to us and walk away on a moral high ground. That's rare."

"Ethics, Charlie, ethics. He talks the talk and walks the walk," Tim concurred.

"You sure he won't sue us?" asked Charlie.

"No, Charlie. I know this kid. He won't even think about it," Tim assured him. "He has this Indian saying he attributes to his mother: Just because you choose to be in a toilet doesn't mean that I have to join you!"

"So now we are all in a toilet?"

"Yes, Charlie. In his eyes, this place is a toilet. An unflushed one," he added politely.

"I can't believe that he walked away from his green card. What'll he do next?"

"Oh, I don't think he'll go to a competitor. He'll probably go back to U of H for a PhD, or move to northern California."

A smile broke across Charlie's face. He laughed as he said, "Hmm. We have a good young man, a bright engineer with great principles and ethics, who has held a mirror up and showed us that we are filthy and live in an unflushed toilet."

He then paused and continued, "Do you think he learned all this from Gandhi? You know the movie we saw last year?"

"Don't know where he gets it from, but it's not from a movie," replied Tim. "This kid is different. We have to salvage him."

"Let me see what I can do," he said as he picked up the phone and called his secretary.

"Sandy," he said, "Please call all the divisional presidents and tell them to be here at six o'clock. Yes, today, this evening."

He then listened to Sandy and added, "No, no agenda. I want to see all eight of them. Tell Billy I want to see him earlier, but not later than five thirty. Thank you, Sandy. And yes, order some sandwiches too. It's going to be a long meeting."

Turning to Tim, he said, "You too, Tim. Be here at five thirty."

As Satish emerged from a satisfying movie, Billy Stanton and Tim walked into Charlie's office.

"Thank you, Billy, for coming at such short notice," Charlie said. He stepped forward to shake hands with this extraordinarily tall, weather-beaten man from West Texas. Charlie could feel the absence of Billy's missing index finger when he shook his hand.

Billy looked more like a scientist or a scholar than the roughneck he had been all his life. He wore serious, dark-rimmed glasses with thick lenses. His silver hair was slicked back, and he wore a dark blue suit with a white shirt and a vintage polyester tie. On his feet were expensive, dark gray Ostrich boots that had seen some wear. The dirt on the heels of his boots said that he had recently visited his ranch.

He was Charlie's father's right-hand man, a trusted lieutenant, and had been with the firm for almost forty years when he retired. Just recently, with the change in industry dynamics, the retired Charles Sr. had asked him to come back to help his son manage the sudden transition. "Help Charlie, Billy. It will be like 1958 all over again," assured Charles Sr. Billy complied and came back to run Clark's largest division.

"My pleasure, Charlie. What's this all about?" Billy asked as he pulled out a pack of cigarettes. On cue, Sandy walked in with an ashtray.

Charlie looked at Tim, who recounted to Billy what had happened.

"I want this Indian kid, Charlie, if y'all don't want him," Billy exclaimed. "We sure don't want to lose him."

"That's what Tim and I thought," Charlie concurred. "But that's not all. I have some other ideas I want to talk to you about."

Then, turning to his VP of human resources, he lowered his voice to a pleasant tone and politely asked, "Tim, will you please excuse us?"

Even as Tim began to leave the room, Charlie began his conversation with Billy in urgent, hushed tones.

When Satish arrived home from the movie, he was surprised to find Priya waiting for him at the doorstep.

"Where were you all day? I called the office, and Laura said that you were not in all day. You were not home. I left so many messages. I was so worried," she complained.

"I did go to the office," he replied calmly. "I had lunch with Tim, and I turned in my resignation."

"What?"

"Yes, I resigned today. Then I went and saw *Reuben, Reuben*. Nice movie," he said in a lighthearted manner.

"What, you resigned? What about your green card?" she asked, her voice turning uncommonly shrill.

"Oh, don't worry about it. I'll get it sooner or later. For now, I don't have to work for that Pete or his gutless staff anymore. Come, let's make some tea."

As he put the kettle on, she came up behind him and hugged him.

"Now why would you do something so drastic, Satish?" she asked tenderly.

"Because, sweetheart, I don't want to be at a company that condones such behavior, especially from its president," he said, matching her singsong, tender tone, as if talking to a child.

"Be serious, Satish. This is no joke."

"Seriously. This *is* no joke. I have seen enough prejudice and discrimination in my life. First, my grandparents had to leave Tamil Nadu because they were Brahmins. They dropped their last name because it denoted our caste. That did not help, so they came to Bombay hoping for a better life."

He paused, waiting for a response from Priya. She remained silent as she looked down at her task of cutting okra.

As he stirred the boiling pot with split peas, he continued. "Then my parents had to go through prejudice again in Bombay because they were South Indians. This time they changed their last name to Sharma because it was common across most parts of India. We all got nondenominational first names that made our linguistic and ethnic origins impossible to trace, at least in India."

He stared at the lather forming in the pot. When it was about to overflow, he skimmed it and threw it away in the sink a spoonful at a time. After discarding the last spoonful, he reduced the flame. He watched the split peas in the pot dance from the bottom to the top, perceptibly changing their color and texture from solid, golden brown hemispheres to yellow platelets with serrated edges.

"Did you know that at the multinational company I worked for in Bombay, we had three of everything? One for the European whites, one for Indian managers, and one for Indian staff. We had three lunchrooms, three sets of travel plans, and, for heaven's sake, we even had three different toilets. Anyone who had any self-respect and dignity would have found this humiliating."

Priya had finished cutting her vegetables, and she moved toward the range to take her turn at sautéing them. She nudged him aside and poured a few spoonfuls of oil into the pan. She added torn dried red chilies, mustard seeds, and other spices before the oil could heat up. He stood near the doorway and watched her.

As the pan of okra simmered down, she stepped back from the range. He came forward and poured into the pasty, yellow split peas a reddish-black concoction of boiled tomatoes with *rasam* (South Indian soup) powder, tamarind, and salt.

"I think you should call Tim and take back you resignation," she said.

"No. You know I cannot do that. It's done. It's an irreversible action. It's final! There's no going back."

"You have to," she pushed.

"No, Priya. I came to this country because I believed it to be the last bastion of principles and equality. People would value me for my values and my work, and not the color of my skin or my ethnicity."

"But, Satish, what about your green card?"

"It's not worth it. If I have to fight back, I might as well go back to India and fight my battles. That's my home turf, and I know the lay of the land better. Screw this place," he said testily.

"Don't get excited. Take it easy." She tried to calm him. She filled a plate with vegetables and rice and poured some *rasam* on the rice. "Do you want some potato chips?" she asked.

"No, thanks," he said as he poured some cold water into glasses, took them to the living room, and placed them on the end tables.

Priya soon joined him with two plates of food, both with potato chips. She smiled at him and said, "I know you are upset. But don't show your anger at your food. You never eat *rasam* and rice without some potato chips, so I brought some for you. If you don't want them, I'll take them."

Priya was right. He loved potato chips with *rasam* and he was glad that she added some. As they dug into the *rasam*, rice, okra, and potato chips, Priya asked, "Why don't you play some music? Stan Getz?" She knew that it would soothe him.

In moments, as the soft strumming of Charlie Byrd's guitar began strumming the first chords of "Samba De Una Nota Só" and a tenor sax joined in, he calmed down and began enjoying their joint culinary effort.

"This is great," he said as he took another tablespoonful of an Indian version of Cajun gumbo—rice, *rasam*, beans, and fragmented potato chips for that added crunchiness in the otherwise semi-viscous mass.

They ate quietly as Brazilian music filled the still calm of the garage apartment.

"Do you realize that you have put our future in jeopardy, too?" she asked softly.

"What do you mean?" he asked.

"Satish, you know I love you and I would do anything for you, but without your green card my future in this country is in jeopardy, too."

He did not say a word. He knew there was more to come.

She set her plate aside and continued. "I was hoping that we would get married after you got your green card."

"Why did you not tell me this earlier?" he asked.

"I thought it was obvious. I did not think you would want to move back to India."

As Astrud Gilberto sang the One Note Samba, he put his plate aside and turned to a distraught Priya. "Don't you want to go back to India?" he asked.

"No, I absolutely don't want to go back to India. I want to stay here, do my PhD, and raise my family here. I don't want to go back," she replied, close to tears.

"Sweetheart, I don't see a life without you. If it's important for you to stay here, I can look for a job at another company that will sponsor me for my green card," he assured her.

"Be realistic," she said. "In this economy? Oil companies are laying off thousands of people. Who would hire you at a time like this? Besides, you are technically out of status. You are required to leave the country immediately."

He recognized the truth in Priya's words. He remained quiet, thinking about his limited alternatives.

"What should I do?" he asked Priya.

Brushing back her welling tears with the back of her palm, she sniffed and said, "There's only one thing you can do. You have to go back to Clark and get them to take back your resignation."

He remained silent. He was not about to go back to the firm and beg them to take him back.

He argued, "Priya, even if Clark took back my resignation, it would stay on my records, and this is the end of my career at the firm. They'll fire me the first chance they get. That, too, on their terms, not mine."

"What would you rather have? No green card, head back home, leaving me behind? Or would you like to get your green card, get married, and settle here? And if you think your career is going nowhere, change jobs when you want to, but get your green card first."

Priya had this uncanny ability to bring things into perspective very quickly. While he was prone to consider a situation logically, generate seemingly infinite alternatives, and slowly throw out unrealistic ones, she could intuitively bring things into focus faster than he could.

Over the past seventeen months, he had learned that her instincts were rarely wrong. Time and time again, he had quietly tested her intuitive conclusions with his slow, tedious ones and found that they were not too far apart. The processes were different but the conclusions were the same. He did not have time to go through his analysis and synthesis, so he conceded to her alternatives, with their obvious choice.

"The choice is clear, Priya. On one hand, I have no green card, I have to leave the country, and I may lose you. On the other hand, I get my green card, stay here, and continue to be with you. What do you think I will choose?" he teased, delicately wiping away a remnant of a tear from her cheek.

"I hope you choose to go back to India. Then I don't have to deal with you and your impulsive acts," she said, still distraught.

He hugged her, gently stroked her hair, and said softly, "It's not going to be that easy to get rid of me, sweetheart. I'll call Tim tomorrow and take my resignation back."

She got up and walked to the kitchen, sniffing along the way. "Come, let's clean the dishes," she said.

It was about six thirty the next morning when the phone rang. Still in a deep slumber after a long night of discussing how to get his resignation back, Satish, without getting up, groped for the phone in the dark.

"Hello?"

"This is Tim," said a familiar, raspy voice.

"Who?" asked a disoriented Satish as he tried to raise himself.

"This is Tim; I want you to bring your ass in my office by eight o'clock."

"What?" he asked, still unable to comprehend the situation.

"I want to see you at eight o'clock. In my office. Bring your security badge."

"Eight o'clock?"

"Yes, eight o'clock. In my office. Wake up. I gotta go. Be there," he said, and before hanging up he added, "Wear a decent tie."

Satish drowsily put the phone in its cradle and reluctantly got out of bed.

He was confused and nervous when he arrived at Clark's parking lot fifteen minutes before his appointment. He walked hesitantly to the security device at the entrance to Tim's office building. Till then, he had taken his entry into this building for granted, but today was different. The security card scanner was a threat.

He nervously swiped his card and waited for the tiny green bulb to light up, followed by the metallic sounds of locks unlatching. Nothing happened.

He anxiously swiped his card again, trying to recall the instructions during his orientation session when he joined the company on how to swipe correctly swipe security cards. Nothing happened.

He cleaned the magnetic strip on the card with saliva on his fingertips; still no access.

"It's just dirty," he said with a sheepish smile to the secretary who stood behind him.

"It's okay, Satish," she said. "If your card don't work, you can go in with me. I know who you are."

"Thank you, ma'am," he replied just as he heard the sounds of his card's acceptance. He pushed the door with relief and ran up the stairs to Tim's office.

Liz waved him in, saying, "Go on in. He's waiting for you."

"Hi, Tim. What's up?"

As soon as Tim saw Satish, he stubbed his half-smoked cigarette, grabbed his coat from behind his chair, and said, "Let's go. We are going to be late. There's a meeting in a few minutes."

"What meeting?" he asked.

"Just come with me. No questions," Tim instructed in a firm tone that he had not heard before. "I'll explain on the way."

The pair went briskly down the stairs and left the building. When they were on the sidewalk to the corporate building, Tim said, "Last night Charlie had a meeting with all the divisional presidents. It went on till way past midnight. They are going to make some announcements this morning."

A puzzled Satish asked, "Why me? Why am I going to this meeting?"

"Beats me. Charlie called me at two in the morning and asked me to call John and Steve to come to this meeting. Billy called a few minutes later asking that you be present, too!"

"Billy asked for me?"

"Yes, Billy. The very same Billy who Pete said would not accept you as a manager."

"What's going on, Tim?" asked a breathless Satish, trying to keep pace with the older man.

"I've told you all I know," Tim said as he swiped his card and gained immediate entrance to the building. Satish followed him in. Charlie Clark's office was at the far end of the hallway with the grim portraits, one door past Pete's.

Tim rushed into Charlie's office with Satish following a step behind, and both turned into the adjoining conference room. Surrounding the large oval mahogany conference table were twelve well-upholstered chairs occupied by people in suits. Along the inner wall of the room were additional chairs. Tim and Satish sat on the periphery with other unknown faces.

Looking around the room, Satish recognized the cheerful Charlie, a sullen Pete, his recent nemesis, and John and Steve, who seemed to be exchanging small talk. He had never seen the rest of the people before. Seated near Charlie was Sandy, his assistant, with a stenographer's pad and pencil ready, poised to take notes.

"Good morning," said Charlie as he rose from his seat after a brief sip of coffee from a mug.

"Good morning," mumbled the room in response.

He continued, "Sorry for the short notice, but I have some announcements."

There was stony silence in the room. Nobody moved, and all eyes were on Charlie as he continued, "As y'all know, our industry is in a recession, and we have to continually look for ways to be more effective in this market."

He paused and took a sip of coffee. Like everyone else in the room, Satish waited for the other shoe to fall.

Charlie put his coffee mug down, stood upright, and looked around, making eye contact with everyone at the table but ignoring those seated on the periphery.

He said, "We met last evening to review our revenue and P and L forecasts for the year." He paused briefly before adding, "They don't look good."

Satish noticed that Charlie's cheerful disposition had now morphed into a cold, steely one as he said, "We are losing cash every month, and we cannot let this continue. So the management team has come up with a plan to generate positive cash flow by the end of the next quarter."

He paused, took another sip of his coffee, and surveyed the room, including the periphery. He stopped briefly at Satish's unfamiliar face and moved on.

"First of all, we will be consolidating our eight divisions into three: a drilling division, a production division, and a logging division. Pete and Paul's organizations will now report to Billy, who will be an executive vice president of Clark Oilfield Technologies, as well as president of the drilling division. Pete and Paul will report to me and work on special projects."

He paused, looked at Billy, and asked, "Billy, do you want to say something?"

While Billy readied his papers and glanced at his notes, Satish looked to Tim as if asking, "What's going on?"

"Not now!" was his silent reply as he looked intensely at Billy and focused on what he had to say.

Satish looked at Pete and saw that he still had his superior grin on his face. This demotion had not affected his demeanor a bit. As he caught Satish's eye, his smirk turned into a sneer.

Billy stayed seated. He looked around the room with a wide grin that displayed a gold molar and said, "Thank you, Charlie. I b'lieve I do have somethin' to say. I always do!"

As Charlie sat down, Billy stood up and said to him, "Thank you, Charlie, for the trust and confidence."

He then raised his hand with the missing index finger and added, "We have serious challenges ahead of us, and I am not going to do this alone. The only way we can come out ahead in this recession is by attracting and keeping the best brains in the world, with the best can-do hustlers in the world. And let me tell ya, nobody has a monopoly on brains or hustle." He paused and added lightheartedly, "Not even people from West Texas!"

The room responded with a polite, subdued laughter of nervous relief that soon subsided.

He continued, "Seriously, this downturn is going to be a long one, and we need to work smart if we are going to beat it."

He sat down, looked at his notes, and said, "Just a few quick announcements. John and Steve will be my vice presidents for engineering and operations, and Tim will be my VP of human resources.

"I will work with these gentlemen to define the rest of the organization, but I do have one more announcement."

He paused, pointed at him with his clenched fist and added, "That young man out there next to Tim, Satish Sharma, will be engineering manager, reporting to John."

Satish was oblivious to Tim shaking and pumping his hand. He barely heard Billy continue, "Clark got here by attracting the best people in the world, and by keeping them. We are a service company, and we are as good as our people."

Satish looked at Pete, who stared back at him with a disapproving nod. While feigning attention to and pleasure over what was being said, he leaned over, nudged Tim, and whispered, "Tim, can I have my resignation letter back?"

"No," whispered back Tim, as he pretended to pay rapt attention to the proceedings.

"Why?" he asked.

"Because I want to keep it," hissed Tim, stressing "keep" the best he could.

"Why?"

"Because it's the stone that shattered this fickle glass house," Tim said earnestly.

However, he was puzzled at Satish's unexpected response. Something was missing. His reactions were not typical of a victor.

Tim paused, and when the meeting agenda had moved to other reorganization issues, he nudged Satish and asked, "Why do you want your letter back?"

Satish sat up straight, slowly removed his tie, and neatly folded it. He stuffed it in his shirt pocket and said, "Because I want to change the date on the letter. My resignation still stands, Tim, but I want to make sure you know that it was today's meeting that pushed it over the edge."

Staring icily in the direction of the head of the conference table, he added, "And that malignant cancer, Pete, is still here, sitting right next to Charlie!"

With that, he quietly rose and politely excused himself from the meeting. With every eye in the room on him, he left the conference room, walked through Charlie's office and down the gloomy hallway with the grim portraits, and exited the building.

He took deep breaths of fresh air, and collected himself. As he walked to his car, he began digging deep in his pockets for Tom's card, which had his attorney's telephone number written on it.

The Touch

Satish was early for his date with Priya, who had avoided meeting or talking with him for two weeks. As his eyes adjusted from the sunny Houston exterior to a dim, oriental interior, the owner of the Thai restaurant, Jimmy, came up.

The restaurateur took his barely extended right hand, shook it heartily, and said, "So good to see you, sir, after such a long time. Table for two?"

"Yes," he nodded. He was led to a corner booth. From there he could observe Priya and the rest of the patrons as they ate and filled the evening with whispered chatter.

"Will your young lady friend be joining you?" Jimmy asked as he picked up the extra settings of silver and placemats from the table.

"Yes, Jimmy," he replied.

Jimmy went away and returned quickly with a tall glass of Thai iced coffee.

"You need some energy, my friend. On the house, from me," he said as he ran to welcome a couple who had just entered the otherwise empty restaurant.

Satish stared at the sugary concoction, the coffee separated from the cream on top by a misty, light brown phase that quickly disappeared when he stirred the contents with a straw. While he sipped his coffee, he stared blankly at the couple; the man and woman were entranced by each other, whispering, oblivious to their surroundings.

He recalled his early days with Priya. Both were commencing new professional beginnings, and despite pressures at work and school, they found scraps of time, adjusting and juggling their schedules, to share with each other.

Mutual friends recognized that they were very different. She portrayed an image of a professional woman, focused on her graduate program, her career, and her independence. What he saw was an affectionate and kind woman who would be a good partner for the rest of his life. She saw him as a slightly flawed man who could be molded into her ideal, and with whom she could be feminine without losing her equality.

Often, observers erroneously concluded that she was the more aggressive, chatty, confrontational person of the two, and that he was the strong, silent type. Neither perception was entirely true. She liked to debate orally, while he preferred to indulge in silent, mental dialectic processes, and then share the results if he chose to do so.

She was a student with limited funds, while he was newly employed, with a sudden, dramatic increase in his disposable income. He spent it freely, mostly taking her out for dinner at nice restaurants at the end of exhausting workdays.

So restaurants were their usual meeting places. He would create humorous stories about other couples in the restaurant and their relationship's current state, creating mock dialogues from a distance. She listened in awe to her favorite engineer's lighthearted, frivolous tales. They made her smile at first, and then laugh, as the stories grew wacky and hilarious.

It was in the darkness of a movie theater that he first felt her touch—he was engrossed in the movie when he sensed her hand slip into his. He did not take his eyes off the screen as he reciprocated with a firm clasp; not too tight, not too loose. He did not forget the sensations of that touch as she put her hand in his, and how he had taken hers and held it lovingly, silently promising her never to let it go.

That first touch was a universe in itself, and he reminded himself of it by taking every opportunity to gently slide a hand over one of hers and holding it tenderly, recalling that moment when their fingers first touched, interlocked, and merged into each other. Every time they were together in his car and it came to a standstill, he would faithfully reach out for her left hand and hold it for a brief moment. It was to reassure her of his promise not to let go.

They constantly sought each other's company, moments when they could bask in the sunshine that they seemed to carry around with them. There were no dark clouds in their skies. Houston's hurricanes and thunderstorms were mere faint manifestations of their senses, on the extreme edges of their paradise for two.

Though he had regular hours working an eight-to-five job and she worked the late, irregular hours of a graduate student, they spent at least a few minutes with each other every day in his Spartan garage apartment. It was their fortress of solitude, away from her dormitory and her roommate, Dora, a fellow graduate student.

Gradually, their lives in their respective work became more strenuous and challenging. To save time they began cooking their meals at his apartment—quick, twenty-minute affairs that produced somewhat edible but spicy Indian food. However, they always had at least one meal a week at a restaurant, where they sat for hours with their hands enfolded in each other's. The touch transmitted their affection for each other, while other senses enjoyed the dizziness of the moment.

From the way Priya responded to his touch, he could sense how she felt. It was all in the way her palm and fingers behaved. If she was seated parallel to him, as in a car or a movie theater, when all was well, she would manipulate her wrist so that the inside of her palm and her fingers would touch his. After a few moments, she would place her fingers between his and bend them, creating a single mingled fist.

If she was mildly disturbed about something, she would not create the fist but instead rub her palm and fingers against his, with Satish seeking the clasping position. If her discomfort was extreme, she did not reach out for his hands, and when he reached for hers, she would expose only the top of her palm and fingers in a casual, unresponsive manner.

He recognized these signs. Whenever she seemed to be out of sorts, his usual frolicsome and playful nature cajoled her out of her discomfort zone. It usually had something to do with her work or colleagues at school, or some bad news from home about her parents' minor health problems or her brother's ill-conceived marriage, which was on the rocks.

However, during the past month, he found that she was in an inconsolable funk. Every attempt to persuade or wheedle her out of it seemed to be futile. She seemed troubled. Through their dinner at Jimmy's two weeks earlier, she had seemed indifferent and distant.

She uncharacteristically pushed away an unfinished Pad Thai, her favorite at the restaurant. Every attempt he made to hold her hands was gracefully evaded. At the end of the dinner, she atypically asked to be dropped off at her dorm room instead of accompanying him to his apartment.

For the past year, she had visited him regularly and talked with him every day on the telephone. But during the past two weeks, he had not seen her, nor had she returned any of his calls except the one that morning when she asked, "How about dinner tonight at Jimmy's?" He tried to push her for an explanation about why she had not returned his calls during the week.

Her response was a tepid, "I have some assignments due today, and I really did not have the time. Can we talk this evening? No, you don't have to pick me up. I'll come there by myself."

He tried to engage her in a conversation to give her the latest news of the day, but she courteously told him that she had to get back to her assignment. He had suggested that he'd come and pick her up—she did not own a car. How was she going to get to the restaurant? She told him that she would manage, and politely ended the conversation.

As he sat in his lonely booth in the corner of Jimmy's restaurant, stirring and sipping his iced coffee, he wondered if his recent decision to resign from Clark and legally confront their discriminatory practices had something to do with her sudden change in behavior.

He had discussed with her his resolution to confront the firm that condoned discriminatory behavior by its senior executive. She felt that since he was only a few weeks away from getting his green card, he should have waited before resigning from his job and taking legal action.

He told her that it was a matter of principle. He was quite prepared to face the consequences, and to go back to India and work there. She argued that his impulsive and dramatic action, in full view of the senior management of the firm, had put their future together in jeopardy.

What he could not share with her was that during the past two weeks, when she was inaccessible, the firm had fired the bigoted executive, Pete Peterson.

Clark had negotiated with his attorney terms of his return to the firm. Not only was his permanent residency assured, but also with his new visibility, his career path at the firm was as secure as possible in an industry in a severe downturn. He was going to return to work the next day.

Only murky ice remained at the bottom of his glass. He waited till some of the ice had melted, tilted his glass, and sucked the liquid noisily through his straw. Jimmy heard the sound, brought another glass of the refreshing drink, and sat across from him. "Young lady is coming, no?"

"Yes, she said she was coming," he replied.

"Can I get you some appetizers? Tiger Cries or Sate?" asked Jimmy.

"No, thank you, Jimmy. I think I'll wait," he said.

While he stirred his fresh glass of iced coffee, he stared in the direction of the restaurant door or looked vacantly at the couple in the distance as they ate their appetizers, their eyes still glued on each other. He waited for that crack in the door that would let the bright Houston sunlight into the dim restaurant, silhouetting his Priya.

Instead, when the door opened, an unfamiliar woman entered. As she stepped into the lit area of the room, he recognized her. It was Dora, Priya's roommate. He instinctively stood up. She saw him in the far corner, came up to him, and sat across from him. He sat down and asked, "Is Priya okay?"

"She couldn't come, Satish," she said.

"Why? Is she okay?"

"She is fine. She wanted to come but could not, and asked me to tell you that she had to finish some assignments."

"She could have called the restaurant and told me personally," he suggested.

"Yeah, but she did not know how to tell you what she wanted to tell you, so she sent me."

On various occasions when Satish had called Priya in her dorm room, Dora would answer and take messages. Over time, this led to comfortable telephone conversations between the two. He had met Dora several times, and the two of them were at ease with each other.

She was an African American from Atlanta and an accomplished student who had educated herself with scholarships and work programs for the gifted. Like Priya, she was slight in build. She had sharp, well-etched features, and behind the John Lennon glasses she wore, she had large, expressive eyes that were complimented by long, dark hair that she tied into a simple ponytail. She was always well-groomed, though her outfits were almost identical. She wore colorful T-shirts and blue jeans, with a pair of well-worn sneakers on her feet.

Dora was focused on her academics and had little time for socializing. She welcomed his brief visits, and when Priya ran late for her date with him and he had to wait for her, the two of them would chat. Initially, they indulged in polite conversations. After a few months, they engaged in discussions about politics, social currents, and environmental issues pertaining to the oil and gas industry.

After a period of growing familiarity, he shared with her cautiously that she did not look like a typical African American. She laughed, and told him that she was not offended by the observation. She explained to this soon-to-be-immigrant that, since the later seventeenth century, people in the United States were socially categorized as African American if they had virtually any sub-Saharan African ancestry.

She was a "sang-mêlé," someone with 125 to 127 parts white blood out of a possible 128. Yet she was classified as a "black African American" because of the "one drop of blood" rule. She quickly assured him that she had not received fellowships because of affirmative action programs, but because of her accomplishments.

Brushing aside the commonly held misperception, she went on to explain African American terms that he had never heard of: griffe, mulatto, quadroon, octoroon, mamelouc, demi-mamelouc, and sang-mel, an American version of 'sang-mêlé'. Each one described a racial mix of a child based on its previous seven generations.

He shared with her the Indian caste system of Brahmin, Kshatriya, Vaishya, and Shudra—each one describing the profession of the family. When he told Dora that he and Priya were Brahmins, she responded with, "Ah, you are at the top of the food chain in India. Why are you here?"

He just shrugged his shoulders and replied, "To gain knowledge?" Sensing his uneasiness, she let the topic slide and skillfully segued to another one.

He found Dora warm, intelligent, socially conscious, and a terrific non-confrontational conversationalist. She found him to be bright, sincere, and committed to Priya. She often shared her opinion about him with her roommate. During the previous two weeks of Priya's forced isolation from him, she told her repeatedly that she was making a big mistake in even contemplating dumping him because he had resigned from his job.

"Girl, Satish is a good man, and he adores you. You are crazy, letting him slip out of your hands. At least talk to him, engage him. Discuss things with him," she implored.

"No. I told him that it was the wrong step. He made his impulsive decision, and now I have made mine," was Priya's consistent response. "I don't need to talk with him. I don't want to be tied to an unemployed man without a green card."

Dora persistently told her that he was doing the right thing. This was the United States, and discrimination, especially such blatant behavior, should not be tolerated.

"Trust me," Dora said, "I know what it is like, and your man is doing the right thing."

Seeing her roommate's stubborn insistence on severing all contact with her boyfriend, Dora volunteered to break the bad news to him, on the condition that Priya call him and set a time and place for their date. She hoped that the telephone conversation would possibly reignite some of the affection that Priya had had for him. It did not.

When Dora saw Satish in the corner of Jimmy's restaurant, she felt sorry for him. She saw how he politely stood up while she came up to him, and stepped out of the cubicle and waited till she inched in and sat down before he took his seat. He was gracious. She knew that he was genuinely concerned about her roommate's well-being when he asked, "Is Priya okay?"

She had an unpleasant task to perform. She could sense that he knew what was to follow, but that did not stop him from being genial while signaling to Jimmy for a menu.

"The food here is terrific, Dora" he said.

"I've had my dinner at the dorm, Satish. But you can go ahead; I'll just watch you eat," she said, smiling.

"Oh no, you've got to have something," he insisted as he handed over the menu. "I am sure you still have some room for good food."

Dora peered through her glasses that had slipped down the bridge of her nose, as if she had bifocals, and asked him if she could have some spring rolls. He added cashew chicken as an entrée, and Jimmy rushed to the kitchen to fill the order. He came back with a glass of Thai iced coffee, placed it in front of Dora and said, "Hot day. This will cool you. On the house. Enjoy."

Dora had never seen a Thai iced coffee before and did not know what to expect. She sampled it through a straw, and got a shot of strong coffee, which startled her. She smiled apologetically at her own ignorance, and looked at him for help.

"You have to mix it up first, Dora," he said. "It will taste like a coffee milk shake, only sweeter and stronger."

"Do I get a spoon or do I use the straw?" she asked, slightly amused at her own awkward helplessness at a simple task.

"You can use the straw," he replied.

She stirred the coffee and, with her eyes focused on the drink, she uncomfortably began. "I don't know how to tell you this, but Priya does not want to see you anymore."

Despite having foreseen this as one of the possible scenarios, he was not quite prepared for it. He held his coffee glass with both hands, sipped from it and put it down without taking his eyes away from it.

"I know that it is hard for you to hear this, Satish," she continued, "but Priya is under a lot of pressure at school, and she probably has no idea what she is doing. Maybe in a week or two she'll realize that it was all a big mistake and come back to you."

He shook his head in disagreement. "You know her by now. She'll never do that."

Dora wanted to reach out and console this heartbroken man when Jimmy came to table with a plate of spring rolls.

"Sweet and sour sauce? Peanut sauce?" he asked.

"Yes, Jimmy. Thank you," Satish said. "Please have some, Dora. They are delicious."

As they ate their crispy spring rolls, she explained to him that Priya had been disappointed in his decision to resign from the firm, quickly adding that in her opinion, he did the right thing. She went on to talk about how discrimination had no place in society. He, in his turn, lauded the civil rights struggle of African Americans, without which Indians like him would not have had the opportunities that were now available to them.

As the entrée arrived, he asked for an extra plate for Dora, and they served themselves some jasmine rice and cashew chicken. She seemed pleased with the flavor of the food she had never eaten before, and complimented him on his choice of entrée.

Slowly, she steered the conversation to the principal reason behind the breakup. Priya intended to quit her career path after graduation and become a homemaker, but not in India. Without his green card and his inability to work and stay in the United States legally, she could not imagine a life with him.

Earlier, Priya had told him that she preferred to be a dink (double income, no kids), at least for a few years, and then raise kids while she continued to work. He said that he was unaware of this change in intentions. If Priya had shared her new plans with him, he would have readily accepted them and acted accordingly.

Dora sensed that somewhere in his mind lurked a thought that his green card was more important to Priya than he was. When that thought reached the forefront of his mind, his disappointment was complete. His shoulders collapsed, his head hung low, and he stared at his plate, unwilling to let Dora see the intense cloud of disillusionment that had settled on him. Pardoning himself, he went to the rest room. He came back after he had washed his face of any traces of tears that may have welled up in his eyes.

Dora saw the refreshed face and recognized its significance. Despite every bite of the chicken exposing a bouquet of unexpected but pleasant flavors, her appetite had disappeared. She just stared at the weary man across the table and wondered what she could do to help him. Then she saw his slight smile.

"It is ironic," he said.

"Ironic?" she asked.

"Yes, ironic," He told her that during the very period Priya had decided to go silent on him, he had won his first major victory of his career. He had not lost his green card, he still had his job, he got a significant promotion, and he was going back to work the next day. But his triumph seemed hollow without Priya.

"That stubborn woman did not realize that I did this for her, so that she and I could have a great future in this country. I knew I would win, or why else would I take such a major step? Shoot, if she wasn't there, I would have just left and gone back to India on the next flight. It makes no difference to me where I live, as long as I can have my dignity."

"Did you share this with her?" Dora asked.

"Sure, I did; many times. But she was convinced that I would not win. Speaks volumes of her confidence in me."

"If I call her and tell her all this, will you ask her out again?" Dora asked.

"Maybe I will, maybe I won't. Most probably I won't."

"Why not?"

The blood vessels in his forehead bulged when he said in a steely whisper, "Because she dumped me when I needed her the most. I used to call her the sunshine of my life, and she turned out to be a fair-weather friend."

Without looking up to Dora, he continued, "How can I trust her to be my pillar of support when I go through another bad patch? I need a partner, for better or for worse. If she can abandon me today, she can do it to me again."

Dora listened to this intense man's inconsolable grief take on a tinge of anger. When he rationalized his intention to end the relationship, behind every statement she could sense his ache of regret that Priya would not be part of his life anymore. It was no longer Priya's decision alone, but a mutual one. They both decided to end their relationship for different reasons and at different times.

Slowly, his rational mind began to wear out, and his emotions began to bare themselves. Yes, he told Dora, he was sad, perhaps inconsolable, maybe even devastated by the death of this relationship. He had grown to love the feeling of being in love and caring for someone. It had taken him to heights of unimagined joy. This sudden, unanticipated loss made an equivalent depth of despondency inevitable.

Moved, Dora gradually stretched out her hand, took his forefingers and held them tenderly. Her consoling gesture had a reassuring touch of friendship.

Going Home

Satish was about 30,000 feet above the Arabian Sea, his six-foot frame uncomfortable in the economy class seat of a Boeing 747 that was stingy with leg room. It was eleven PM local time. A boor sitting in the seat behind him had just grabbed the top of his seat for support, vibrating it while raising himself from his seat and awakening him from his deep but disturbed sleep.

Satish was tired, having been on this transcontinental journey from the U.S. to India for almost twenty-four hours. He would have welcomed another fifteen minutes of sleep, but instead he smiled and said, "It's OK," to the apologetic man who had shaken his seat and woken him up. "No problem," he added when the apologies and the seat shaking continued until the perpetrator had squeezed himself from the window seat to the aisle, disturbing every passenger in his vicinity.

Now awakened, he peeked out of the window. He could see nothing beyond the faint blinking of the red lights at the tip of the wing that gave the airplane's silver structure an eerie sense of Christmas and celebration. Just then, the plane's fluorescent lights came on, and instinctively he knew that he was a little over an hour away from Bombay, his home.

Wishing he had not put his sleep mask away, he shut his eyes and tried to anticipate what lay ahead on this two-week vacation in Bombay. His parents, sister, and friends were all going to meet him for the first time in a decade. He looked forward to spending time with them and seeing his friends.

Normally, he would have looked forward to a laid-back, relaxed two weeks of doing nothing. However, since he was now a divorced man, everyone, especially his parents, would be curious and he would have to answer many difficult questions.

Why, after so many years of dating the same woman, had his marriage ended so quickly in divorce? And why had he not remarried so many years later? There would definitely be questions about his preferences in an "arranged marriage." Going through immigration and customs in Bombay would be a breeze compared to the inquisition that lay in store for him when he got home.

Before he could drift off into a reverie, he smelled the mixed aroma of Indian food and spices, so different from the early morning smells of baked goods and eggs on a flight across the Atlantic. This cabin smelled like an Indian restaurant with invisible, low-hanging clouds of pungent spices.

Soon, stewardesses began distributing a happy meal for Indians. Warm, rolled *chapatis* (Indian bread) in aluminum foil, small helpings of spicy vegetables, artificially colored red chicken curry, yellow rice with peas and traces of cilantro, a cup of fruits, and *gulab jamun* (fried milk balls in a sweet syrup). Everything was in Saran-wrapped cups and placed in receptacles on a plastic tray. In the corner of that tray, was an empty cup for tea or coffee.

Satish's neighbor, the poor soul in the middle seat who had to endure a nine-hour flight stuck between two adults, turned to him and asked, "Don't you love the food on this airline?"

Satish smiled and nodded. The middle-seater lunged into his meal, tearing a *chapati*, using each torn piece as an impromptu spoon to pick up some of the vegetables and chicken, and shoveling the combination into his eager mouth.

"I don't need a fork or a spoon," he proudly said, chewing his food with obvious relish. "See, look at the food. They even have lemon pickles, *raita* (yogurt with minced cucumbers and onions), and *supari* (betel nut based digestif). I like this airline's food. It is the best." Satish left his food untouched.

A few minutes later, stewardesses reappeared in two synchronized waves: the first one to collect food trays, and the second to offer tea or coffee.

"Is it Indian tea, you know, *chai*?" said the middle-seater.

"Yes sir," replied the pleasant stewardess, who seemed to be of Indian origin, though her name, Monica, was globally nondenominational. If she was an Indian, she could be a Hindu, or she could be a Catholic, like the majority of Indian Christians.

"See?" said the middle-seater. "That's why I love this airline: good food and Indian tea." Turning to Monica, he said, "This airline has the most beautiful stewardesses in the world!"

She ignored the compliment and asked Satish, "Tea or coffee, sir?"

"Coffee, please," he responded.

"Milk and sugar?" she asked.

"No, thank you," he said.

"So, you like black coffee, huh?" asked his inquisitive neighbor. "You must be from America. They drink coffee without milk or sugar. Of course, American coffee is like water, dark brown water. There is nothing like our South Indian coffee."

Satish smiled and acknowledged the comments. He sipped his coffee, which was dark, strong, and had a definite European flavor to it. It was similar to café au lait from New Orleans, except without the lait. Chickory gave it a nice bitter bite.

While he sipped his coffee, he noticed that the 747 had perceptibly slowed down. The drone of the jets had become a bit subdued, and it felt as if the giant bird was gliding quietly through the dark skies. Peeking out of the window, he saw the lights of the city of his birth slowly emerging on the horizon.

In the distance, Bombay shone like an antique gold necklace laid along the Arabian Sea, its streetlights like strands of dull gold beads, thicker in the middle, tapering off at the ends into unseen threads that would meet at the nape of the neck of a princess.

As the mammoth, droning bird and its exhausted passengers approached this golden city from the west, he saw it go past the sliver of lights to turn around over the Sahyadri Mountains and land from the east against the westerly sea breeze.

He checked his seat belt and brought his seat to the upright position while a hurried stewardess picked up the remnants of trash from passengers. She balanced herself as the plane tilted steeply to make its U-turn for the final approach.

"Good to be home, huh?" asked his co-passenger.

Satish smiled and nodded.

"I went to London on business," the middle-seater volunteered. "We manufacture valves, all kinds. If you need valves, call me," he continued, thrusting a card into his reluctant palm.

"Oh, by the way, my name is Ralph. Ralph D'Souza."

"Satish Sharma. Thank you for your card. I am sorry I don't have a card on me," he said.

"Where are you from, in America?" asked Ralph.

"Texas," he replied, wanting to hold on to the exact location a while, until it was relevant.

"Ah, Texas," said Ralph. "Yes, so you are an Indian from cowboy country, huh?" he chuckled.

Ralph continued, "Texas is a big state for valves, but they always want high-quality valves. We cannot make those. Tolerances are too fine and we get too many rejections. I have to build fifty valves before one passes your quality tests. Very difficult to sell in Texas, but they'll come around some day, when they find that they are paying too much for no improvement in performance."

"Yes," Satish responded, waiting impatiently for that telltale screech, bump, and taxiing that would end this long journey.

Ralph made a sign of the cross and closed his eyes when he heard the familiar rumble of the plane lowering its wheels. He kept his eyes closed till the plane was safely on the ground, had taxied for a few minutes, and stopped at the gate. As soon as the plane came to a standstill with a slight jerk, Ralph's eyes popped open.

"We always have to thank God for everything. It's all God's grace," Ralph said. He got up immediately and began to nudge his way past the passenger in the aisle seat. He turned back to him, smiled, rubbed his oversized stomach, and said, "Someday I would like to eat Texas beef. I heard you have great barbecue."

"The best," replied Satish, beginning to take a liking to this large, friendly Ralph, who reminded him of Ralph Cramden.

"Call me. You have my card. I know this place in Bandra that has the best Goanese food, the best Sarpotel!" Ralph said as he squeezed himself through the crowd in the aisle.

Satish sat in his seat, watching the scene. Slowly the unkempt, uncomfortable, unshaven, unbathed mass began to move a step at a time, with great patience and politeness—allowing passengers in the middle and window seats to merge in, like brooks to a river. When his turn came, he pulled out his briefcase and joined the stream of exiting passengers, extending courtesies to stragglers trapped in their seats, unable to secure their luggage.

As he approached the exit, he got his first whiff of comforting Indian air, cool and humid, with a strong, salty flavor of the nearby sea and a hint of an undesirable aroma that he could not quite place.

Progressing through the corridors, he finally reached the immigration hall and stood in the line marked "Visitors," feeling slightly awkward at first for not being in the Indian Citizens' line. That sense disappeared when he noticed that almost everyone in his line was of Indian origin. He assumed that, like him, they too held passports of other countries.

Moving one slow step at a time, he gradually reached an immigration officer in a brown uniform, who gave him an unsmiling but not quite stern once-over. He rapidly typed on his computer keyboard, stamped and returned his American passport, and waved him on with a nod in the direction of the luggage carousels. Satish said, "Thank you" to the officer, who ignored the courtesy and waved his hand for the next passenger to come forward.

Satish put his passport in his shirt pocket as he walked to the luggage carousel, praying that his bags had arrived with him. A slight man, dressed in civilian clothes with a badge dangling from his shirt pocket asked him in Marathi, "Saheb, do you need help with your bags?"

He answered in chaste Marathi, "No, I don't need help," adding in English, "Thank you."

"No mention," replied the porter in English. He smiled sheepishly and went away.

Satish realized instantly that he had committed his first faux pas in India. He had been spotted as an NRI—a non-resident Indian. He had said "Thank you" in English, a habit only NRIs seemed to possess. Soon every porter and customs officer would know that he was an NRI, a target to make a quick buck. He now needed to be on guard.

When he heard a loud alarm, he went to his assigned luggage carousel and stood there with an empty cart. Soon, an opening with a black curtain of rubber slits began to spit bags onto the back of a creaking, serpentine conveyor belt.

Bag after bag came out. Some fancy designer bags that had been mauled, some hard suitcases with missing wheels, some with ropes tied around them for insurance. There were many almost identical huge, black, soft suitcases, each with a ribbon, rope, name tag, or simply a huge colored letter for easy identification.

He waited and watched as porters and men helped women haul oversized suitcases to waiting carts. Exhausted children stood guard at carts while parents dragged one bag after another to them. He was amazed at the volume and weight of luggage that came out of the bowels of his plane. Ralph was right. It was only because of God's grace that they had arrived safely.

Normally, he survived his travels with carry-on bags; he rarely checked his bags. His trips were short business trips, and he could not afford even the remote possibility of losing his bags. For this trip, he borrowed suitcases from his friend, Indrajit, who traveled every year to India. He loaned him the perfect bags for the trip, deeply discounted black, soft luggage that was discarded after a few round-trips to India.

He now had to pluck out his suitcases, indistinguishable from the hundreds of similar ones that went round and round on the carousel. He hoped that the "Premium Service" suitcase tags from his airline platinum card would be adequate. They were.

Placing his suitcases on his cart, he pushed it in the direction of the green channel, which had a large X-ray machine. His bags emerged from the machine, and as he reloaded them on his cart, a customs officer dressed in white came to him and asked, "You have anything electronics?"

"No," he replied in English.

"What do you have in the bags?" asked the man in white.

His nametag suggested that he was a Maharashtrian, a local, so Satish switched over to Marathi and replied, "It is after ten years that I have come home to see my parents and family. For them, I have brought some clothes, chocolates, and toys for my newborn neighbors. No drinks. Nobody touches alcohol in my family."

"So why did you not tell me that in the first place?" said the customs officer in Marathi. He waved him on with a smile.

Thankful that he had gone through three hurdles—immigration, baggage claim, and customs—without a hitch, he pushed his cart toward the airport exit. Glancing at his watch, he noticed that the whole process had taken less than thirty minutes from the moment his plane had landed. As he grew closer to the exit, he saw an expectant mass, of hundreds of people waving their arms, waiting to greet passengers in the middle of a pleasant, cool January night.

As Satish emerged into the night from the fluorescent hallway of Bombay airport, he was greeted by a sight he had not seen for ten years: hundreds of people behind barricades, with police controlling crowds to keep them from swarming into the facility. Controlling his ill-mannered cart from rolling down the handicap ramp, he turned onto the sidewalk, looking for a familiar face in the crowd.

In the distance, he thought he noticed his brother-in-law, Krishna. His sister had married him a few years after he had left for the U.S. He had seen wedding photographs and had a few telephone conversations with him, but he was not quite sure until he saw his sister's reassuring, beaming face behind her husband.

He waved to them and then proceeded past people holding placards for hotels and private taxis. At the end of the ramp, he merged into the crowd, pushing, shoving, saying, "Excuse me, excuse me." Finally, after making it through the ten-deep crowd, he reached his kin.

"Hi, what took you so long?" asked Lata, his sister.

"The flight was about ten minutes late, but I think I made it out in good time," he replied.

"I am Krishna," said her husband, shaking his hand. "If we wait for your sister to introduce us, we will be senior citizens by then," chided the brother-in-law, almost all in one breath.

"Come, let's go to the car," said Lata. "How was the flight? How was the food? Did you meet any pretty air hostesses?" she continued.

"The flight was fine and plane food is plain food," he replied.

"I heard that your airline has pretty air hostesses. At least, if not food for the stomach, they must have had food for the eyes, huh?" asked Krishna with a laugh. He shrugged off a fleeting thought that Krishna and Ralph were the same person.

"No. I slept most of the way," he replied. "How far is the car?" he asked as they walked past the crowd and crossed the noisy street. It was jammed with honking cars trying to catch the attention of pedestrians who were navigating overloaded luggage carts. They squeezed through narrow gaps with surprising ease.

Satish was astonished how easily his Bombay road sense came back to him. He had no trouble traversing to the parking lot. Realizing that despite the long absence from Bombay his instincts were still intact, he pushed his cart with a sense of aggression that surprised both Lata and Krishna.

"Hey, take it easy," warned Krishna. "You have just come back from America. You may not be used to all this 'hulla-gulla,' the commotion, this chaos, this traffic."

"Yeah," added Lata. "Be careful. These taxiwallas and drivers are different from the ones when you were here. They may hit you and your cart."

"Not to worry. If these bags can handle airline baggage handlers, they can handle Bombay taxis," he said.

After what appeared to be a few close calls, and a few searches in the wrong lanes of the dimly illuminated parking lot, the trio and the uncontrollable cart reached the car. They barely managed to fit the two suitcases in its trunk. The hand luggage was placed in the rear seat.

"Come sit in the front," said Krishna.

"No, no. It's okay. I'll sit at the back. Let Lata sit in the front," he replied.

"See, this is what happens to people when they go to America. They forget that this is India. Men sit in the front, especially special guests. Listen, I spend the whole day with my wife, so I also want a little change, even if it is with her brother," he laughed.

Lata opened the rear door and sat in the back seat, and her brother went to the passenger door, only to discover that there was a steering wheel there!

"We are all right-hand drive, Satish," announced Krishna. "Get used to it. We drive on the left side of the road! It is our British legacy."

Krishna started the car and asked, "You need air-conditioning?"

"No, it's okay," he replied.

"Hey, I need it in the back," piped in Lata, casually asking, "So, are you going to get married on this trip?"

Krishna intervened before Satish could respond. "First things first, Lata. Let him go home, meet his parents, chat with them, and then get a good night's sleep. We can talk tomorrow. He is here for two weeks; what's the hurry?" asked Krishna. He gave a slip of paper to the parking lot attendant, who saluted him.

"Yes, let's wait and talk tomorrow," he said, and settled in his seat. "Nice car," he added. "What brand is it?"

"Maruti," replied Krishna. "Remember Sanjay Gandhi, Indira Gandhi's son? This is his legacy," he added with a laugh. Satish sat back and eased into his seat as his brother-in-law gave a quick update on the Indian economy.

Krishna was an engineer. He had a booming voice that belied his slight build and added to his presence in any situation. His ability to project his voice, his confident air, and his swagger made people either step back or stay put, but rarely come forward in an aggressive manner.

He was the perfect foil for Lata's introverted nature. She rarely spoke, and when she did, it was only after she had carefully weighed the pros and cons of her words. She was petite, barely five feet tall and slim, with what Indians called a wheat complexion, neither fair nor dark by Indian standards.

She dressed carefully, with calculated casualness, making sure that her attire was just appropriate for the occasion. That night, she was in her blue jeans, a dark blue long-sleeved silk shirt, and tennis shoes. Her long hair was tied into a casual bun that seemed to stay put despite the delicate way in which she had tied the knot. Of course, she had to have her traditional *bindi* on her forehead, but with a modern twist—its color matched the color of her shirt.

Krishna, on the other hand, was a natural slob who had not quite outgrown his sophomoric dressing habits. However, Lata's relentless focus on how he looked, especially at work, seemed to have made some difference. He really did not care how he looked, what car he drove, or what clothes he wore. Like a good engineer, he looked for good quality and neat, good lines, but aesthetics and color sense were beyond him. He particularly detested designer products, and thought little of people who preferred them.

Krishna rambled on about the state of the Indian economy and Lata sat quietly in the rear seat as the Maruti pulled out of the airport and made its way to the city.

In the dark night, dimly lit by sodium lights, Satish could see that Bombay and India had changed some. He saw a few large, well-lit, fancy hotels, but surrounding them were shantytowns that almost encroached on the main road. It was almost one AM, yet there were people, mostly men, on the sidewalks. Some were walking; some huddled under their bedsheets in groups, under a streetlight, holding dialectic conversations.

The Maruti then turned south onto the Western Express highway and began to achieve speeds he had never seen before in Bombay. Comfortable with the velocity, he dozed off. He was rudely awakened when the car came to an urgent, screeching halt.

"What happened?" he asked.

"Oh, nothing. There is a huge pothole ahead. I almost forgot about it. In this town, we have to remember where the potholes are if our cars are to survive," laughed Krishna.

The car sped up and Satish closed his eyes again, not from fatigue, but from not wanting to participate in this live video game of barely visible shadows of pedestrians trying to avoid speeding cars and hurtling trucks on the highway. He opened his eyes only after the car had come to a halt at a traffic light and he heard Krishna ask, "Should I take our friend through the scenic route, through Dharavi? Or through Mahim and Shivaji Park?"

"Mahim," was Lata's single-word answer.

Soon the highway terminated and merged into Ghodbunder Road, one of the two main arteries of the city.

"What's this road called now?" he asked.

"Swami Vivekananda Road," said Krishna. "But we call it SV Road for short. I don't know why we come up with such long names. But if we had called it Vivekananda Road, we would have shortened it to VA road, or something with two syllables," he added.

Satish recognized the familiar smell at this juncture, from the fishing village on the right of the causeway that bridged the creek that turned Bombay into an island. A familiar landmark, Mahim Church, soon appeared. He recalled how every Wednesday evening, this busy intersection was clogged with traffic, because of the large number of devout Catholics and people of other faiths who came to seek the blessings of the novena.

He had made a few trips with his mother to this church, and to Mount Mary in Bandra, carrying candles of various shapes that were later lit in a solemn interior.

Within minutes, the car turned on to Tilak Bridge, speeding past the Plaza movie theater with its huge billboards. He could not recognize the movie or the actors on the billboards. He liked Bollywood movies, but had seen very few since he migrated to the U.S.

"So, how are Hindi movies today?" asked Satish.

"What Hindi movies? They are all the same," said Krishna. "Rich girl meets poor boy, father hates poor boy, wants her to marry a rich, good-for-nothing fellow who is doing something nasty with the bad guys who hurt the father when our hero jumps in and saves him. The father relents and gives his daughter's hand in marriage to our lad, but only after giving him a big job in his factory, with a huge chair and desk in an opulent office!"

"Wait," said Lata, not to be outdone. "Don't forget that our hero is actually the long-lost son of another rich guy, who was actually the girl's father's best friend, and had extracted a deathbed promise that their children would be someday married to each other."

"So, the formula has not changed yet?" he asked.

"No, it has not. Except that people like you, NRIs, are the bad guys. In Hindi movies, they return home to India from abroad after picking up all those bad western habits like smoking, drinking, and dancing with strange women at nightclubs. These are not traits of a good Hindi hero. He is a good local boy with a golden heart, and preferably from an Indian village!" said Krishna.

"So people are going to look at me as if I am a villain?" he asked with an incredulous laugh.

"No," said Lata, as the car turned north on Ambedkar Road, another major artery of Bombay. He was less than a minute away from his parents and his home.

"No, no one is going to look at you like a villain. You are a good man, and people will recognize you for what you are. Don't worry about it. First, meet and spend some time with our parents, Amma and Appa. Then we'll meet some girls," she said quietly.

"What? Meet what girls?" asked a shocked Satish as the car stopped on the main road.

"Come. Come," said Krishna. "Let's go in. Your parents have been waiting for a long time for you to come home. There they are, on the balcony upstairs. Can you see them?"

Satish looked up and saw that only his flat had its lights on. The rest of the building was dark; its inhabitants were presumably fast asleep. As he pulled the suitcases out of the trunk of the car, he saw the faint outlines of his mother and father on the balcony that overlooked the street. He waved to them, and they waved back.

Pulling a suitcase with one hand and hand luggage with the other, he paused briefly, opened the squeaky metal gate, and took quick, impatient, but familiar steps to the building. The staircase was dark, but he remembered exactly where the light switch was in the seventy-year-old building's fuse box.

"Hey, don't put your hand there in the dark. It is all 220 volts; you'll die if you get electrocuted," warned Krishna in a near panic-stricken whisper.

"Don't worry. I know where the light switch is," whispered back Satish.

"Krishna, he is the only one in the building besides the caretaker who knows where this switch is. He can find it with his eyes closed!" said Lata.

Moments later the staircase was lit up and the three of them began their laborious journey, carrying the heavy suitcases up one floor. Satish had no problem carrying his load. He took two steps at a time, as he had for over twenty-two years up and down these stairs. His ascent was effortless due to his excitement of being home and the help of a little adrenaline. He paused briefly at an intermediate landing to see if Krishna was handling his share of the load.

"Krishna, leave that suitcase downstairs. Let me drop these at home, and I'll come back for that one," he said in a low voice. He took five double steps and he was standing in front of his home, the light from within creating silhouettes of his parents.

"Come, Satish," said Appa, his father, while Amma, his mother, simply stood nearby and smiled, her hands clutching the ends of her *sari*.

He went in and promptly touched his parents' feet. When he came up and stood in front of them, his mother hugged him. She was speechless, her eyes swelling with tears.

"Why did you take so long to come home?" she asked, expecting no reply.

He realized that he had been gone for a long time. Over the years, his parents had grown smaller, and they appeared to be frail. While they did not show their age, they seemed fragile, like delicate petals of flowers. They walked with slower, measured steps, and their voices were not as strong, with words trickling out rather than flowing.

His father, who had recently retired as a senior accountant at a major Indian conglomerate, was immaculately dressed, as usual. A stark white, long-sleeved *kurta* covered his upper body, and he wore a neat, white, handloom *vayshti* for pajamas. His mother wore a delicate cotton voile *sari* and blouse, old comfortable ones that had been relegated to sleepwear.

"Hey, Satish, where are you?" said a loud voice in this quiet night. "You had to bring up one more suitcase!" Satish quickly turned around to see Krishna on the landing, sweating and in breathless agony. "What do you have in there? Rocks?" Krishna asked, while Lata rescued him and wheeled in the suitcase. Satish shut the front door behind her and sat down on a nearby chair to remove his shoes. Krishna and Lata followed.

"Don't go around in your bare feet; it's too dusty here. Here, I got your favorite rubber sandals for you to wear at home," said his mother as she gave him a pair of new yet very familiar flip flops with blue straps, the type he had worn for all those years in Bombay.

These had been his constant, preferred footwear, and he had taken a couple of pairs with him to the U.S. when he had departed for graduate studies. However, these did not last more than four years. Year after expectant year he had hoped to make a trip home but could not. It seemed silly to request a pair of flip flops in the regular care packages that came from Bombay, carried by obliging friends and relatives. For years he had missed wearing them. Now, sitting at the entrance hallway of his home, he was glad to see another pair.

He slipped them on. They were instantly familiar and reassuring.

Satish picked up the suitcases in the passage and asked, "Where should I put these?" There were only two choices, the bedroom or the living room, also called the hall. The third room in this small, eight hundred square-feet flat was a kitchen.

"Put them in the hall. That's where you are going to sleep. It has an air-conditioner. You might want it," said his mother.

"Amma, it is about sixty degrees now. It is comfortable. I don't need an air-conditioner," he said.

"Then you can sleep in the bedroom if it is too noisy for you being on the main road," continued his mother.

"It's okay, Amma. I am too tired for the noise to disturb my sleep," he said as he carried the suitcases to the hall. He placed the suitcases in a corner and said, "Can you give me a towel? I need to wash my face."

Krishna, Lata, and his parents made themselves comfortable in the living room as he went to the sink to wash his face. It was tinier than he had imagined.

It was the same old sink. He had some difficulty cupping his hands in it to collect enough water to splash on his face to refresh himself. Nevertheless, he was thankful for running water; that dribble would have seemed substantial just ten years earlier when there was a permanent water shortage.

Drying himself with a thin cotton towel that had amazing absorbency, he went back to the hall to discover that it was empty. Everyone had moved to the kitchen. They were seated around a dining table.

In the far corner of the kitchen was a bookshelf-like structure laminated to match the dining table. On the shelves were miniature figurines and framed pictures of various deities and enlightened men, including the picture of Shirdi Sai Baba he had brought home many years ago. The pictures on the shelves were small compared to the large prints of Raja Ravi Varma's spiritual paintings that adorned the walls.

All icons had the golden-yellow markings of dried sandalwood paste and red, powdered *kumkum* that Hindu women wore on their foreheads. A faint smell of *agarbatti* (incense) was in the air, but also a stronger aroma that he recognized as that of his mother's cooking.

"Sit. Have something to eat. I have made some *rasam* and some French beans *poriyal* (stir fried vegetables)," Amma said as she placed a stainless steel plate in front of him.

"With coconut?" he asked joyfully.

"Yes, yes. It's with coconut. You know we stopped using coconut after Appa had his heart attack. So I don't know how it will taste," said Amma.

"So, all this special cooking is for your son only. Here I am, your son-in-law, coming and eating in your home for all these years, and not once have I had beans *poriyal* with coconut. Now your son comes here and you make some. Amma, you always say that I am like a son to you. Then how come you don't make beans *poriyal* with coconut for me too?" teased Krishna.

"Come, come. I have made enough for you too," said Amma as she placed another plate in front of him.

Lata added, "But first go wash your hands."

"My God, her brother comes to town and suddenly my wife is giving me orders," said Krishna, shaking his head in disbelief as he went to the sink.

"I hope he's not upset," said Amma.

"No. No. He's fine. He's just joking. You know how he is. He is always like that. Never talking seriously," Lata said.

Satish rolled up his sleeves and waited expectantly to be served.

"What, have you forgotten how to serve yourself? Remember, never put rice on an empty plate. It's a bad omen. Here, start with some *poriyal*," said Lata as she put a large spoonful of sautéed beans on his plate.

"Enough. Enough!" he protested, instinctively placing his inverted right palm between his plate and the serving spoon.

"If he doesn't want it, you can give it to me," said Krishna as he sat down to eat. "What, are you not going to join us?" he asked his in-laws and his wife.

"No," said Appa. "We cannot eat now. It's almost two o'clock, and we have to wake up in a few hours."

"How about you? You must be hungry?" Krishna asked his wife.

"No, I am not hungry. You eat. I am fine," she said, serving him some *poriyal* and following it with a serving of rice.

"Where's the *karandi* (serving spoon) for the *rasam*?" she asked. She found it on top of the stainless steel plate that covered the *rasam* vessel. When she removed the cover, Satish could see the memorable brownish-red liquid with cilantro leaves and a few tiny mustard seeds floating on the top. Mild steam, loaded with spicy aromas, escaped the pot and reached him. Yes, this was his mother's *rasam*, and he looked forward to consuming it after all these years.

"Do you want just the light top layer, or all mixed up?" asked Lata.

"Mix it up. I think I can handle the heat. I still eat spicy food in Houston. We have jalapenos, cayenne and serrano peppers, and habaneros, which are the hottest chilies you can find," he said.

Lata gently stirred the pot and poured a ladleful of *rasam* on the white mass of rice that Satish had mashed with his fingertips. The mix first turned a reddish-yellow from the entrapped turmeric and the boiled blonde lentils of the solution, while a stream of unencumbered brownish-red liquid, colored by tamarind, tomatoes, and spices in the *rasam* powder lightly flowed out to test the boundaries of the plate, encountering a green mound of beans *poriyal* at the periphery.

"What, you don't need a spoon?" kidded Krishna. "I thought you foreign-returned people always ate with forks, spoons, knives, and chopsticks."

"No. I don't need a spoon. Besides, you can't eat *rasam*-rice with chopsticks, especially on this flat plate. Maybe in a bowl," he said. He continued the pleasurable task of using the bottom edge of his right palm as a squeegee to stop the *rasam* from migrating too far, bringing the dispersing fluid back to the mass of rice that was becoming increasingly absorbent.

"Just a little more, please," he said. He continued until the mixture was just right—rice saturated with *rasam* and its lentils, with pieces of sliced tomatoes, cilantro leaves, and lentils captured by the rice. Some fluid flowed past its boundaries, but nowhere near the domain of the beans *poriyal*.

With the tips of his fingers, he mixed a few pieces of the stir-fried French beans and coconut with the rice and rasam. With one swift move, he picked up a portion of the runny mass, and deftly placed it on his four forefingers, drawn together to create a spoon. Quickly, before the liquid could drain out from the cracks between his fingers, he used his thumb to gently push the mass into his mouth, noiselessly sucking in the accompanying liquid. He instantly brought his fingers down to the plate to avoid any remnant rasam on his fingers from trickling onto his palm.

Flavors exploded in his mouth. Behind the sharp, piquant sensations were others: mildly salty, gently sour, and countless spices, all slightly neutralized by the bland rice and lentils and the distant sweetness of beans and freshly grated coconut.

Ten years in Houston, Texas, and despite his encounters with local peppers, his tongue was still sensitive. He could sense a gush of forgotten flavors overcoming his mouth, instantaneously reactivating his dormant taste buds. His tear glands and sinuses instantly awoke!

"Water," he cried, and his mother quickly brought him a glass of cold water.

"I've boiled the water, and there is a separate bottle for you in the fridge. We use only aqua guard, but we don't want to take any risk with you. After all, you are here only for two weeks," she explained.

"Is it too hot for you?" asked Krishna.

"I think I ate a red chili," he said.

"Do you want some *appalam* (large South Indian flatbread chips)? I can fry some for you," volunteered his mother. "We don't fry too much nowadays because of Appa's heart," she added.

"It's okay. I can manage. Do you have some *ghee* (clarified butter)?" he asked.

"Yes, let me look for it," said his mother. She went to the pantry to fetch it. She came back with an apologetic look and said, "There is very little, and it's all solid because of the cold weather. Do you want me to heat it?"

"No, the *rasam* and rice are hot. That will melt the *ghee* anyway," he replied.

Turning to Krishna, who was busily engrossed in his food, he asked, "Krishna, do you want some *ghee* in your *rasam* rice?"

"What, add *ghee* and spoil the taste of this fabulous *rasam*? I tell you, you have lost your mind. How can you add ghee to *rasam*?" he exclaimed.

Satish added a tiny spoonful of *ghee*, and while it rapidly melted in the hot concoction on his plate, he mixed it and took another bite.

"Better?" asked Lata.

"Yes," he said, smiling. "This is terrific. I did not realize how much I missed this *rasam*, and the beans *poriyal*, of course."

He finished his portion.

When Lata reached out to serve him more rice, he said, "No. No more. Thanks. That's it for me. I just wanted *rasam* and rice. Nothing more."

"What, is that all you are going to eat? How about rice and yogurt? I have some good *aavakai*, mango pickles that you like," his mother said.

"No, that's it. I ate on the plane one hour before we landed, and this is enough," he lied. "I'll have a better appetite tomorrow."

"Okay. I'll keep all this in the fridge. You must finish it tomorrow for lunch. You know we don't waste food," said his thrifty mother.

"When you've made such especially tasty food, how can it go to waste, Amma?" he asked as he picked up the plate and took it the kitchen sink to rinse it and wash his hands.

"Just rinse it. Pandu will come tomorrow morning to wash the utensils," Amma said.

"Who wants *chai*? I am going to make some for me," chimed Lata. "Amma, you sit down and talk with your son. I'll make the tea."

"I'll have some," said Krishna and Satish in chorus.

"No, you cannot have any," Lata said to her husband. Then, addressing her brother, she said, "If he has tea at five o'clock in the evening, he cannot sleep all night and has trouble waking up in the morning. And he wants tea now! You'll be up all night and all day tomorrow if you drink *chai* now."

"Does she know how to make tea?" Satish asked in jest to Krishna.

"The best," said Krishna. "It is even better than your mother's. I have trained her to make it right," he retorted.

"When I left for the U.S., she was such a spoiled kid. Knew nothing about cooking or where anything was in the kitchen. Could not even make *chai*," he said. "And now look, she volunteered to make some."

"Marriage is a miracle worker, my friend," said Krishna. "She had to learn everything fast. She was on the phone to her mother every day at least five times, asking for recipes!"

"Talking about marriage, what happened to your marriage? Why did you get divorced?" his father asked. Satish knew from the tone of the voice that it was now time for some serious talk; his father had just ended the casual, good-humored banter.

"We were all wondering when you called to give us the news. Why did this marriage fail? She was such a good girl," said his mother sympathetically. "Satish, if you don't want to talk about it now, it's okay. We can talk tomorrow morning."

"Yes," said Krishna. "If you are uncomfortable talking in front of me, you can do it later with just your parents. After all, you just met me."

"No, it's okay. Let's talk about it right now and get it out of the way," he said. He paused, took a breath, and, looking down at the table, said, "My marriage failed because our differences were too much."

"But that happens in all marriages. Marriage is all about adjustment and compromises. As they say in Bangalore, '*Solpa Adjust Maadi*.' Adjust a little," said his father.

"Yes, Appa," he replied softly, not wanting to seem argumentative to his father. "But the key word is 'solpa,' a little. But you cannot adjust values, can you? When the differences go beyond a limit, one has to stop, take a stand, and let go if necessary."

Lata brought him a hot cup of tea. He looked up at her, smiled, and said, "Thanks." Lata smiled back, recognizing that this moment was a difficult one for her strong brother, who had never seemed so vulnerable.

"What happened, Satish?" she asked.

He looked at his piping hot tea and fiddled with his mug for a moment, and then took a sip. "Hey, this is good tea, Lata," he said. Krishna sipped at his tea quietly, looking at his cup, not wanting to catch Satish's eye, while Lata excused herself and left the room.

"What happened, Satish?" asked his mother. "All you've told us since you telephoned to give us this news was, I don't remember the exact words, but something like 'not working out.' What does that mean?" asked Amma.

"The marriage did not work out, Amma, meaning it failed and died. We did not see ourselves living with each other for the rest of our lives," he said.

"But why?" asked Appa.

"Appa, it is too complicated to explain and, honestly, I am a little too tired to tell you all the events that led to the reasons for the break-up. After four years, they all seem so irrelevant. Slowly, year after year, the bad memories fade away and the good ones remain. All that remains now is the fact that my marriage did not work out. I really don't want to rake up those memories."

"But people will ask, won't they?" said his mother.

"Yes, they will ask, and they have asked. I have the same answer for them. She was my wife. We are now divorced. Why we split is our business, no one else's," he said. He paused and took a sip of his tea, hoping that he had not, in the heat of the moment, impolitely conveyed to his parents to stay off his turf.

He continued in a softer voice, "Amma, Appa, she is a good woman. I think I am a good man. She will make someone else a good wife, and I will make someone else a good husband, but we were not made for each other.

"We were blinded by each other. We were first attracted to each other by our similarities, and then we were addicted to each other. However, our similarities became trivial; they were on the surface. We liked the same movies, the same songs and arts, the same food, but we differed so much at a deeper level."

As he paused and sipped at his tea, he wondered if he should tell his traditional Indian parents that when his career did not comply with Priya's expectations of a rocket-like trajectory into the stratosphere, she slowly fell out of love with him. He should have recognized the signs early on, when she left him twice before they were married.

The first time, she dumped him when he resigned and confronted his firm for its discriminatory practices and was on the verge of losing his green card. They reconciled soon thereafter. The second time was when she felt that his career was going nowhere, and that she would have to work to support her preferred lifestyle. They reconciled again and got married to forge stronger ties.

The third and final time, she left him after her visiting mother, unimpressed with Satish and his career, reinforced her daughter's suspicions. She told her that if she intended to leave him, she should do so before she had a child by him.

"Amma, Appa, she was a good daughter-in-law to you. Lata, she loved you like a sister. Why do you all want to take all those happy, thoughtful moments and actions and muddy them with what happened between the two of us? You had good memories of her and our marriage. Keep those, even though the marriage is dead!"

His parents had not expected this response. Krishna was stunned into silence. Lata, on the other hand, knew her brother well and was pleased with his idealistic answer.

"I understand what you're saying, Satish," said his father. "Let bygones be bygones. I like that. It is important to think and act that way to start afresh, to turn a new leaf."

"Oh, you men are all alike," said Amma. "It's always a game. If someone breaks a rule, you give a penalty or a fine and quickly continue the game. Forgive and forget the mistake, the penalty, and move on."

Krishna, sensing familiar turf, jumped in. "Yes, Amma, it is a game. If someone trips me once during a game of football—soccer to you, Satish—and the referee does not penalize him, then I forgive that player if it was not intentional. But if he does it again, just because I am smaller than the other players, then I make sure that he does it no more.

"I am sure something like that had happened in the marriage. His partner turned into an opponent, and hurt him once too often. So they left the game," surmised Krishna. "Yes, Amma, it is all a game, but the important thing is for Satish to get back into it, not stay out just because he lost."

"I don't think I lost. The marriage and the companionship were great when we were on the same side. It was wonderful, but then it had its sorry side, too," he said politely.

"Enough talking about the past," declared Appa. "Let's talk about the present and the future. I am sure you've learned some lessons here. Let me ask you this point-blank: Do you want to get married again?"

"Yes, Appa," he replied.

"Good. So, let's focus on that," said Krishna.

"See, I told you he would say yes," Lata announced to everyone. "That's why I placed some ads in *The Times of India* matrimonial column." Turning to her brother, she added, "I got so many replies."

"What? Yes, I am interested in getting married, but I did not say I wanted to get married on this trip!" he protested.

"What are you waiting for? It's been three years since your divorce and you're still single. You are not getting any younger. Do you have a girlfriend in Houston you want to get married to?" asked Krishna.

"No, no," he replied, glancing at this mother. "No girlfriends. No one even on the horizon."

"What happened to all those girls that your friends recommended in the U.S.?" asked Amma.

"Amma, these are women, not girls, though you see them that way," he kidded with his mother. "Nothing came out of them. It was always the same story. First, they were divorced women, and, yes, there were two widows. All of them had the same story. Each was married to a horrid man who was a philanderer or beat her. Or, in the case of one of the widows, the husband came home one day and shot himself in the presence of his wife and child!"

"What?" Lata asked, echoing every listener's response.

"Yes, he came home one day, pulled out a gun, and shot himself. No explanations, nothing. The wife is a doctor. They had wonderful one-year-old child, and this woman is still in a state of shock. She is not yet ready for remarriage, but her friends forced her to meet me.

"The others were the same. They were walking wounded, whose concept of marriage was tainted by their recent experiences. Besides, I was not about to trust my own judgment in selecting another partner. For all the failure analyses I do at work, I could not predict the failure of my own marriage. My judgment was flawed. I made a blunder."

"I like that," said Krishna. "I like that attitude. When something fails, analyze it so that it does not happen again. So, what are you going to do different this time?"

"I am going to rely on the old fashioned way—an arranged marriage. I am going to depend on all of you and my Bombay friends to help me in my choice," he replied. After a pause, with a smile creeping up the edges of his mouth, he added, "That way, if this marriage fails too, I can blame it on all of you!"

"Hey, I have a few women who would like to meet you. I have talked to them and they all seem nice on the phone," said Lata. "I even have photographs for all of them. Do you want to see them?"

"Satish, before you see any woman, I have some advice for you—make sure that she can cook!" Krishna interjected. "After the physical attraction vanishes, it's her cooking that keeps the marriage together. A hungry husband is an angry husband!"

"But then how did you marry Lata?" he asked. "She did not know how to cook when you married her."

"Yes, but Lata had a mother in the same town who was an excellent cook. She used to send us *tiffin carriers* (steel boxes for light lunches) full of food every day till Lata learned the art. She learned fast, and I think today we have a happy marriage," Krishna said.

As an afterthought he added, "Don't you think so, Lata?"

"Yes, we have a happy marriage," Lata agreed. "Krishna has this habit of analyzing everything. So if he has reached this conclusion, it means that he has thought about it for some time. Okay, let's look for someone who can cook."

"Anything else I should look for?" Satish asked, amused. "What cuisine should I be looking for? Telugu, Tamil, Kannada, Gujarati, Marathi, Punjabi, Moghlai? There are so many in India."

"Vegetarian," piped in his mother. "Do you still eat beef and meat and fish?"

"Yes, Amma, but I try to keep it to a minimum. I eat mostly vegetarian food at home," he said, turning to his father. When he was in high school, his father was very displeased with him when he told him that he had eaten meat at his Parsi friend Jimmy's home and he had enjoyed it a lot.

His mother was more understanding and had said, "It's okay. God knows where he will have to go in his life. He will have to eat whatever is available there. Besides, you need the protein."

"Please try to be vegetarian now. You get all our groceries and spices in Houston. Why do you need to eat meat?" she asked.

"Because, Amma, I do not eat at home all the time, and those Indian restaurants serve only Moghlai food that is heavy with cream and floating in oil," he replied.

Krishna interjected, "Why is it that every time we Indians get together the topic always comes to food?

"I said that you need to make sure that the woman can cook, and suddenly we are talking about food—not women, and certainly not Satish. Amma, he leads a very different life there. Texas beef is one of the best in world. Your son has good taste."

"Whatever you say, Krishna, this time I want him to marry a girl who is a vegetarian—a *Saatvic* girl. Not *Rajasic*, not *Tamasic*." announced Amma, with a tone and vigor in her voice that all at the table were so familiar with. She used it when she wanted to get her way.

Satish, Krishna, and Lata looked puzzled. They had not heard these terms before. Sensing this, Appa said, "*Rajasic, Tamasic* and *Saatvic* are the three states of a human being. The simple explanation is, *Rajasic* is a hyperactive state, *Tamasic* is an extremely lazy state, and *Saatvic* is just right, balanced. The reason why Amma wants a vegetarian daughter-in-law is because you will find that *Saatvic* people eat *Saatvic* food, vegetarian food."

"Okay, Appa. Sounds good. But how do I recognize one?" he asked.

"That's easy," said Amma. "You can see from her family, food, and friends whether or not she is *Saatvic*."

Appa volunteered, "I will make a list of attributes for you, if you want." He was fond of and good at making lists of helpful hints.

"Okay, Appa," he said.

Lata asked, "I have photos of six women for you to see. Do you want to see them now?"

Before he could respond, Krishna got up from the seat and said, "Listen, I have to go the plant at six-thirty in the morning, and I want at least a few hours of sleep. Lata, why don't you leave behind the pictures and he can see them at his leisure? Let's go."

As soon as the son-in-law got up, so did all the other people at the table, out of deference that Krishna abhorred.

"Sit. Sit. Why are all of you getting up? Only Lata and I are leaving. You all sit and talk some more."

Turning to his brother-in-law and shaking his hand while simultaneously patting him on the back, he said, "I'll see you tomorrow evening, but Lata will be here in the morning. Don't worry; everything will be all right. We'll find a good girl for you. We are all miserable in marriage, why should you alone be single and happy?" he joked as he left for the passage to get his shoes.

"Hey, do you want to come down and switch off the staircase light?" Krishna asked him.

"Sure," said Satish. He walked out with them, down the stairs and past the gate, to their car. His sister and brother-in-law looked up to the front balcony and waved to his parents.

"Bye," said Krishna as he got into the car.

"Bye. See you later," he said.

"Don't worry, everything will be fine. You are still a hero, not a Hindi movie villain!" reassured his sister. "Good night."

As the car speeded away, Satish stood and waved at it for some time. Then he turned back, walked past the gate, closed it, switched off the staircase light, and made it to his front door in quick bounds.

Sliding sideward past the half-open door that was the entrance to his flat, he turned around, shut it, and secured its six latches. He went into the kitchen, where his mother was clearing up the last remnants of the late dinner.

"Can I help?" he asked.

"No. No. You go ahead and go to sleep. And sleep as late as you want. I will ask Pandu to clean that room later in the day."

"Okay, Amma, I am going to sleep. Where's Appa?"

"Oh, Appa went to bed as soon as Lata got into her car. He was very tired. He must be fast asleep now."

"Okay, Amma. Good night," he said as he gave her a warm hug.

"Goodnight, *Kanna*. Go to sleep" she said.

She had an afterthought. As if in a conspiracy, she said in a whisper, "I have seen this girl. She will be a good wife for you. She is a vegetarian. Do you remember Appa's friend Dr. Sastri, from Chembur?"

"Do you mean the one who married a Catholic woman?" Satish asked.

"Yes. Unfortunately, about three years ago, Angel—Mrs. Sastri—died of a heart attack."

"I am so sorry to hear that. She was such a sweet woman," he said.

He had liked Mrs. Sastri and had been somewhat close to her. She reminded him of one of his favorite teachers at school. As a child, he loved going to her place in Chembur, especially during Christmas, when she made her delicious cake and entertained him with her stories about her childhood Christmases in Goa. But he had not seen the family for almost eighteen years, since his high school days, when he had divorced himself from his parents' friends and spent time with his own.

"The reason I brought it up is because they have a daughter, Mona. You remember her?"

"It's been so long, Amma. I remember nothing except that she was a pest and kept bothering and teasing me and running to you for protection. But if you and Appa like her, that's fine by me," he responded quickly.

His mother continued, "Poor girl is a widow. She lost her husband in a motorcycle accident a few years ago."

He was glad to see that his mother had not lost her balanced touch of simultaneously being a traditionalist and a radical. He was confident that his mother had investigated all aspects and facets quite thoroughly before coming up with a recommendation for her son. But Amma was surprised at her son's immediate consent. That was so unlike him.

She stepped back and said, "No, first you meet her and see if you like her. Go to a nice restaurant. Go to the Taj, to Sea Lounge, and talk with her there. See for yourself. If that's okay, then we will go and meet her father. Remember, she has to like you too!" She smiled and added, "I think she will like my little *Kanna*. I think the two of you will be happy together and have a good family."

"Okay, Amma," said the tired, drained son.

"What do you want for breakfast?" she asked.

"Amma, go get some sleep. We'll talk about breakfast in the morning," he chided. He made his way to the hall, switching off the kitchen light behind him.

He went to the hall, switched on the fluorescent light, and opened his hand luggage, where he had packed his pajamas, just in case the airline lost his checked baggage. After a quick change, he switched off the fluorescent light and lay down on his familiar bed, the one he had used for decades.

As he covered himself with a light cotton sheet, he realized that he was uncomfortably warm. He went to the bank of switches and turned on the ceiling fan, which instantly came on with full power, creating a mild hurricane in the room. He turned it down to a soft breeze setting, went back to bed, and lay down.

As his eyes acclimated to the darkness, he noticed that the sodium streetlights of Ambedkar Road gave the room a dull, dusk-like glow. He saw the hypnotic, slow-moving blades of the old ceiling fan, a gift from his grandparents to his parents on his birth. The night was quiet, unusually quiet, and he could hear the tick-tock of the eighty-year-old clock that hung on the wall below the unlit fluorescent light.

For decades, these two, the fan and the clock, sang rhythmic, mechanical lullabies to him. This night, after another decade, was no different. Mesmerized by these old companions, he sank into a deep, welcome sleep.

Bride Hunting in Bombay

When Satish woke up on his first day in Bombay, his sister, Lata, was already at their parents' home, organized and prepared to discuss women who had responded to her matrimonial advertisements in local papers. By the time he had his first cup of tea and some *idlis* for breakfast, she had showed him pictures and resumes of the six women who she had chosen for him to meet over the next two weeks.

Each one was from a different state of India. Each one had a different linguistic and cultural background with a common element—they belonged to the same economic strata as his parents. The fathers were all senior managers employed in private enterprises, and most mothers were homemakers. Most of the women had siblings; one did not. Without a doubt, all parents were anxious to get their daughters married to someone who had permanent residency in the U.S.

In his eyes, all women were pretty. "There is something beautiful about every woman," he used to say to his friends when they made snide remarks about a woman's looks. "It's in your mind. All you have to do is focus on her beautiful attribute, and the rest will disappear." He had a generous perspective about women's looks, and he was often teased by his buddies that, since he did not care about how a woman looked, he would marry an unattractive one.

He had learned the hard way that there was a fine balance between modesty and narcissism, and he chose to stay away from beautiful women, who did not know how to tip the balance in favor of humility. He also shied away from those whose self-perceptions were exaggerated. The six women under consideration were pretty, gracious, modest, and polite.

He met all of them for lunch or tea, because his evenings were taken up with dinner invitations from his IIT friends, who had not seen him for a decade. There were spouses and children to meet, and friendships to be reenergized.

He met the women at a restaurant in the Taj Mahal Hotel or at the Oberoi in south Bombay. Almost all of them brought along either a father or an uncle as a chaperone and, sometimes, a sister. There were no brothers in these discussions. He went with his sister, Lata, his parents preferring to stay out of the first meeting.

Satish made reservations at these elegant restaurants and made sure that they occupied a quiet corner. After the first visit to a restaurant, the maitre d' recognized his name and knew exactly which table to set aside for him. These restaurants were common matrimonial meeting grounds, and the staff was sensitive about interrupting the proceedings. He always paid the check.

Lata had the initial discussions with the family and set up the meetings. The first time Satish spoke to a woman was in person, but it was only after the guardian had talked at the beginning, asking questions about him and his family, attempting to see if there were any common links that could possibly connect the families. Then came the delicate phase where polite questions were asked about his failed marriage and his divorce.

In one instance, when the queries came close to being an inquisition, the woman stopped her father politely and suggested that she wanted to have a word with Satish alone. She apologized for her father's behavior, but Satish's mind was made up. The father reminded him of his former mother-in-law and he was reluctant to marry into that family.

At every meeting, after they finished understanding each other's family backgrounds, he and the woman were left alone. He suggested to his prospective wife that they go for a walk along the Gateway of India or Marine Drive. All except one preferred to stay and talk at the restaurant. Later, Lata shared with him that the women did not want to mess up their hair in the strong breeze from the sea, nor did they want seen in public alone with a man.

Every chaperone volunteered information about their wards. They talked about their educational backgrounds. According to the accompanying elders, all were top students, educated at English medium schools and colleges, with exemplary culinary skills. All women he talked with were professionals, and each of them held an executive position in a multinational company, a bank, or a major Indian corporation. Their resumes seemed perfect.

He wondered why the families were so keen in talking to a flawed man who was divorced. Folklore in India was rampant with stories and urban legends about how Indians who go abroad had lower moral standards than the puritan standards that the local males seemed to possess. Each family's first choice would have been to pick a never-married bachelor rather than a divorced one like him.

So what was the catch? What was the flaw that made the families lessen their standards? Lata was too polite to ask these questions, and so was he, in the presence of the families. Their guess was that the lure of America was a great equalizer.

At times, the guardians volunteered their wards' limitations, and during the initial conversations on the phone, Lata always shared that her brother had been married before and had been single for four years.

All except one had been married before, and had divorced their husbands for various reasons—inability to consummate the marriage, infidelity, and mental cruelty. None volunteered information about physical abuse.

He was sympathetic to the individual tragedies that each one had been through, and his sister warned him about marrying someone out of pity. "You'll suffer again if you marry the wrong person for the wrong reason," cautioned his younger sibling.

After an hour of private conversation, the siblings thanked the families and the woman. He, prone to introspection, did not speak till they were in a taxi headed home. Lata, unable to stand the growing suspense, would ask, "So, what did you think of her?"

Usually his answer was, "I don't think she is the right one," except in the case of Kripa, when he said, "I'd like to meet her again."

Two days before his scheduled departure from Bombay, Satish met Kripa over lunch on a workday. She came alone and was amazed to see that Lata had tagged along with her brother. However, Kripa did not let her surprise show and was courteous to her. The three-way conversation was delightful. She was charming and, at first blush, both he and Lata liked her.

She was a Bombayite, and her ancestors came from many parts of India; her mother was from the south, and her father from the east. She was tall, dark, and handsome in a very feminine way, with pretty features on spotless, unblemished skin that showed no makeup except the mascara that highlighted her large eyes. For her first meeting with him, she wore jeans, a colorful top, and elegant high-heeled shoes that matched her purse.

She was a South Bombay cosmopolitan, an only child, and her parents had large families in the city. She seemed to have stronger connections and familiarity with Anglo-American culture than the rest of the women he had met during the week. She had enjoyed her childhood in the city, she loved her parents and they her, and there were no demons lurking in the dark shadows of her mind. She enjoyed her work and spent a good deal of time with her friends.

She was an architect, and worked at a local firm of national repute. She reminded him that she was not an engineer. In an organized, articulate manner, she went on to explain why architecture was different from engineering, segueing into the city's delightful, undiscovered little eating-places, theaters, and used-book and music stores.

They talked about friends and colleagues, and soon discovered that their networks overlapped. Lata made a mental note of them, to remind her brother to talk to them about her. She could see that her brother liked Kripa and, at an appropriate moment, excused herself, saying that she had to visit the hotel's bookstore.

On cue, he suggested they could continue sitting in the restaurant or go for a walk along the seashore, from the Gateway to Colaba. She liked that idea and told Lata, with a sly wink and a disarming smile, that she would bring her brother back in an hour or so.

She was pleasantly open and candid in providing information about herself. She had studied at the JJ School of Architecture and had done a stint at the National Institute of Design in Ahmedabad. There she had met her boyfriend of seven years, who suddenly, when the subject of marriage was broached, left her. They had been living together for more than five years.

She was generous in her perspective about divorced men. "You were stupid to get married to the wrong woman and realized it after you had signed the papers," she joked. "I did not get married, so I don't have the stamp of 'divorced woman' on my forehead. Technically, you and I are the same. We both lived with someone for some time, enjoyed some conjugal bliss, and then the relationship ended. You have a court decree to show for it; I escaped one."

She confessed that she had called up a few friends to see if anyone knew of Satish. His name and year of graduation from IIT provided the coordinates to research and track down contemporaries, who unanimously agreed that he was a decent chap. She did not share the names of people she had talked with, and he did not push her. He confessed that he had made no inquiries about her and, interspersed in her life story, he recounted his own.

"Why don't we meet again soon?" she asked when she noticed that the hour was up. "I have to get back to work. Besides, Lata will be waiting for us."

He would have suggested that they meet that evening, but he did not want to be hasty. He wanted Lata's opinion before taking the next step. He told her he would call her later that afternoon to set a time to meet again. She said, "Bye. See you soon," as she hailed a cab to get back to work.

During the cab ride home, Satish waited for his sister to ask her standard question, and he was ready with a different answer. She shared with him that the two of them would make a good couple, she would like her as a sister-in-law, and she would be a good daughter-in-law to their parents, though she was "more Western than Indian." His parents were pleased to hear about Kripa, especially after Lata shared her opinion.

"Go meet her again, Satish," his mother said. "She was honest with you, and open about her past. Maybe she has changed her ways and learned her lesson."

His father was silent initially, but after his wife's concession he said, "I think her behavior was not the kind we expect in our circles. Living with someone for so long without being married is difficult for us to accept, but these are different times. Satish, if you think she has changed and is sincere and genuine, talk to her again. But be cautious." He heard his father loud and clear.

He called Kripa at work and suggested that they meet again. "Can we meet this evening?" he asked.

"Sure," she said. "How about a place closer to my home in Bandra? I'd love to try this new Goanese restaurant on Hill Road."

Satish arrived early. He was pleased to see the elegant interior of the restaurant, decorated like a Goan village with boats and nets on the ceiling and walls and waiters dressed in typical costumes of different Goanese professions. They were respectful to the roles of priests and nuns; they just went around blessing patrons.

In a remote corner on a stage were two young men with guitars, taking requests from patrons. Their specialty was that they could mimic the original artists in the performance of their songs; all they needed was a few seconds to change into appropriate costumes and wigs.

It was as if he had entered a time warp and was back in his childhood, listening to *Saturday Date* and *Wednesday Choice*, the two late-night hours of western pop music programs on local radio. The only difference was that the acoustics were better than the AM radio he listened to clandestinely and softly at night.

The talented duo was like a live jukebox, with a varied repertoire, singing songs by Jim Reeves, Elvis Presley, Cliff Richard, Buck Owens, the Beatles, Trini Lopez, Neil Diamond, Simon and Garfunkel, Abba, the Village People, John

Denver, Tom Jones, Englebert Humperdinck, Bread, Everly Brothers, Don McLean, Frank Sinatra, and Nancy Sinatra.

The duo sang their songs well, but was nowhere close to the live performances of the original artists. Nevertheless, it was good enough for the audience, who enthusiastically and raucously applauded every number.

He enjoyed the outpouring of nostalgic music, despite the vaudevillian veneer to the act. As the evening progressed, it took on the atmosphere of a country and western bar in Houston, with couples on the dance floor.

Kripa came up to him and apologized for being late, blaming Bombay traffic for her tardiness. He politely stood up and waited till she sat down on a chair that a thoughtful waiter had pulled back.

He noticed that she had refreshed herself. She wore black pants and a dark lavender silk top with a set of matching shoes and a very small purse. Her subtle and subdued makeup was barely visible in the dimly lit restaurant.

He had a delightful evening. "Wine, women, and song," he mused as they clinked glasses of Indian red wine. Satish was unfamiliar with Goanese cuisine, so she took charge. She ordered many dishes so that he could sample and appreciate its range.

Over dinner, she talked about her life as a single working woman in Bombay, with humorous anecdotes about her life with her recent boyfriend and how she had suffered scorn from a majority of her family and friends.

Only after they broke up did she realize how widespread the disdain had been, and how forgiving people were—many who had avoided her for five years began warming up to her again. She said that she had learned her lesson and was not keen on having a relationship outside of a marriage.

He talked about his life in Houston, his work, and volunteered information about his life with Priya, offering no details about the reasons behind the breakup except, "It just didn't work out." He felt guilty about not being forthcoming when she was so obliging with the details of her breakup. He confessed that it had taken him a long time to get over the breakup, but he felt that he was now ready to make a commitment and to begin another chapter in his life.

The past behind them, they moved on to comfortable turf and talked about their aspirations and their expectations in life. They talked for hours, unaware of their noisy surroundings until the duo on the stage began to wind down and, for their last song, asked people in the audience to collect in groups by the Catholic schools they attended.

Almost everyone stood up and so did Satish, who requested Kripa to join him as the restaurant patrons formed different groups. Then the singers asked everyone to join in to sing Carole King's "You've Got a Friend."

Both Satish and Kripa were touched by the warm manner in which their dinner ended. He hailed a cab, dropped her at her nearby apartment, shook hands, and promised her to call the next day. He went home, let himself in without waking up his parents, and went to bed.

"Wake up, sleepyhead!" were the first words he heard the next morning. He woke up with a start to discover Lata looking over him. "Wake up. Tell us what happened. We are all anxiously waiting."

"Go away!" he said.

"Satish, wake up. I am serious. Amma and Appa are waiting for you."

"Okay," he said, and begrudgingly got out of bed.

When he had brushed his teeth and refreshed himself, a fresh cup of tea was waiting for him.

"Have some *upma*," his mother said as she placed an empty plate in front of him. He served himself some of the savory, semolina-based dish that was in a serving bowl on the table. It was like salty grits, except more flavorful and drier. There were spices, chilies, and vegetables such as peas, tomatoes, and onions in it. It was garnished with cilantro leaves.

"Did you like her?" Lata asked, unable to curb her enthusiasm. He could see that his parents were anxious, too. So after he had a consumed a spoonful of the *upma* and taken a sip of tea, he answered, looking down at his plate. "Yes, I liked her a lot, but I don't think she's the right one."

"Why?" asked his father.

"Appa, she is a good, kind, warmhearted woman, but I see her more as a friend than a wife."

"What does that mean?" his mother asked. "I don't understand."

"I can't quite express how I feel. For some reason, I feel that she'll be an excellent friend, but once we cross that line and get married, we will not last together too long. The marriage will be tumultuous and disharmonious."

"I understand," Appa said.

"It's all for the best," Amma said. She asked him to eat his *upma* before it got cold.

"I don't understand, Satish. Can you explain it to me?" Lata asked.

"Sure," he said, "But can I first finish my *upma* and have some tea?"

A few minutes later, while their parents were in the bedroom watching TV, the siblings were on the balcony with teacups in their hands, watching the traffic and uniformed school kids go by.

Lata prompted him that he had a little explaining to do. He confided with his younger sister that in marrying and divorcing Priya, he had lost a very good friend.

"Wives are good friends, but not all women friends can be good wives," he said.

He said that Kripa was very similar to Priya in many ways, and he was not going to make the same mistake twice and lose a friend, if Kripa could be one. As soon as she heard her brother compare Kripa to Priya, she stopped asking him questions. They silently watched the ever-changing scene on the street below.

Unprompted, he continued, "Last night, I finally discovered what these six women were missing and why I felt they were not right for me. Women nurture human life, Lata, and I could not sense a strong nurturing instinct in them."

Lata asked her brother, "Am I good nurturer, Satish?"

"Of course you are," assured her brother, and added in jest, "Look at the way you baby your husband!"

She gave him a mock slap for ribbing her and asked her tea-addicted brother if he needed a refill. When she went to make a fresh batch, he went to the living room to phone Kripa.

"So how did she take it?" Lata asked when he hung up.

"She took it as well as she could, I think. She understood what I said, but it took some explaining to tell her that I was not judging her past. I told her that was God's business on judgment day, not mine. I even volunteered to meet her again to explain things. She said that it was not necessary to meet, considering that I was leaving for Houston tomorrow and needed to spend time with the family."

"That was nice of her."

"That Kripa is a terrific woman and will someday make someone a great wife, but I don't think she is right for me today. Often, timing is everything," he said, disappointed in the outcome but finding consolation in having done the right thing.

"So, what should we do now? Do you want me to call anyone else?"

"No, I think I've met enough women on this trip. I think I am going to go around town, do some shopping, and generally hang loose," he said.

"Do you want the car? It's air-conditioned, and Bikram, the driver, is here, too," she volunteered.

Despite her brother's reluctance, she told him that she was going to leave her car behind for his use till about ten PM, when the driver had to go to the airport to pick up Krishna, who was on a business trip.

For the next two hours, until lunchtime, Amma, Appa, and their children sat in the bedroom and watched Marathi and Hindi soap operas on TV. Satish found them amusing. During commercial breaks, he caught snippets of CNN and BBC news, which prompted his sister to tease him about "overdramatizing and propaganda" in American news reporting.

After a relaxed lunch, so absent during the past two weeks of bride hunting, he got into the car and asked Bikram to take him to his school. There he visited its church and sat for a few minutes of solace, as he had for almost twelve years of his school life.

He wandered around the old grounds, and instantly recalled the crowds and the excitement when Pope Paul VI visited his school during the Eucharistic Congress in Bombay. He had felt overjoyed and blessed that the pope had passed just two feet away from him. Satish had stood at attention, holding up a Vatican flag, on the papal route around the grounds that were barricaded with bamboo structures to hold back the fervent faithful.

He walked past the new buildings that had cropped up on this vast campus, to the giant banyan tree near the basketball court where he and his friends had gathered every morning before school and after lunch. He entered the secondary section building. When he was stopped by a staff member, he simply said, "Past pupil," and carried on.

He walked through from the back entrance to the front, pausing in front of a Bombay newspaper on a notice board, as he had for five years, to glance at the front page and back page headlines and the daily comic strip of Tarzan. He then left the building.

He requested Bikram to take him to Fanaswadi, in the heart of old Bombay, to the Venkateswara temple that he and his family frequented. After buying offerings for an *abhisekham* (offering), he walked into the temple barefoot.

Stunning seclusion, in the midst of the noisy, crowded city surroundings, greeted him. A bare-chested priest performed a *pooja* to bless him and his family and returned half a broken coconut, a fruit, and some flowers as *prasadam*. The priest gave him some *teertham* (holy water) in his palm. He sipped it, and ran his wet palm over his head. The priest then took a silver crown and placed it on his head to bless him.

Next stop was Kala Ghoda—literally, black horse—so named because a huge black statue of King Edward VIII astride a horse used to grace the area. It was the art district of Bombay, and he enjoyed visiting the art galleries, museums, restaurants, and his favorite music store. He spent hours browsing through an art exhibition at the Jehangir Art Gallery, taking breaks for some tea and *samosas* (fried pyramid shaped stuffed pastries) at its outdoor café.

While the gallery was peaceful and tranquil, the music store was crowded and congested. After a decade of expansive personal space in Houston, he was no longer accustomed to people standing so close to him. He rapidly bought a dozen CDs, charged them to his credit card, and escaped the store.

He told Bikram that he had to make one last stop at a bookstore near Mahalaxmi temple, and asked him to take the scenic route along Marine Drive and Breach Candy.

As he went past the U.S. consulate and saw its huge iron gates, he shuddered as he recalled that early monsoon morning, a decade ago, when he had stood in line for his student visa.

He was now a U.S. citizen, and he felt a perverse pleasure that his tax money now sustained that White House and the staff within.

His stop at the bookstore was short. It was crammed with books and patrons, with little room to maneuver without jostling somebody or knocking over a display of books. In an hour he bought a dozen books, fiction and non-fiction, then ran out of the claustrophobic store to the private space of his car. He asked Bikram to drive him home.

He was now caught in Friday rush-hour traffic, and it took him almost half an hour to traverse Haji Ali. On Fridays, people came in large numbers to pray at the tomb of a Muslim saint who died while on pilgrimage to Mecca. A casket containing his mortal remains floated and came to rest on a rocky bed in the Arabian Sea, where devotees constructed a tomb that could be visited only during low tide.

Thirty minutes later, he was home. He tipped Bikram, collected his purchases and *prasadam*, and released him. After a quick, light meal with his parents, he went to bed and instantly fell asleep.

Morning had not yet broken, but in the faint distance, Satish heard the familiar, pleasant sounds of sparrows chirping, intermingled with the grudging, crunching sounds of BEST buses changing gears as they left nearby bus stops and attempted to accelerate.

He opened his eyes slightly, to see if daylight had seeped through the opaque glass of the shut windows and doors. It was still dark outside, yet the city was already awake. So were his parents. He could hear some activity within his home: water running in the sink, accompanied by vigorous teeth brushing and mouth rinsing. He got out of bed, folded the sheets, and put them and the pillows in a wooden cupboard. When he stepped out of the room into the passage, he saw his mother at the sink.

She turned around and whispered, "Why did you wake up so early? It is only five thirty."

"I will have enough time to sleep on the flight tonight," he whispered back, realizing that his father was still asleep.

"Come, let's have some tea," she said. She went into the kitchen.

He brushed his teeth at the sink, washed and wiped his face, went past the kitchen and unlatched the door to the front balcony. He gave it a slight but deft kick at the bottom to open it.

"You haven't forgotten this house, have you?" asked his mother.

"No, Amma. How can I? This is where I grew up. I know every inch of it," he said. He stretched his hands on the wooden balcony banister and looked up to the slightly blue sky that silhouetted the buildings of Parsee Colony, across the street.

He saw his old friend, the morning star, in the sky of the emerging dawn and realized how much he had missed this familiar sight. For more than ten years, ever since he first learned the nursery rhyme "Twinkle, Twinkle Little Star," he had stared at Venus almost every morning.

As a child, he was enamored by its steady brightness and puzzled that it did not twinkle, as stars did in his poem. Later, when he learned that his heavenly friend was a planet, it became the first object that he sought when he awoke, but as his teenage years progressed, he often awoke late in the morning, when the sun shone bright in the sky.

When he moved to the IIT Bombay campus, and then to the U.S., both with their vast, unhindered views of the night sky, he was too distracted and disoriented to seek out his old friend in the morning sky.

But not this morning. As the sun, hidden first by the distant hills of the Sahyadri and the buildings across the street, began to strip the firmament of its lesser players, Venus persisted. As he softly whispered, "Twinkle, Twinkle Little Star," his mother, a witness to countless renditions and recitations that matured over the years, brought him his cup of tea in a familiar mug. It had the inscription "Houston" on one side, and "Don't Mess with Texas" on the other.

She stood alongside him on the balcony, as she had so often, watching the world go by. She said, "It's so nice to have you at home. Finally."

"Yes, Amma. So am I. It has been a long ten years."

"I don't know when you'll come home again. I wish you had found someone you liked in the last two weeks," she said as she sat down on the stool at the edge of the balcony.

"It was not my time, Amma. Maybe next time. I promise you I will be back next year."

"Next year? Next year you will be one year older, and it will be harder for you to find someone," she complained.

"Yes, Amma. I know. We have a saying in America: 'All the good ones are taken,'" he said.

"I really wished you had liked that girl, Kripa. Lata liked her but I don't know why you felt she was not right for you."

"It was just my intuition, Amma. I cannot put a finger on it and explain to you exactly why I felt that she was not right for me," he replied.

Despite his reluctance to share this with his mother, he blurted out, "She was too much like Priya."

"Why didn't you say that in the first place? That's a good decision. That would have been bad for your marriage," she said in a matter-of-fact tone as she went to the kitchen to make some coffee for Appa, who had just woken up.

Satish volunteered to get some breakfast from their favorite restaurant, Mani's Lunch Home, and overcame his mother's objections, aided by Appa's mischievous tacit approval. "Go ahead. Till you come back from the U.S., this will be the last time I will be able to eat this kind of food. After you leave, I'll have to go back to my no-salt, low-fat diet!"

Amma's disapproval melted and he stepped out of his home for a walk through the tree-lined streets of Hindu Colony, recalling friends and moments of his childhood. He came to the restaurant just as its cashier was completing his morning prayers. He was waving incense fumes and rattling steel shutters to ward off demons and evil eyes while early patrons, senior citizens in shorts and tennis shoes, waited patiently for breakfast and fresh South Indian filter coffee.

He stood outside, acknowledged the cashier's greeting of recognition, and ordered *dosais, idlis,* and *vadas* for the family, anticipating that Lata would come over soon. The cashier, who was a childhood playmate, asked him his whereabouts. When he told him that he was in the U.S. and was returning that night, the cashier called a waiter and asked him give his friend a cup of coffee on the house.

Satish declined, but the cashier insisted. Within seconds, he had two sticky, stainless steel glasses, one with coffee and milk, and the other with sugar. He mixed the two, creating a frothy concoction, and enjoyed the familiar flavored coffee. By the time he was done, the waiter returned with paper packages of his takeout order.

Lata arrived a few minutes after he and his parents were into their breakfast and joined them. She could see that her brother was not depressed with the futile two weeks of bride hunting.

"So, when are you coming again?" she asked.

"In a year," he replied.

"In a year you'll be a year older," she said, sounding like her mother.

"Yes, Einstein, I will be a year older in a year," he countered.

"Next time when you come, I'll do better. I have a good idea about what you like and don't. If I meet someone I like, will you talk to her on the phone before you come?"

"Sure," he said.

"Then I'll start looking right now," she said.

"First, finish your *dosai*. Then you can begin the search," he suggested. He dipped his *dosai* into the fresh coconut *chutney* on his plate and swallowed a generous portion.

"Where's Krishna?" Satish asked, noticing the absence of his brother-in-law.

"Oh, his flight got cancelled last night; he is arriving this morning. He'll go straight to the office for some time, and then come here in the evening to see you," Lata said.

After breakfast they retired to the bedroom to see their parents' favorite show. After a few minutes of watching TV, Satish excused himself and went to the living room to pack his bags. Lata followed him there, curious about what he had purchased the previous day. She was disappointed when she saw that he had only books and CDs to show for his two weeks in Bombay.

"You are boring, Satish," she said. "You do need to get married."

"So my wife can buy interesting things in Bombay when she visits?" he asked.

"Yes," she said, and left the room to rejoin her parents. He packed his bags hastily and joined them, anxious to see CNN and catch the weather forecast for

Houston at the time of his arrival. He was ready to board his flight and return to Houston, his home.

Addressing him, his mother said, "I know you don't like it, but I took your horoscope to a very reliable astrologer, and she told me that the stars were all aligned correctly. She has never been wrong before, especially with your horoscope. Right from birth, she told me that you would have two marriages."

"Not yet, Amma," he said, with a smile. "The second marriage is yet to occur."

"Maybe this is not the right time," Appa said. "When the right time comes along, you'll be happily married. Don't worry about anything. You go back to Houston and let your karma flow."

"Please, can I watch CNN, just for a moment? I want to see the weather forecast in Houston," he asked his father, who held the remote tightly in his hand.

"Wait. This is the interesting part of this episode, where the mother-in-law discovers that the daughter-in-law is going to have a baby, and she is going to be a grandmother," Appa responded.

"What? You are watching a rerun, you know the story, and you won't let me watch CNN?"

"Yes. Amma and I watched it last night, and they repeat it the next day for people who missed it. If the plot is interesting, we see it again. Watch, this is where the mother-in-law comes in," Appa said.

His mother said, "Satish, we don't want you to see CNN because we don't want you to leave. You are physically here, but mentally you are already in Houston. Can you stay with us physically and mentally for at least the rest of your last day here?"

After the episode ended, Appa gave him the remote and said, "Now you can watch CNN." He went with the ladies to the kitchen to prepare for lunch. After his mother's guilt-ridden request, he decided to switch off the TV and join them. It was not a big deal; he could handle any weather Houston had to offer in January.

If he was anxious about leaving town, he did not show it. He joined the rest of the family in the kitchen and began to nervously contribute to setting the table.

"Sit down. You are making everyone nervous," his sister commanded. "Just sit down and eat. You don't have to do anything. Just eat." He sat at his usual place, next to his father, and waited for everyone to join him.

The menu was the same as it was when he had arrived, plus *saambaar*. He realized that he had forgotten to wash his hands. He went to the sink and came back just when his father served everyone samples of the food that was offered to God, when it was first cooked, a few hours ago. He looked out the doorway in the direction of the other balcony to the kitchen and saw that crows were feasting on their lunch, sometimes disturbed by bothersome sparrows.

He watched his father take the first bite from the consecrated food, and then everyone joined in. This was not a proscribed ritual, but everyone waited for Appa to take the first bite. The pecking order was, God first, then ancestors, who were represented by the crows, then Appa, and then the rest at the table.

Just then the doorbell rang, and Satish sprang up from his chair to open the door.

"Why has Pandu come so early?" his mother wondered aloud.

When he opened the door, Satish could see the outlines of a man and woman in the dark passage outside. "Yes?" he asked

The man approached him and said, "Is this Mr. Sharma's house?"

"Yes, it is. Please come in," he said. Leaving the door ajar, he went into the kitchen and announced that a couple had come to see them.

"Who is it?" his father asked him.

"I don't know," he said. "I don't recognize them."

"And you let them in?"

"Yeah, they looked decent," he said, hoping it would be an adequate expla-nation. As a child he was notorious for keeping the door ajar for strangers, who sometimes stole their footwear from the passage.

Just then, a tall, barefoot man with a loud voice entered the kitchen and said, "Hello, Sharma. How are you? Hello, Savitri, how are you?" He sat at the head of the table, close to Appa, in a familiar manner, while Lata and Satish looked on, puzzled.

"Where are you, Sastri?" Appa complained. "I tried to call you for two weeks and nobody answered the phone. So I wrote you a letter."

"Mona and I were in Bangalore. We just came by this morning's flight, and when I checked the post, I saw your letter. We did not even open our bags or have a wash. We came straight here," he said.

"Where's Mona?" Appa asked.

"Oh, I made her sit in the living room. I thought I had come to a stranger's house," he said with a laugh.

"What is this? How can you leave the child sitting there all alone?" Amma said, and left the kitchen to fetch her.

"This is Dr. Sastri, from Chembur. Remember Angel Aunty?" reminded Appa.

"Yes, yes," Satish said as he went over to say hello.

Amma came back with Mona, and when they entered the room, Satish was astonished to see that Mona had grown into a beautiful woman. She wore a smart but simple light green cotton *salwar kameez* (traditional North Indian dress) that complemented her complexion, which was similar to Lata's. Her long black hair was braided, and it curved around her long neck like a dark vine, to rest on the matching *dupatta* (long scarf) thrown carelessly over her shoulder. She looked as if she had taken no pains to look attractive, yet her loveliness shone through.

Lata, who was sitting across from her brother, saw his reaction and kicked his leg under the table. His leg smarted, but he did not show it; he was too enamored by Mona's striking presence.

Instinctively, he stood up and waited till she was seated at the other end of the table from her father, next to him. Amma quickly brought out two more stainless steel plates and placed them in front of their guests. Lata brought out the glasses, and Satish poured water.

"No. No. You were not expecting us; we cannot eat, Savitri. It's okay," Dr. Sastri said.

"Mona, don't listen to your father. There is enough for all of us. Tell me, are you hungry? Would you like to have lunch, my child?" Amma asked in a maternal way.

Mona looked at her father as if asking for permission and said, "Actually, I am very hungry. I did not eat on the plane."

"Okay, okay. Let's eat," said the boisterous man. Both father and daughter went to the sink to wash their hands. When they came back to the table, their plates already had servings of beans *poriyal*, rice and *saambaar*, and a sample of consecrated rice.

"So young man, tell me, ever since you went to high school, you stopped coming to our place," Dr. Sastri said, breaking the ice.

"Yes," he acknowledged shaking his head. "I am sorry about Angel Aunty. She was a wonderful woman. My deepest condolences to you," he said to Dr. Sastri. Then, turning to Mona, he added, "To you too, Mona."

"Thank you," Mona said. "My mother, God bless her soul, was a wonderful woman and we miss her terribly."

"Don't think that way, Mona. We are here for you," Amma consoled her.

"Young man, you went to IIT, did you not? Did you know a Professor Arjun there?" asked the father.

Satish, having gone through six such interrogations about common friends and connections, understood the intent behind the question.

"Yes, I knew him very well. He was my guide and mentor on campus. He has now retired and moved to Madras," he replied, attempting to show the depth of his acquaintance with his teacher.

"He was my classmate at the Indian Institute of Science. I always wondered where he went after he retired," he said. Satish volunteered to give him details.

Lata asked Mona, "Are you working now?"

"I used to work as a stewardess, but the travel was too much, so I just resigned," she said.

"Oh, she enjoys traveling; she resigned so that she could stay here and take care of me," the father retorted. "I told her that I could sell the house and move to Bangalore, but she insisted that Bombay is my home and made me stay back."

"Smart girl, Sastri. You have a smart daughter," Appa said. "This is where you have all your friends and family. What are you going to do in Bangalore? You will be bored to tears. Remember Ramanna? He retired and went to Bangalore, and after one year came back to Bombay. He said that he knew nobody, and he was too old to have the energy to start meeting new people."

Over a warm lunch in a familial atmosphere, with food being passed around and complimented upon, his mother, her father, and Lata asked questions of Mona and Satish. They were attempting to fill in non-sensitive details of the seventeen years that had elapsed since he had last seen her in her pigtails, and she him, wearing shorts. Everyone stayed clear of Satish and Mona's previous marriages.

After a long lunch, when they were about to arise from the table, Amma said, "Please be seated. I just remembered that I had made some *semya payasam* (a sweet vermicelli pudding) for this evening."

When Amma got up to fetch the *payasam*, Lata and Mona simultaneously got up to help her. Mother and daughter exchanged knowing glances, and did not stop Mona from helping them serve the men seated at the table.

After dessert was consumed with obvious relish, the fathers rinsed their plates, placed them in the sink, and left the room. Satish followed suit and rinsed his plate, but when he attempted to stay back in the kitchen to help clean up, Lata shooed him away, saying that he would only get in the way, saying. "You can do the dishes in America. Here, we have Pandu, who'll come and wash them in the next few minutes."

Satish was the odd man out in the living room. His father listened to Dr. Sastri reminiscing about his childhood in Bangalore, and how his sleepy little hometown had transformed into a crowded metropolis with pollution, traffic, and changing weather patterns. A few minutes later, Pandu rang the doorbell and went to the kitchen.

The women came to the living room carrying an exquisitely carved silver plate with traditional digestifs—betel leaves and Mysore *supari*. They sat a while, basking in the dulling aftereffects of a carbohydrate-rich Tamil meal, when Amma suggested that they move to the other room. Everyone arose when Appa said, "Satish, you and Mona sit here and talk."

They sat nervously on two ends of his bed that served as a seat during the day. They were silent for a few moments, then Mona asked, "What should we talk about, Satish?"

"I don't know. Where do we start?"

"How about your life in Houston?"

Feeling unusually at ease with her, he readied himself in a comfortable position. He candidly recounted his life in Houston, describing in some detail his middle management role at Clark Oilfield Technologies, and its challenges.

He emphasized that his career had seen very slow growth, and he was not on a fast track of any kind. However, he enjoyed the people and solving engineering problems at Clark. He also described his multicultural social network and life, his friends and their families, and his activities and interests.

While he spoke, she relaxed, turned toward him, pulled her bare feet on the bed, and sat in rapt attention. When he had finished, she told him, in a composed voice, her story about how she had studied commerce and accounting at a Bombay college. By the time she graduated, she was thoroughly bored with accounting. Her real interest was travel.

When she told her aunt on her mother's side, who worked for a European airline, of her interest, she got her an interview. Mona had worked for the airline for about eight years on the India-Europe route, and used her vacation and travel privileges to see Western Europe and North America.

She said that five years earlier, she had married a colleague, a steward. They had a good married life, but the husband had a drawback—he was an alcoholic. Six months before his death, the airline had dismissed him for being inebriated on the job, which compounded the problem. She said that her late husband was a very nice man when he was sober, but gradually, over the last six months of his life, those temperate moments were few and far between.

When her husband got fired, her mother had just passed away, and she was bereft with grief. The combination of her deep sorrow and his increased alcoholism made those six months a living hell for her. When he died in a gruesome motorcycle accident, he was in an angry, drunken stupor—she had just told him that she was leaving him.

For more than a year, she blamed herself for her husband's death. Gradually, it dawned on her that he had brought it upon himself. Between almost silent sobs, she shared difficult memories with him. He said the kindest words to soothe and console her. Then he began his story.

It was brief. When he reached the part about the reason for the divorce, he told her, "It just did not work out." She did not ask him for details, but said, "It's best that we put these rotten memories behind us and start a new life. No point living in the past." Then she smiled a pretty smile and asked, "So, what new movies have you seen lately?"

After they talked about the movies he had seen on his twenty-hour airplane ride to Bombay, they shared humorous experiences about air travel. She related stories about obnoxious and funny passengers, and he about the idiosyncrasies of the airline industry, particularly its staff.

When Amma came into the room two hours later, around teatime, she was pleased to see that Satish and Mona were talking like old friends who had rediscovered each other.

When Amma asked if they wanted some tea, Mona said, "Amma, do you know that your son is real *buddhu*, a simpleton?"

Amma was pleasantly surprised to see the transformation of this quiet, impeccably polite woman of a few hours ago to a naughty, familiar child.

"Why? Why is he a *buddhu*?" she asked.

Mona burst into a laughing fit and told the mother, "Your son is not only a *buddhu* but a *sadhu*, a saint. Amma, I was the stewardess on his flight to Bombay. He ignored me throughout the trip. Not only that, when he saw me today, he did not recognize me."

Amma was amused and went in to share the coincidence with the rest of the family, seated in the kitchen.

Satish was dumbfounded. "But, I remember that my stewardess's name was Monica," he said.

"My given name is Monica, Satish. Mona is my pet name. My grand-mother's name was Monica, and people did not want to confuse the two Mon-icas in the family, so they called me Mona," she said.

She pressed her fingertips on his forehead and said, "You may be from IIT, but to me you are a real *buddhu*." She ran out of the room to the safety of Amma's presence.

By the time he could reach her, she was firmly behind Amma, who said to her son, "You dare not touch her," in a mock stern tone. Turning to Mona, she said, "If he ever troubles you again, let me know."

"This is exactly how you two behaved when you were children," her father observed. "She would tease you and you would go running after her until she reached your mother for protection."

As everyone sat and drank their tea, Lata was the first to pop the question. "So Mona, what do you think of my brother?"

Amma and Appa were astonished at her unusual boldness. Dr. Sastri seemed pleased with the question.

"I think Satish should answer that question first," Mona said.

Satish said, "Since this woman thinks that I am a *buddhu*, I better make sure that I have thought it through. Dr. Sastri, do you mind if I take Mona to a res-taurant and talk to her some more?"

"I have no objection, young man, but don't you think you should ask her?" he replied.

Mona said yes, and they left immediately. It was four o'clock in the after-noon, and he had about five hours before he left home for the airport and his flight back to Houston. As they got into a cab, he told the taxi driver to take them to a hotel in South Bombay.

They chatted for the entire half-hour ride to the hotel, attempting to pro-vide each other with details of the lost years. Often, she kidded him for not rec-ognizing her. He cautioned her to be on the lookout. Sooner or later, he was going to get even with her for having kept her identity a secret for so long, and for calling him a *buddhu*.

When they reached their destination, instead of walking in the direction of the restaurants, he went instead to the airline ticket office located in the same hotel. The staff at the office immediately recognized her. They gathered around her to say hello and ask about her life on "solid ground." She said that it took some getting used to.

She then turned to him and asked, "What are we doing here?"

Unexpectedly, he took her by the hand and sat her down on a sofa. Under the gaze of her curious colleagues, he asked her, "Will you marry me, Mona? If you say yes, I will change my reservation right now, or else…"

She cut him short and said, "Yes, I'll marry you, you *buddhu*. There is no 'or else.'"

After he postponed his reservation, he called his parents and told them that he had proposed to Mona, and she had accepted. They were ecstatic. So was the airline staff, who applauded the unusual event that had occurred in their office. Monica was a bit embarrassed by the attention she received.

On their cab ride back home, Satish warily reached out to his bride-to-be, held her hand, and said, "I told you I would get even with you." They were married at her home four days later.

When Satish saw his wife in her bridal dress, he could not help but think of what Ralph D'Souza, his friendly middle-seat companion on his flight to Bombay, had said: "This airline has the most beautiful stewardesses in the world."

Two Lines

Friday was a mixed day at work. As soon as Satish arrived in the morning, he received a call from Clark's vice president of operations, Steve Longorio. Their company's equipment had passed a crucial field test at a customer test well. He congratulated Satish and said that the hard work of the previous five years was beginning to show some payoff.

The customer had committed to using their equipment on the next five development wells on an offshore rig in the Gulf of Mexico, but he still had to get past their drilling superintendent, who abhorred unproven equipment in his bottom-hole assembly. Steve asked him to accompany him to Lafayette, Louisiana, to meet this resister and turn him around.

Satish was unaware that over his nine years at Clark, he had built a good reputation in the company and the drilling industry for being not only a good engineer but also a pragmatic one, who understood the motivations, risks and concerns that dictated each action on a drilling rig.

He was famous for a posture he took whenever he was at a lectern. He would hold up his right hand, stretch out four fingers, and say that the top four guidelines for any decision were: "Number one, health, safety, and the environment; number two, quality; number three, schedule; and number four, cost." He was passionate in the pursuit of these objectives and admonished and threatened to fire anyone who would sacrifice or compromise the first two.

Satish was a natural to take to customers. He was a good listener and could communicate succinctly with them, absorbing and using their local accents to make his audience comfortable. Moreover, his reputation for being uncompromising on his first two objectives usually preceded him to meetings, which comforted oil company personnel. In addition, he loved to try local cuisines anywhere on the globe, which also pleased his hosts.

He was most at home in Lafayette, where he enjoyed authentic spicy Cajun cuisine, Zydeco bands, and the Cajuns' unique sense of humor. At times, when Clark's field crews drilled in an area that had extra-hot cayenne peppers, a field hand would remember him and FedEx him some overnight. Laura, his assistant, held these potent packages in her outstretched hand when she brought them to him—their spicy fumes penetrated paper and brought tears to her eyes. She claimed that one package had almost burnt her fingers!

Satish was elated to hear the good news about the field test from Steve. He felt that it would give him substantial leverage when he went in for his annual performance review with his boss, John Boudreaux. Over lunch, John congratulated him for his role in the successful field test and his other accomplishments over the year.

He told him that he was going to receive an above-average increase in his pay, thanked him for the exemplary job he had done, and ended with, "I am sure you'll continue doing a great job over the next year."

He then gave him a performance review document with comments suggesting that he review it and, if he agreed to its contents, sign it. If not, annotate the document and send it back to him, and they could meet again to discuss it.

Satish was happy with the raise, but disappointed that he had not been promoted to director, especially after his significant contributions to the recent successes. Besides, he was the only "manager" in the entire company who reported to a vice president. He shared this thought with John, who told him that his hands were tied, and that he had attempted to compensate the shortcoming with a higher raise.

Satish said little after that. The two had a pleasant lunch, discussing his impending trip to Lafayette and how to handle his first layoff that afternoon in a humane manner, while following company policies and procedures.

It was a depressing task, telling his employee that his services were no longer needed, especially on a Friday afternoon. He fought hard to keep the employee, but John told him that it was a corporate mandate to cut at least ten percent of the headcount. Satish was lucky that he was being asked to cut only one person from his staff of twenty-seven people.

Joe, a Cajun, had been a conscientious company man for more than fifteen years, but had not attempted to stay current with his field of expertise. Over the years, Clark moved him around from one position to another, performing delegated tasks by hand that people could easily perform with personal computers. He had seen the writing on the wall, and had asked to be laid off during the next round. Yet the task was an unpleasant one.

Satish liked Joe, and after he had given him the bad news, he suggested that they meet after hours to see how he could cushion the transition. The "redundant" employee was then escorted by a human resources assistant to his car, after a time was set for him to come to the facilities over the weekend to pick up his personal belongings.

Later that afternoon, Satish declined invitations from his fellow managers to join them for their traditional weekend beer. Instead, he joined Joe to discuss his plans. Then he embarked on his forty-five minute drive home to Monica and their one-year-old daughter, Seeta.

As soon as his car pulled into the garage, the back door of his home opened and Seeta, his infant daughter, ran out, all wobbly. She grabbed his knees and said, "Carry me." He obliged her, and while he was being showered with kisses, he entered his home.

"Want some *chai*?" Monica asked as she poured hot water on tea bags in two mugs. "So, how was your day?"

"We had great news and bad news," he said.

"Bad news?" she asked with concern.

"I had to lay off an employee and, trust me, it is one of the worst acts a manager can do. They don't pay me enough to do such things."

"Is your job safe?" she asked.

"Yes," he said, sounding positive. "We had a successful field test. We now have funds for the next phase." He and Seeta, who was sitting on his lap, sifted the mail. He quickly dispatched junk mail to the recycling bin, separated bills and magazines for his personal attention, and sorted out sale and coupon sheets for his wife.

"Oh, by the way," he said. "I had my performance review today. It was good. I got a good raise but no promotion."

Monica could see that he felt as if he had let her and Seeta down. She had seen her husband give Clark every iota of the physical and mental energy he possessed. When she met his superiors at office parties, she heard nothing but genuine praise for him; yet, an unseen obstacle prevented his ascent in the company. She told her husband that some day he would be rewarded for his efforts.

Soon a cup of hot *chai* arrived at the table, accompanied by some Gluco biscuits, imported from India. On cue, Seeta reached out for one to munch. Husband and wife chatted about various topics, from Monica's excessive dieting to lose the weight she had gained during her pregnancy, to who brought what to a women-only lunch at a friend's place, to how the other women had loved the exotic taste of her version of a Middle Eastern baked dessert.

"Thank God I kept some at home for you. There were no leftovers!" she said. She teased him: "How can you eat that stuff?"

"I love it. It's the best." He went over, kissed his wife, and said abruptly, "I have to go for a haircut."

"Now?"

"Yes! Now! I am overdue for a haircut. Tomorrow we have to go to a wedding reception, and the barbershop will be crowded in the morning. I'll be back in half an hour. You won't even notice that I am gone."

"OK," chimed his wife. Seeta looked up, perhaps puzzled at how easily her mother had granted her father permission to leave the house so soon after he had just arrived.

"Wait," his wife said. "I have a coupon for you, for your haircut." She pointed at the refrigerator. "And, by the way, can you buy milk, and whatever multigrain bread is on sale, and some cheese, the kind with jalapenos and chilies in it?"

Retrieving the coupon, he headed for his favorite barbershop. The one he frequented had a sports theme to it, with a receptionist behind a pastiche of a stadium ticket window. A large-screen TV tuned to a baseball game dominated the lobby. Many sports magazines were clumsily scattered around the sitting area. Every element tried to add some masculinity to this enterprise with only women employees.

"Last four digits of your phone number, please," chimed a perky high school kid.

He gave it to her.

"Any preference for a hairdresser?" she asked.

"I'll just go with first available, please," he said. He proceeded to the waiting area with its stale, dog-eared magazines and its grainy, large-screen projection TV with shrill sportscasters whose looks were marred by the bulging veins of fake enthusiasm in their foreheads and necks.

He really didn't care what the announcers were so excited about, so he sifted through a magazine. Before he could get past the table of contents, a young Oriental woman called out his first name.

For decades, he had heard his name mispronounced in every possible way, and he instantly recognized his name in the jumble of sounds this Asian woman made. He stood up and approached her. This petite Asian woman had a name tag that said "Quynh."

"Hi, my name is Quynh," she said.

"Hi, Quynh," he said.

She led him to a seat and pointed to it with the poise and grace of a model on a TV game show displaying the grand prize. As she wrapped a protective sheet around him, she said, "You say my name correctly." She was visibly pleased that her name was not mispronounced.

"Hey, if I can say Zbigniew Brzezinski, Quynh is a piece of cake," he bragged.

Quynh was puzzled by the comment, and understandably so.

When Satish first came to the America, like any new immigrant to this country, he was given many telephone numbers of people from the old neighborhood who now lived in the U.S.

Vikas, a fifteen-year veteran of this country, living in Manhattan, was one of them. He had one piece of advice for him: "Don't go changing your name to Sat or Stan. If this country can say Zbigniew Brzezinski, it can say Satish. Heck, your name has two vowels in it, and recognizable syllables from the English language!" Zbigniew Brzezinski was the secretary of state in the Carter administration.

"Pardon," exclaimed Quynh. "I don't understand 'speak new?'"

"No, Zbigniew," he said. It was too difficult to explain, so he let it pass.

"You from Vietnam?" he asked as she turned on her clippers.

"Yes," she said, again quite pleased. "How did you know?"

"Easy," he said. "Your name is Vietnamese."

"Yes. You say it so well, but most people find it so hard," she complained. "You know a lot of Vietnamese people?"

"Yes," he said. "Who does not, if you live long in Houston?"

"You live long in Houston?"

"Eleven years. When did you come here?" he asked.

"Two years ago," she said, and then the dam burst open.

She was born in Hanoi, in North Vietnam. Her father had his own business, building boats. In the early eighties, she and her family left Vietnam in a boat, seeking a better life.

"I was nine years old, maybe ten. I don't remember. One hundred and fifty people in a boat, for many days. No food, no water, all smelly and sick. One day we landed in Macao. You know Macao?"

"Yes," he said. "Near Hong Kong. It was a Portuguese colony."

"Yes," said Quynh. "We children go to villages to beg for food, to bring to big people. Children were good for begging for food," she said, pleased with her insight.

"Villagers gave food for a few days, weeks, maybe months, but soon they ask us to leave. We go back to the boat and leave Macao. Again, all smelly and sick and no food till we land in Hong Kong. My father, mother, and all of us sent to camp for Vietnamese refugees.

"I learn English there," she added. She beamed when she said that. Then she cut quickly to how all of them were shipped back to Vietnam from Hong Kong, and her father went back to his boat-building business. Soon she got her visa to come to the U.S. "But only my mother and I come to the U.S. with my brother."

"Your brother? Where did he come from?" he asked

"Yes, I have a four-year-old brother. He was born in Vietnam," she said. "I work to take care of my mother and brother."

Quynh had a slight smile, or so he imagined when he saw her face in the mirror. It was that slight smile of being in the moment, of being aware and happy as she went about cutting his hair. He sensed that she knew that she was better off at that moment than she ever was before. When she was done, he gave her a handsome tip.

With images of sick Vietnamese boat people, a child begging in the villages of Macao, and refugee camps in Hong Kong still swirling in his mind, Satish stepped into the neighborhood's giant grocery store. Usually this errand was a pleasure, but today it was soaked with irony. He grabbed a basket and made his way to the deli, where women and men wearing transparent plastic caps and latex gloves were helping other customers.

He politely took a position in front of the counter, glancing around at the people who were ahead of him in this informal line. There was no organized line; just people scattered along the length of the deli counter, some peering into the glass enclosure that displayed a variety of cold cuts, cheeses, and other refrigerated products. Quynh and the irony persisted as he joined the curious crowd and began walking up and down the display while keeping tabs on his relative position.

Before it was his turn to respond to the query, "Who is next in line?" he was tempted by the *tabouli* salad in the window. A helpful assistant offered him a plastic spoonful sample of the salad, and she closed the sale.

"Half a pound of that *tabouli* salad, please," he found himself saying. The assistant went on to say how it was her favorite salad. She poured out a little more than half a pound and said, "It's a little more; would you like me to remove some?"

"No," he said. A spoonful more would not hurt. As she packed the salad and put a price sticker on it, he remembered, thankfully, the original mission that brought him to this counter.

"Will that be all?" asked the cheerful deli assistant.

"No, I'd like half a pound of pepper jack cheese, please," he said. "The store brand."

She disappeared and came back holding an almost translucent slice.

"Is this okay?" she asked.

"No, a little thicker, please."

She disappeared again and came back with thicker, more acceptable slices.

Again she said, "It's a little more; would you like me to remove a slice?"

"No," he responded, but he was beginning to see a pattern here. "A little more" was about 10 percent more than he had requested.

Before he could mentally compute what 10 percent of everything sold in the deli would amount to, and its impact on the obesity of the local population, not to mention the store's cash flow, he remembered that he had to buy multigrain bread. So he went to the bakery section and pulled from a special display stack a loaf of "whatever low-fat multigrain bread is on sale."

Next, he stopped at the dairy section without getting distracted or tempted by hundreds of food items that were on his path to buying milk. He remembered a sage professor from his executive MBA program saying, "Always place the dairy section at the far end of a grocery store, so customers can see other items in the store. Every customer needs milk and dairy products, so use those as magnets to draw customers through the store so that they can make impulse or other purchases."

"Hah!" he thought as he made his way to the dairy section with singular focus, not even sneaking a glance at his favorite jalapeno potato chips that were strategically positioned on his route.

He grabbed a gallon of milk—2 percent fat, store brand, of course—and rushed past the tempting ice cream section to the "less than five items" checkout counter. He paid cash to the clerk, and when he was ready to dart to his car, he heard a voice call out his name.

It was "Harry," his Sikh friend Harbhajan, who had Americanized his name for Texans. He had migrated to the U.S. during the Ronald Reagan era, and had not heard the Zbigniew Brzezinski story from Vikas. Harry had a large load of groceries, his cart brimming with basic supplies and more.

"Looks like you just moved into a new house and you're stocking up your refrigerator and pantry," Satish said.

Harry's face fell as he said, "We just came back from Bombay. We had a death in the family."

"I am so sorry to hear that, Harry," Satish said. His voice dropped from its former ebullient tone, greeting a good friend, to a softer one, empathetic and sympathetic to the loss he had suffered.

"My nephew, my sister's son suddenly passed away," Harry added, with tears brimming this Sikh's eyes.

As he dropped his face to conceal the tears, Satish reached out and patted his back.

"Oh God, Harry," he said. "This is the worst loss we can face in life. The death of a child. Come, sit here for a moment," Satish said as he guided the visibly shaken man to a nearby bench.

At that moment, it did not matter to him that he was in the U.S., in suburban Sugar Land, Texas, as he held Harry and led him to a nearby bench. He could sense that many people watched curiously the unusual sight of one Indian man holding another, but his friend's grief was intense. He sat next to him, consoling him the best he could.

Harry said, "He was only twenty, doing so well at medical college, so bright and successful, so responsible, and so full of joy and happiness.

"Every parent should be blessed with a child like that. I wish the whole world had children like my nephew, but suddenly he is gone. He went into a coma—no one knows why—and then, a few days later, he was gone!

"My sister is still inconsolable. I tried to tell her that she had a perfect son for twenty full years, and most people don't have that for a lifetime. She enjoyed him all these years.

"But a mother's sadness and grief is simply beyond words. I stayed with her as long as I could. But I could not console my sister. What use is a brother if he cannot help his sister at a time like this? Only God and time can help."

Then he turned to his groceries. "Look at that cart. I can feed a whole village in India for a week," he proclaimed.

"Or a boat full of Vietnamese refugees," Satish thought.

"You bought only milk, cheese, bread, and this green stuff?" Harry asked.

"Tabouli salad," he replied.

Harry abruptly got up, composed himself, and asked, "So, Satish, are we going to help some candidates win some city council elections this year, or what?"

"Yes, of course," he said, attempting to match the regained enthusiasm in his friend's voice.

Grabbing his hand and pumping it, Harry said, "Thanks, my friend." He turned to his cart and rushed out of the store, the automatic door opening barely in time to let him and his cart through.

When Satish reached home and emptied his grocery bags' contents on the kitchen counter, Monica noticed the container with tabouli salad and examined it closely.

"You paid $3.25 for just this much salad?" she asked in a voice tinged with a combination of incredulity and disappointment. "Half of this is water!

"I don't know why I spend so much time looking for coupons and saving money, and I don't know why I send you to the grocery store. All you do is buy useless stuff and waste money." She put the accursed plastic container in the refrigerator with a thud of displeasure. Seeta briefly looked puzzled. She wondered, for an instant, why her mother was so upset but went back to play with her toys on the kitchen floor.

Normally, Satish would have reacted to his wife's well-intended criticism and leaped into a rebuttal, arguing that, occasionally, he was allowed to make some impulsive purchases. Instead, he said nothing. He sat still as a slight, almost invisible smile of awareness crept across his face.

He thought about Harry's loss, Joe's layoff and Quynh's life when a phrase from his native Tamil, "*Iru Kodugal*," crossed his mind. It literally meant "two lines," but was commonly used to convey two unequal lines, one long and one short. The phrase was the idiomatic equivalent of, "I cried because I had no shoes, until I saw a man who had no feet!"

Satish picked up Seeta from the floor and hugged her warmly. With his daughter in his arms, he went over to his displeased wife, embraced her affectionately and whispered in her ear, "I love you!"

Monica wondered why he was acting so strange and pushed him away gently after she tenderly whispered back, "So do I, but next time don't waste money!"

As he put Seeta down on the kitchen floor and walked away to the bathroom for a refreshing post-haircut shower, his slight smile persisted.

The Hunt

When a somber Tim O'Leary, the vice president of human resources of Clark Oilfield Technologies, walked into his office unannounced late Friday afternoon and told him that the firm's president, Billy Stayton, wanted to see him immediately, Satish was not surprised. He had been anticipating this moment, when he would be politely told that his "position had been eliminated," American corporate speak for being fired.

Tim was a good friend and colleague who had supported him through many tumultuous twists and turns in his ten-year career at Clark, but now had to play the role of a reluctant executioner. Industry conditions and the firm's continuous hemorrhaging of cash needed a tourniquet but often reducing headcount by amputating employees was the fastest way to stop the bleeding.

Satish was familiar with the process of being "let go." He had played Tim's role before. For the past year, on several occasions, he had to undertake the loathsome task of informing his employee that his or her services were no longer required, and giving the unfortunate person a formal letter that outlined the details and the background of the dismissal. He also had the repugnant task of informing the ex-employee that he or she had to leave the premises immediately, and that personal belongings could be collected at a later appointed time, unseen by the still-employed, lest it affect employee morale.

Both Tim and Satish knew that this was the last time he would walk these hallways and the campus as an employee. It was a long silent walk to Billy's executive suite on mahogany row in a different building.

As they came out into the open and walked along the pathway around a man-made lake, Tim pulled out a cigarette and lit it nervously, his hands trembling as he tried to bring his lighter's flame to its tip. He inhaled deeply and hurriedly several times, attempting to ingest sufficient nicotine before they reached Billy's office building.

The two walked down the final hallway with portraits of founders of the firm. Liz, Billy's new executive assistant, saw them. She hastily got up and went into Billy's office to announce their arrival. By the time they reached the end of the hallway, she was back to escort them into the conference room adjoining the office, saying that Billy would join them in a moment.

Tim and Satish sat across from each other at the conference table, leaving the seat at the head of the table for Billy. They said nothing until Tim got into a coughing fit and poured himself a glass of water from the pitcher on the table.

"You've got to stop smoking, Tim. It will kill you," Satish said.

"This job and my ulcers will kill me before any cigarette," replied Tim. "This is hell."

"That's not the way it looks from where I am sitting, Tim. You still have your job," he said, with a touch of acidity that was not lost on Tim.

Tim paused, took another gulp of water, and said, "Yes, I have my job, but this part is very stressful. You can't imagine doing this all day long with no end in sight."

Satish tried to empathize with Tim but could not. Not while he was waiting for Billy to walk in and graciously tell him that his services were no longer needed. His mind was engrossed in devising a plan to look for a job immediately, so that Monica and two-year-old Seeta would continue to live the good life.

Still, he advised his friend, "I wish you'd stop smoking, Tim. It does not help you with your stress. I am the one being axed. You are the one who still has a job, and you are more nervous than I am."

Tim took another deep puff and said, "That's because of all that yoga stuff that you Indians practice to remain calm in all situations. Besides, I don't know when my neck will be on the block and I need this job to pay my bills. I cannot afford to lose it."

"No one can afford to lose their job, Tim. Just take it easy. All will be well. And, just in case you do need another job, call me. I'll have a head start on you," he said with a sincere smile that seemed sardonic to his friend.

Just then, Billy walked into the conference room carrying a manila folder that Satish guessed contained his walking papers. Unpredictably, Billy sat next to Tim and both now faced him, as if they were on opposing sides. These subtleties were Tim's style.

After a few pleasantries, Billy got swiftly down to business. He recounted how the industry's severe downturn had affected Clark's bottom line. His board of directors had brought in some consultants who recommended that his division be mothballed, if not shut down, because it was a long-term play and was burning cash that they could ill afford.

"I am sorry Satish, but your product line did not make the cut. As a consequence, your position has been eliminated."

Tim sat silent while Billy spoke but, as if on cue, on the phrase "your position has been eliminated," he jumped in and pulled out some papers from the folder that Billy had brought in. He read the terms of their disengagement aloud, highlighting various confidentiality- and non-compete agreements that Satish had signed.

After Tim was done, Billy said, "Satish, this was a very difficult decision for us. I mean it. We tried to find you a position somewhere else in the firm, or at least an advisory role on my staff, but we have many more good people than we have slots. We are now cutting into the bone. There is no fat, there is no flesh, only bone."

"I am sorry to hear that, Billy," he replied. "Clark has been an excellent company to work with and I have good memories here. I enjoyed working with the people here. They are the best, and I will miss them. Thank you, Billy and Tim, for the opportunity and the support. Trust me; my gratitude comes from the bottom of my heart."

With that, he rose from his seat, shook hands with Billy and Tim, and left the conference room. He passed Liz, who had a sympathetic face when she said, "We'll miss you, Satish. God bless you, your wife, and your darling little baby."

He smiled momentarily as he thanked her for her best wishes. He walked down mahogany row, and as he was about to step out of the building, Tim came panting up to him and said, "Wait, I've got to talk with you."

"I am listening," he replied as he walked to his car in the parking lot. "You don't have to walk me to my car. I know the drill."

"Listen, you, you, Indian," Tim stammered, as he was prone to do when he was upset with him. "What the hell was that all about? Jesus, nobody gives up on a ten-year career like that, so courteously. You just left without asking for anything."

"What should I have asked for?"

"A severance package, for instance?"

"A severance package? I thought that was only for senior executives. I am just a manager, Tim. Not even a director."

"Well, my friend, we had one ready for you, in case you asked for one. Now you don't."

"Sounds good, Tim. Anything else? I have to get home and let Monica know about this. She has been worried for months, and now that it has happened, we can move on. Thank you for everything, Tim. You are a good friend."

"Will you please stop hurrying to your car? I have one last favor for you, Satish. Just walk with me to the cafeteria. I want to talk with you."

The post-lunch cafeteria was empty. Without people, it looked like a morgue for molded plastic and steel furniture—the sets of chairs and tables perfectly aligned with each other, creating an antiseptic but geometric design that Tim shattered by yanking out a chair and clumsily setting it at an angle to the table. He pulled out a cigarette as Satish sat down and crossed his arms. He positioned his chair away from the table.

"I don't give a whit who sees me," Tim muttered as he lit his cigarette in this nonsmoking area.

"Well," Satish said, "What favor were you talking about?"

"Even though you did not ask for a severance package, we are going to give you one. Billy has always liked you, and when you left his office, he insisted that I run after you and let you know that you have one," Tim said.

Satish, his arms still crossed and his chair slightly tilted back, said, "So, what's my severance package? Two weeks?"

Tim, who was perturbed that he and his good friend were on opposite sides of the table, said, "No, you get six months."

He almost lost his balance on the tilted chair. "What? Six months? I thought that's what people with employment contracts were given. Senior executives."

Tim looked down at the table and whispered, "It does not end there, Satish."

"We are also going to give you access to an outplacement service that will help you in your job search," he added.

"Pour moi? For poor little Satish? What have I done to deserve this benevolence? Why the magnanimity, Tim?" he asked suspiciously.

Tim inhaled deeply. After a brief moment, he exhaled and intently watched the miniature cloud of smoke around him dissipate. He knew that this was Tim's nervous habit when he needed a moment to think about a response to a question.

Tim dropped his cigarette to the floor and squashed the butt with his foot. He turned to him and asked, "Do you want the stated reason or the real reason?"

"Both," was his immediate response.

"Well, the stated reason is that you have contributed a lot to the company over the last ten years, and we value what you've done for us."

"And the real reason?" he asked.

"The real reason is that they are scared shitless that you will bring in an attorney and charge racial discrimination, like you did nine years ago. Corporate memories die hard, and you get the additional benefit of this severance package because of it."

Satish went back to his cross-armed, tilted-chair position. He thought for a moment and asked, "Does this mean I won't get good references from Clark?"

"That won't happen as long as I am here and responsible for human resources. We HR folks contact each other for references; I'll make sure you are okay," Tim said.

"Thanks, Tim. Appreciate the candor and all the help. Don't know if I would have lasted this long at Clark without you running interference for me, especially in high places." Satish got up from his chair and extended his hand to his friend.

Tim got up and clasped his friend's hand in a firm handshake and as the two left the cafeteria, he patted Satish on his shoulder and said, "Come, let me walk you to your car."

Satish was quite relaxed and relieved as he drove home. The last six months had been torturous at work, with weekly announcements of layoffs and the pressure of delivering results on schedule despite a constant reduction in people. It had a reached a point where frustrated and deflated employees just threw their arms in the air and gave up, and sat around doing nothing, waiting to be led to the guillotine.

Satish's project was a significant part of a revolutionary new technology that would have changed the way oil and gas companies produced from their reservoirs. Despite several engineering breakthroughs that significantly reduced the product's development time, the team was not fast enough to avoid the inevitable downward cycle that afflicted this hyper-cyclical industry.

He often compared himself to a surfer trying to ride the upward cyclical wave and staying on top of his board as long as he could. When a cycle came crashing down, he hoped to find a "tube" to course through for at least some time.

The six-month ride in this tube was harsh, ruthless, and draining; he was glad that it was over. He breathed easier when he drove up his driveway and parked his car in the garage. Monica and Seeta were pleased to see him home so early.

Seeta grabbed him at his knees and thighs, hugged him, and began singing, "Daddy's home, Daddy's home." He picked up his gleeful daughter and placed her on his lap as he sat at the breakfast table.

"You are home early," Monica said. She went to the faucet for some water to brew his tea.

"It finally happened, Monica. They let me go," he said. Seeta tugged at his tie and tried to catch his attention. Satish kissed her on her ample cheeks, which set off joyful laughter.

"They fired you after all these years of dedicated work?" she asked sternly from the direction of cooking range.

"Yes, they fired me, but they had no choice. They are going to shut down my division," he tried to rationalize.

"So what do we do now?" she asked in a cool, matter-of-fact manner, her eyes focused on the tea leaves that were floating on the simmering water.

"Well, on Monday, I'll start looking for a new job. They gave me six months severance and the services of an outplacement firm," he said.

"So, you'll get a paycheck for six months while you are looking for a job?" she asked in disbelief.

"Yes," he replied simply as he played with Seeta.

Monica placed a cup of tea on a coaster in front of him and asked, "Do you want Gluco biscuits? I just got some."

"Sure," he said. He took one from the opened packet that she placed on the table, dipped it in his tea for a split second, and popped the soggy cookie into his mouth before it could collapse under its own weight.

"Daddy, can I 'ave a biscuit? Please?" asked the daughter on his lap as she tried to grab a few for herself. He gave her one, and turned to Monica and said, "Yes, I will get a paycheck deposited directly into my bank account every pay period for six months."

"That's very magnanimous of them," Monica said.

"Oh, I think it's all Tim's doing. He told me that the firm was afraid that I would take them to court, and that this was a peace offering. But I think Tim must have scared them into giving me this package. He's a good friend."

"Did you really have any enemies at work, Satish?" Monica asked her husband. She knew that he was good with people and rarely did anything that would hurt anyone. The last six months of laying off his team had been excruciatingly painful. He had agonized over every person he let go, talking often with Monica about how much suffering he was unleashing on his people and their families.

"I don't think so, Monica. I don't think I have enemies." He gave Seeta, who was still comfortably seated on his lap, another cookie to eat. As he reached to take his first sip, Monica came over and picked her daughter out of harm's way of the scalding hot tea.

"So, what are you going to do now?" she asked.

"Well, I thought about it on the way home, and I have decided that I am going to take the weekend off, relax a bit, and then go to the outplacement office on Monday to start a new adventure."

"That's it? Don't we have to stop newspapers, reduce our expenses for the next six months or something?" she asked, bewildered that her husband was so blasé about not having a job after ten years of continuous employment.

"No. We live as we have so far. No change. I just lost my job. It is not the end of the world. Come, let's take Seeta for a walk," he said as he laid down his empty cup.

Satish pushed the stroller with Seeta seated in it while Monica walked alongside. The family walked quietly to their neighborhood park on a lake. He could tell from Monica's unusual silence that the recent change was bothering her.

"Monica, you really shouldn't be worried about my getting another job in the next six months," he said. "All will be fine; just you wait and see."

"Satish," said his soft-spoken wife as she reached out for his hand on the stroller handle. "I have full confidence in your abilities, but the market is so bad. What if there are no jobs? What if it takes a little longer? Do we have enough savings for a long job hunt?"

"Monica, I cannot go job-hunting assuming that there are no jobs—that is self-defeating. I have already lost the game before I started playing it if I think that way. I can certainly assume that there are only a few jobs, and my challenge is to find one or more of them in the next six months," he said.

"You know me by now," he continued. "I need to have the right attitude in whatever I pursue, and usually I am successful at it. That has worked in the past, and I don't see any reason why that attitude cannot be successful in the future."

"I understand what you're saying but this is so different than anything that I have experienced before. In India, I don't think anybody in your family or my family ever lost their jobs and had to look for a new one. Your father retired from his first job; same for my father. This is all new to me," she said.

"It's new to me too, Monica, but with a big difference. I have seen how people recover from job losses in this country. People here are resilient, and I've seen how they do it. I am not entirely ignorant about how to go about it. Trust me, Monica. We will be fine. My goal is clear—a job in six months, come hell or high water."

Monica held her husband's hand tightly all the way to the park, where she watched the father take his daughter out of the stroller and place her on a swing. She made her way to the gazebo to get out of the mild spring sun and found a seat on a bench. From there she watched him stand behind his child and give her seat a slight push to begin the oscillations.

At Seeta's urging, "Higher, Daddy, higher," Satish complied, his hands pushing his daughter to newer heights and shriller shrieks of excitement. But his eyes were on his wife in the distance, whose morale had ebbed.

A few hours later, after dinner, when he had lulled Seeta to sleep and gently placed her on her Little Mermaid bed, he went to Monica, who was cleaning up the kitchen, and hugged her tightly from behind. She was taken aback by the warmth and strength of the embrace.

"What is it?" she asked as she struggled out of the hold to continue loading the dishwasher.

"I've got to tell you something," he said as he swung her around to face him.

He hugged her again tightly and whispered, "Monica, I may not have said this to you, but you are my pillar of support."

"Go away," said Monica as she struggled to get out of his hold, assuming that this was yet another romantic ploy.

"No, I am serious. Without your strong support, I will have a hard time finding a job."

"Do you want me to look for a job, Satish?" she asked.

"No, that's not what I meant. I want you to be strong at home so that I can focus on hunting. If I have to focus on two fronts, I will not be as successful as I want to be."

"Oh, don't worry about me, Satish. I'll be fine," she said as the dishwasher roared into action. "Give me a day or two and I'll be back to normal. Come, let's watch some mindless TV."

They sat on the sofa in the living room, cuddled up, and watched a sitcom at barely audible volume so that they would not wake up their sleeping daughter. Soon, the only sounds that filled the home that night were his loud, resounding laughter. It overpowered Monica's sparse chuckles at punch lines and the drone of the dishwasher.

At first, he was depressed when he saw his new surroundings. The outplacement service's accouterments seemed cheap, with plastic and particleboard fabricated furniture. Their aesthetics seemed to diminish further in the poor but adequate lighting in the premises.

He was thankful, though, that he had a superior package that assured him a private office. And his gratitude for Tim's efforts multiplied when he saw that his new temporary workplace, on a tenth floor of a high-rise, had a large window.

Basking and working in natural sunlight more than compensated for the other shortcomings of his new office. He rationalized that this was a brief, passing phase and that he could survive the minor discomforts.

The staff was polite and pleasant, speaking in sensitive, hushed, and encouraging tones, as if he was in a sanatorium, undergoing therapy to recover from a corporate injury. He was assigned a counselor, Scott, an expert at helping the corporate wounded in recuperating from their recent little "accident" or "career hiccup."

Scott was an organizational development expert who had had a long career at human resources departments at many Fortune 100 companies. When his last position was eliminated, he changed his career track and decided to join the outplacement industry, which, in his opinion, was a growth industry.

Scott was in his late fifties, six feet five, and lean. Every day, he wore a predictable red tie on a white shirt enveloped in a blue blazer; only the color of his pants changed daily, from blue to gray to tan. He always wore black wingtip shoes that were worn out at the heels.

He had sparse hair that was perhaps blond in his youth, and he wore thick, gold-rimmed glasses on his hawkish nose. He had a deep, booming voice that he curbed into a whisper when he spoke, as if he wanted his voice to barely reach his intended subject and no one else. Though Satish thought that Scott's empathy was a little artificial, verging on condescension, he still found him congenial and competent.

"I have been doing this for five years, and the truisms behind successful job hunting have not changed, Satish. Am I saying that right?" Scott said from behind his clean, modest desk.

He nodded and Scott leaned forward, as if he had been trained in body language and needed to appear friendly. He continued, "All my successful candidates have followed my step-by-step process and gotten out of here before their outplacement term ran out. Tim tells me that you are as smart as they come. I am sure you'll be out of here in a jiffy."

Then he sat back with a practiced smile that lacked sincerity—the edges of his eyes did not crinkle to display any of his ample crow's feet.

Satish felt as if he was in a correctional facility, doing time, and Scott was his benevolent parole officer, giving him hints about how to reduce his stay. He shrugged off the thought and concentrated on what Scott had to say.

"Let me tell you this first: more than 85 percent of jobs, especially at your level, are not advertised. They are filled through personal referrals and recruiting firms. Second, it is a numbers game; the more people you meet and network with, the better are your chances of success. Third, looking for a job is a full-time job. It is an eight-to-five endeavor; you can't take vacations. But before we get into all that, we have to first get ready and aim. I'd like you to take a few psychological tests."

He had never taken a job-related psychological test before, and was somewhat reluctant to take one. He had heard from his friends that these tests did not transfer well across cultures; his Indian upbringing could skew his profile in an undesirable direction and scuttle his career.

Scott persisted, "Even if the tests are skewed or inaccurate, it will give you some insights, Satish. I have seen many people come here and look for the next job that looked just like their last job. When they got it, they were fired again. Why? Because it was the wrong job for them."

He paused to let Satish ponder what he had just said.

"The people with the most successful careers are those who by accident or design are playing to their strengths. Repeatedly, I have seen successful careers built around just aptitude, and not strength. We all have aptitudes in several areas, many of which guarantee good careers, but what happens over time is that satisfaction from work begins to diminish and we start living lives of quiet desperation."

"Thoreau," piped in Satish. "I understand what you're saying, Scott. Go on."

"Good, I am glad you understand. Tim told me you were smart," Scott said, cracking that artificial smile.

"Here's the deal. You have a God-given opportunity to understand yourself on someone else's penny. Make use of it. If you take time and do these tests seriously, they will reveal things about yourself that neither you nor your friends have seen about you.

"It will also confirm how you see yourself, and you can share it with your friends to see if they agree. We do not make an extra dime by doing these tests, my friend. Of course, it's all confidential. We don't even keep any of your records. We give them all to you, for your safekeeping. Shucks, we don't have the room here to keep any of your paperwork."

"I understand, Scott. I have a question. What makes an aptitude a strength?"

"Terrific question," cried out a buoyant Scott as he stood up, pulled up his pants, and came around the desk to a seated Satish. He bent down and whispered, "A strength is an aptitude that you have great interest in."

He went back to his chair, leaned over, and said, "You are an engineering manager, right? I don't care how good you are in engineering, Satish. If you are not interested in it, it is not a strength! Sure, your career will progress nicely, till one fine day you ask yourself, 'What the hell am I doing with my life? How did I get here?'"

He paused and answered his own question, "By compromising. By compromising. But we all do that, and there's nothing wrong with it. However, it is a whole lot better when you compromise knowingly, rather than out of ignorance. Self-awareness, Satish, it is all about self-awareness. The earlier you gain it, the faster you are on a path to a meaningful life."

Then he stood up and extended his hand, indicating that the meeting was over. "For the next ten days or so, spend some time doing these tests, which are quite detailed. Relax; have a good time doing them. Take some time off and spend it with the family. But next Monday, and every subsequent Monday, I'd like you to attend our meetings, where you get to meet other candidates and listen to their progress and experiences."

He shook Scott's extended hand. He left the office and went to his own. A well-dressed office assistant, Lucy, came by a few minutes later with test packages. Going through the documents, she gave him instructions on how to fill them.

It was about noon, and Satish was hungry. He asked Lucy for some recommendations to nearby restaurants. She suggested a Chinese restaurant, but as she stepped out of his office, she turned around and volunteered, "Let me see if the Lunch Bunch is still around. Maybe you can join them."

Half an hour later, he was at the recommended Chinese restaurant with four other candidates from the outplacement center.

"Hi, I am Dan Benjamin," said the first one, who appeared to be friendly. "Former VP of sales at Brumliere. This here is Samuel Bartlett, former CFO of Brumliere; that's Darrell Kennedy, president of Trustmink, and that's Clyde Perrin from Texinveste Bank."

"Satish Sharma, engineering manager, Clark Oilfield Technologies," he said as he stood up and shook hands, reaching out across the round table. "Pleased to meet you," he said to each one.

So began his association with the Lunch Bunch. He was the latest and the youngest addition; Dan was about his age, and the rest were at least ten years older.

They saw themselves as being very different from the Brown Baggers, their thrifty colleagues at the outplacement office who brought predictable sack lunches: a sandwich, some chips, and a piece of fruit or a yogurt. However, Satish had a different point of view. The Lunch Bunchers were senior executives, while the Brown Baggers were mid-level managers. He fell somewhere in between, but preferred to hang around with the Lunch Bunch, who treated him like an equal.

Dan was Jewish and had served in the Israeli Air Force as a fighter pilot. He was lanky yet muscular, and the nattily dressed aviator had that-in-your face, go-for-the-jugular attitude of a good "closer". He was outspoken and easy to read, sharing with Satish that he was a superb salesman but a lousy manager. He preferred to close huge, complex deals and not be bothered with "piss-assed" administrative details. "I began closing my salesmen's deals myself, rather than managing them," he shared with the group as the reason for his departure from Brumliere.

He had that cavalier attitude that camouflaged his perceptive powers and quick, sharp judgment. He was the most successful of the bunch in his job search because of his networking ability, aided by the strength of his connections. He was aggressive and relentless in his job pursuit, and once he picked up the scent of an opportunity, he honed in on his target with the tenacity of a hound after its prey.

However, every job he had pursued was a small fish, which he shared with his colleagues at the outplacement center. He coached some of the candidates on how to land these jobs, and the successful ones and their families were ever grateful to him. "Think nothing about it," he would say when they gave him minor tokens of gratitude. When some were over-effusive in their gratefulness he said, "If you feel so grateful, just send me your first paycheck." This quickly tempered their appreciation.

Twice-divorced, with a wife and child on the Atlantic and Pacific coasts, he joked that his life would not be complete without a wife and child on America's third coastline along the Gulf of Mexico. Driving the latest model German sports cars was his passion, and he changed his automobiles every year. He had more speeding tickets and dated more women than any person Satish knew.

Sam was a rotund African American who had a soft-spoken, sophisticated demeanor about him. He was always polite and well-groomed, oozing quiet confidence and somewhat introverted. However, when he got on a podium or was center stage, he transformed into a powerful motivational speaker. He had a thundering voice and a rhythmic, alliterative speech pattern that could resonate and move anyone who heard him.

His father was a preacher in a small town in neighboring Louisiana, which explained some of Sam's commanding presence under the spotlight. But his career was built around accounting and financial engineering, a low-risk, high-reward path that his father had chosen for him and encouraged him to pursue.

He had the etiquette and demeanor of a cultured person and presented himself professionally at all times. He was always immaculately dressed in well-fitted dark suits, white shirts, and designer ties that complemented his perfect haircut, trimmed moustache, and well-shined and relatively new Italian shoes.

Sam did not leave any of his job-search papers at the outplacement office. He carried a designer briefcase with a security code lock that contained his confidential papers. At the end of the day he carried home a four-inch, three-ring binder that contained all his correspondence.

He was disciplined and methodical in his search. He came in punctually at eight AM and left a little after five PM to be with his wife of twenty years. This childless couple had adopted children from a Fifth Ward neighborhood, and every weekday evening, at a church, they helped primary school kids with their homework.

Darrell had an impeccable New England pedigree and his family would have preferred him to stay in the area, married one of their kindred, and propagated their species. He followed the family track and, after his masters in engineering from MIT, joined a local engineering firm that was developing new drilling technologies for the oil and gas industry.

In the late seventies, the U.S. was in a sustained recession due to OPEC's machination of oil prices. Challenging engineering jobs that Darrell preferred were amply available only in the exploration and production industry. He compromised with his family that he would not move out of New England and chose to work for Trustmink. But his constant travels to Houston and other centers of oilfield activity exposed him to an adventuresome life that he had never seen in the Gatsby-like, croquet and country club environs of his birth.

During one of his frequent trips to Houston, he met a Mexican American woman and, to the consternation of his family, married her. He fulfilled his family's perception of being a black sheep when he moved to Houston after a major oilfield services company acquired Trustmink. He went on to become the president of his product division.

About six months earlier, he had refused to lay off any more of his staff and offered to resign instead so that, "You can do your own dirty work." The conglomerate moved in one of its own hatchet men and gave him a generous package that included one year of outplacement services.

Clyde was the only native Houstonian in the Lunch Bunch. He was called a banker, but he saw himself as a senior salesman, selling financial instruments to the oil industry. He had spent almost thirty years with the same bank, starting as a part-time employee when he was an undergraduate student at the University of Houston's accounting program.

His father had been employed by a petrochemical plant, and he grew up with his sisters and brothers in the modest neighborhood of Pasadena, Texas, immortalized by the film *Urban Cowboy*.

His family was originally from West Texas and he had a raw, deeply creased face with a weather-beaten look, a laid-back swagger, and a drawl to prove it.

Despite his triple bypass heart surgery, he loved beer and barbecue. A large belt with a shiny buckle the size of his palm kept his pants from slipping down his portly midriff. He wore cowboy boots with his suit, and an Indian bolo tie.

He enjoyed his work, the camaraderie, and wining and dining with clients. He had been very successful in his career until his bank had been acquired by a New York multinational bank that had determined that he did not fit the profile of their "customer-facing" executives.

The official reason for his departure was that he had retired after thirty years of service, but the exit package he negotiated included outplacement service for a year. At his retirement party, when he received his gold Rolex watch, he smiled wryly and told his audience that he was too young to spend the rest of his life golfing, fishing, and hunting. Instead, he was hoping that a silver fox like him could have a second career with another small Texas bank, and that he looked forward to competing with "them young Yankee pups from New York."

A devout Baptist, he donated his Rolex watch to his local church auction. He continued to wear his trusted, twenty-year old Timex that, like his heart, took a licking but kept on ticking. His personable, "Aw shucks, I'm just a country boy from West Texas," deportment made people underestimate him. He exploited this during negotiations of complex oil and gas financing deals.

Satish spent the first ten days, as predicted by Scott, his counselor, completing his self-evaluation tests at an easy pace. The last six months had worn him out, and he enjoyed the unhurried pace in the outplacement world. He would reach the office at about 9:30 AM and leave at three PM, both to beat the horrendous traffic jams that clogged Houston freeways. In between, he took off an hour and a half to be with his Lunch Bunch. The rest of the time, he meticulously wrote detailed answers to his test questions.

When he returned home, he sat with Monica and Seeta and watched children's shows on the local PBS station. After a quick dinner, the trio would amble to the park and back, talking as if they had just discovered each other. After Seeta went to sleep, they would sit with each other and watch some sitcoms on TV before retiring for the night.

To Monica, it was as if a new Satish was awakening. He was relaxed and calm, and had lost the sharp edginess that was building during the last year. This was the first time in their three-year marriage when they were together, doing nothing but quietly enjoying each other's company. In one week, a soft solace descended on the family—until Satish saw the results of his tests. They rattled him.

While Satish believed that his strengths were his analysis and synthesis skills, the test showed that his strengths lay elsewhere, in a much larger scope than he had imagined—in leadership and execution. His major strength was leading professionals in complex situations, which in his myopic way he had applied to his engineering group.

Another test revealed that he was on the borderline between introversion and extroversion, though he thought himself to be inhibited. The biggest surprise was that the tests showed him that he was stronger in his intuitive and perceptive powers than in the analytical prowess that he admired in himself.

At first, he was disturbed by the results. He shared the findings with Monica, who dissuaded him from dismissing them. During their now frequent walks to the park with their daughter, they talked about the implications of these findings, but there were no obvious directions in his job search. He was confused, but his wife was not.

As their daughter played with her pail and shovel in a sandbox in the park, Monica took her uncertain husband's hand and held it caringly.

Both said nothing until he said, "It's like I've discovered a whole new person that I never knew."

"Well, Satish, that's the person I have known and grown to love. You just saw yourself differently," she said.

"I can understand being slightly off, but this is drastic."

"No, it is not," retorted his wife. "It just happens to be larger than what you thought of yourself. You don't know this, but there are certain chores you enjoy doing. There are others you don't, but you do them with the same diligence that you do anything," Monica said.

"I learned it by observing my father. He has two simple rules. One, anything worth doing is worth doing well. Two, do it right the first time; you won't have time to do it again," he said.

Monica continued, "And that's why you took the tests, and did them honestly. Now we have the results, and I am sure you want to take advantage of them. That's you, Satish; you will focus and do things well, not half-heartedly, even if you don't enjoy it. But how long will you do things you don't enjoy? Think about it."

She held his hand firmly to show her support, and that she was not being judgmental.

"Satish, your marriage to Priya showed commitment and persistence. Your divorce from Priya forced you to rethink everything related to marriage and family life; commitment alone was not enough. You told me that you went into years of introspection, discovered yourself, and slowly changed.

"When you met me, you were a different person than when you met Priya. You got closer to your own true self. I think your self-awareness makes our marriage a happy and satisfying one."

"Yes, I had to change, because something was drastically wrong with my old rules." he said.

Monica laughed softly and said, "You know Satish, for all the brains God has given you, you can be quite a *buddhu*."

They had had this discussion many times, and before they could go off on a tangent, he quickly said, "Yes, I am."

She smiled at the minor victory he had conceded to her.

She continued, "Similarly, your parting with Clark is like another divorce, except they gave you an anesthesia when they said good-bye. They thought that the package made the severance humane, but I think you would have been better off if you had seen this as a personal tragedy. It would have forced you to think and look at this differently, as you did after your divorce."

Satish was not surprised by Monica's insights. He expected nothing less from her. He listened.

"I think that the tests are the biggest blessing of your package. It would have taken you years to figure this out by yourself."

"I guess you are right," he conceded. He gave her a slight, sideways hug in appreciation of her insights. She shrank and moved away; embarrassed at her husband's public exhibition of affection, looking around to see if anyone had noticed.

Just then, Seeta came up to them and asked them to come see the sand hill she had built. Monica seized this opportunity to get away from her amorous husband. She was still very Indian in her Victorian mores of not displaying affection in public.

On their walk back home from the park, he told her that he was still going to pursue the fastest path to employment and cash flow. He would look for a job similar to the one he had at Clark. Then, once he was firmly established, he would work on maneuvering his career in the direction of his newly discovered strengths. Monica concurred that it was the prudent path, at least until there was a steady stream of income buffered by savings.

The Lunch Bunch's reaction to Satish's evaluation results and his decision to go down the same old beaten path was varied. It was evenly split between the yeas and nays.

"Shoot, Satish," Clyde said when he heard about his decision. "Someone just told you that you were a big game hunter, and you're telling me that you are going back to shooting in a penny arcade to win some stuffed animals?"

"Life's too short not to be true to yourself," Dan suggested. "I understand money problems; I've seen my share of them. But everything cannot be just about money, can it?"

"You're right, Satish," was Sam's reaction. "Take care of the home front and everything else falls into place. We all have to make some small sacrifices to keep the home fires burning."

Darrell was surprisingly supportive of Satish. "I like the way you think: short term and long term simultaneously, and meeting both seemingly contradictory goals. That's not easy to do, guys," he said, addressing the rest of the group. "In everything we do, we cannot be one to the exclusion of the other; we have to do both concurrently. I like that attitude; I really do."

After hearing Darrell's opinion, Clyde and Dan hurriedly compromised, and all four offered Satish full support in his job search. Encouraged, he began his search in earnest.

He created a mental map of the whole process. There was a job out there for him. He had to reach the decision maker through his network and convince this senior executive, initially through his cover letter and later through interviews and references, that he was the best person for the job.

The process was simple, except that these jobs were hidden. He had to be at the right place at the right time when they were being filled. He had to play with probabilities and speed to be successful before his severance ran out.

Books were often his first source of information. He checked out a few job-hunting bestsellers from the center's library, and gave them short shrift. They were anecdotal, simplistic, and talked down to the job hunter. They mimicked each other and revealed no new principles or revelations that could give him that extra edge in his search. It was very clear that he had to be innovative and different on this hunt.

He began to execute the basic, commonly practiced principles of networking. He called it his ABCD strategy: associates, bridges, customers, and decision makers. He built a list of his associates, who could introduce him to bridges to customer organizations where decision makers resided.

He spent several weeks scouring his card files, and computer to create an exhaustive list of all his industry contacts. He then informed each one, via letters and fledgling e-mail services, that he was on a job search and would be contacting them to get referrals.

A week after the letters went out, he systematically called every person and asked them for references to people who might know about job opportunities. It was not adequate to just learn about a firm; it was of primary importance to get a name and telephone number.

He was insistent in getting at least three names of bridges from each of his associates. During week ten, he sent them a carefully crafted resume and a cover letter with a proactive last line that stated, "I will call your office for an appointment."

When he called bridges and reached them, he asked for an appointment. If an associate had a strong relationship with a bridge, the request was granted instantly. If not, there was a telltale hawing, if not reluctance. He backed off immediately, thanked the person, and went on to the next bridge on the list.

By week thirteen, the halfway mark, Satish was mired in the minutiae of meeting assorted Bs and Cs at different stages of cooperation. Some Bs were polite and offered to meet him to please an A, but within minutes, he could sense that he had walked into a dead end. This was also true of polite Cs who did not want to upset the Bs in their link.

He scrupulously avoided lunch appointments—he would be obliged to pay the check, since he had requested the meeting. He preferred to get back to the office and be with his Lunch Bunch to compare notes and to listen to their suggestions. They were all encouraging, noting that his progress was impressive. They wished that they had his dogged persistence and organization, and, most importantly, the stamina he displayed in seeing at least six people each day.

"I'd be happier than a hog knee-deep in slop if I could meet three people in a day," commented Clyde as he sipped his beer. "Boy, you're somethin'. Let me tell ya, I've seen many urban cowboys, but you're the first Indian who can ride!"

Everyone at the table laughed, except Satish. He was clueless that Clyde had just paid him a compliment.

He went on, "Son, this ain't my first rodeo, and let me tell you that jobs today are rarer than hen's teeth. But the way you are sniffing around like a hound dog, sooner or later you're gonna find one."

Satish was not satisfied. He leaned over, looked into this chili con queso thoughtfully, and stirred in the Tabasco sauce, creating a fiery red mix with rings of melted cheese.

"What's wrong, cowboy?" asked Clyde.

"I think I am doing it all wrong," he replied.

"Why do you say that?" Dan asked.

"Because I am at the halfway point, and all I have are some Bs, a few Cs, and no Ds in sight. I need to be talking to a few hiring managers by now. I am doing all the right things, but it feels like I am driving my cattle from here to Laredo via the Grand Canyon," he said, extending Clyde's analogy. "I need to get to hiring managers, and this is not the smartest way of getting there from here."

Sam, the diligent practitioner, suggested, "Satish, you have to be disciplined about it. It has worked for so many people before you, and people who recommend it have many examples and success stories behind them."

"Yeah," Dan joined in. "Networking is the secret to success in any sales job. This is selling. You are selling your services, and you have to network to get to the right people."

Darrell sat back and said nothing, observing the young man struggle with his Lunch Bunch partners.

"I respectfully disagree, gentlemen," Satish said, smarting from the latest spoonful of chili that had a mean slice of jalapeno in it. He grabbed his beer, took a long sip to soothe his palate, and continued. "I think I am making a mistake, but I can't put my finger on it. There must be an easier way of doing this; there must be a short cut. This process is not rocket science. There must be a better way of executing it."

Satish was in a state of quiet agitation when Darrell pitched in and said, "Just listen to what Dan just said. You have to network to get to the right people. The key term he used is 'right people.' Are you talking to the right people?"

"Yes," Satish said.

Darrell continued, "Maybe not. Let's test that premise. Who are your targets?"

"Engineering directors and some VPs of engineering," he said.

"Why engineering directors?" Darrell asked.

"Because I am looking for an engineering manager's position, and it typically reports to an engineering director or VP of engineering."

Darrell was pensive for a moment or two. Then he said, "Satish, there's a bigger problem here. I think we may have made a mistake. You may be aiming too low.

"I think we all make errors in targeting positions for ourselves, especially early in our careers. We believe that we are not ready for senior positions when we are, and we hold ourselves back. Tell me, Sam, could you have been CFO several years before you actually became one?"

"You are right, Darrell. I was ready two, maybe three years before I was finally promoted, but those times were different. The industry was hitting bottom. I wanted to stay out of the limelight so that when the reaper came along, I was below the radar. Look at me now. The thresher got me anyway. I guess I was a little scared to ask for the senior position."

"How about you, Dan? Were you promoted before or after your time?" Darrell asked.

"Before my time, Darrell, before my time. I did not want to be promoted to manager or vice-president; I just wanted to be a plain old salesman, but they would not let me do that. They wanted me to be part of management and help the underperformers get better. I wasted four years trying to create silk purses out of sows' ears.

"Selling is inside you. Either you have it or you don't. I was happy where I was, making a lot of money; then they promoted me, and then they fired me for not performing!"

He shrugged his shoulders as if he did not care about the outcome.

"I am sorry to hear that, Dan. But generally, do you believe that we hold ourselves back a little bit and see ourselves smaller than others see us?

"I think we do. I can tell you, when I was in my pilot's uniform, women told me that I looked ten feet tall," he said, laughing. "Shoot, I am only five ten, shorter than Satish here, but he thinks I am taller than him. Isn't that true, Satish?"

"Yeah, you're right," Satish conceded.

"How about you, Clyde? Your experience?" Darrell asked.

"True. I always thought that I was a country bumpkin and that I was not as good as them Yankees from them Ivy League schools. It held me back some," he confessed. "I probably lost about ten years or so. Humility is a good thing, but if you wear it on your sleeve, it will hold you down and sink you like an anchor."

Darrell gulped down the rest of his beer, and laid the empty mug on the table. Staring at it, he said, "Satish, I am going to ask you a tough question, and I want you think before you give me an honest answer." Then he leaned forward, looked him in the eye, and asked him, "Satish, do you think you were treated fairly at Clark?"

He promptly answered, "Yes. I think I was treated fairly at Clark. Why do you ask?"

Darrell drew a deep breath, shook his head, and said, "In my opinion, you were not treated fairly at Clark. I have read your technical papers, and I have seen you present them at conferences and participate in industry workshops. We did not compete directly, but I often heard my counterparts—presidents and vice-presidents of engineering and other divisions—pay you compliments, especially when they heard about a successful field test or when they heard that your schedule had accelerated because of one of your breakthroughs.

"We wondered why you were never made a director or a vice president. And why you did not leave the firm, even when headhunters offered you lucrative, enticing positions. It is a small industry and company boundaries are porous. Your reputation preceded you when you joined the Lunch Bunch."

"Darrell's right, Satish. Sam and I knew you by reputation before you joined us," Dan added.

Sam said, "That's what your evaluation tests revealed to you. Unknown to you, you had transcended from execution alone to strategy and execution to leadership. You were being underutilized at Clark, and if you had been there any longer, your growth would have been stunted. You were a tall man in a low-ceilinged room, and if you had continued to hunch over to fit, it would have deformed you."

"Let me tell ya something, Satish. You're a lot taller than you think you are," Clyde said.

"Wow, gentlemen. Thank you so much for the compliments. Can I buy you all a round of beer? And then perhaps you can explain what all this means in how I go about looking for my job."

"I'll drink free beer anytime," Clyde said with a grin. "If you've got the beer, I've got the time."

"Damn fine rule," Dan said, and signaled to the waiter for another round of beer.

The five of them then huddled and, over several rounds of beer and nachos, helped Satish with a plan to accelerate his search. The premise was simple. He needed to target senior executives, CEOs, and presidents of firms who constantly looked for engineering leadership skills.

These executives were visible and could be reached by a letter from him, but he needed to recast his letter, resume, and calling techniques to move these executives to quick action.

Finally, Dan added, "You need new clothes. You dress like a bloody engineer, not an executive. Get rid of those pens from your pockets."

When the waiter brought the check, Clyde signaled for it. He took the check, and as he pulled out his credit card over the protests of his lunch buddies, he looked around the table and said, beaming with pleasure, "Gentlemen, this one's on me. I am now an employed man, unlike your sorry asses!"

Clyde's compadres jumped from their seats to congratulate him. "You poker-faced son of a gun," Dan said, slapping Clyde's back hard.

"Hey, the fat lady just sang a few minutes before we left for lunch," he protested.

The rest congratulated him. Darrell ordered another round of beer, over which Clyde gave details of his new position.

"Executive vice president of Translaniar Bank. It's just a small local bank, and the title don't mean nothing—you know how banks are with titles. Shoot, this bank has a VP of internal communications who just delivers the mail!"

He paused, put his hands on the table, raised himself, and said, "Well gentlemen, my free ride is over. It's back to the grind." When the Lunch Bunch came around to congratulate him, he said nothing. After the last handshake, he silently went for the exit, but just before he pulled the door handle, he turned back and said, "Adios, amigos! The pleasure was all mine." He then exited the building, waving to no one in particular.

When Satish watched Clyde leave the building, memories of all the western movies he had seen, where cowboys rode into the sunset, came rushing to him. None was as majestic as Clyde's unrehearsed exit.

When Satish went home that afternoon, Monica noticed that he was unusually calm. She had seen him engage in frenetic activity, wearing himself out driving all over town, meeting people to reach his aggressive targets of what he called a "numbers game." That evening, he dropped his briefcase carelessly on the floor and hugged her firmly, all the while with a silly grin on his face.

"Did you get a job?" asked the suspicious wife.

"No," he replied. "Something better."

"What's better than finding a job at this time?"

"Finding the right job," he said.

"And?" Monica asked.

"Let's take Seeta to the park and I'll tell you all about it," he replied.

"In this heat?" she asked. "Have you forgotten that it is almost July in Houston? It is almost ninety-five degrees out there. I am not going for a walk. Seeta will get dehydrated."

"How about if we go to the swimming pool?" he suggested. "I know Seeta will love playing in the water, and it will cool her down, too."

"Okay, as long as you don't expect me to go swimming," she said. She was still bashful about wearing a swimsuit in public.

On the way to the pool, he gave Monica a synopsis of what had transpired that afternoon. He shared the Lunch Bunch's opinion about how Clark had 'screwed' him all those years. He told her that he had a terrific reputation in the industry, that he had been aiming low, and that his compatriots were convinced that he had to aim higher to fulfill the results of his tests.

"I am going after a vice president position, Monica. From now on, my targets are only CEOs and presidents of companies."

Monica was pleased with what she heard. She conveyed her admiration by squeezing his hand and saying, "I am so proud of you, Satish." She gave him a peck of encouragement and support on his cheek. Though he wanted to, he could not reciprocate; he was focused on turning his car into a parking spot in the crowded neighborhood swimming pool lot.

A few minutes later, Seeta, protected with "floaties," and her father, with a large, bright orange "noodle," descended into the shallow end of the swimming pool and played around in the warm water. Monica watched, pleased with the scene.

The oppressive combination of the summer heat and humidity in Houston did not slow Satish in his job search. He systematically analyzed and created a list of target companies, excluding Clark's competitors. He sifted through industry directories and discovered the names of their senior executives. Aided by Dan, he recast his cover letter and resume.

Like a shrewd direct mailer, he sent succinct and polite requests for meetings, with a handwritten "personal" inscribed on the envelope, a tactic Dan suggested. This was to prevent an overzealous executive assistant from opening his letter and making the decision to either reject it or reroute it to the human resources department, from whom he could only expect a standard "thank you but no thank you" missive.

He was pleasantly surprised with the results. His Lunch Bunch was right—he was undershooting, and he did have a credible reputation in the industry. His requests for interviews were often granted. Dan had cautioned him that he needed to schedule fewer meetings in a day. This would allow the executives the flexibility of extending the interview to call in colleagues to meet him and, perhaps, take him out for lunch or supper to test his social graces and etiquette.

The Lunch Bunch held mock interviews with him, sensitizing him to major management concerns and smoothening his rough edges. Dan took him to his favorite clothier and picked out suits for him. Satish blanched at seeing the price tags, but Dan comforted him. "Think about it as an investment, not an expense. It's CAPEX, not OPEX," he said, referring to industry acronyms for capital expenditures and operating expenditures.

During the first two weeks of August, Satish entered a new universe of experience. Though they had different personalities, the executives all had similar concerns about sustaining the value delivered to shareholders, and how to get the right people and organization to deliver this value. They were uniformly polite and courteous, making inquiries about his family and background, and were appreciative that he had written to them when there were so many employment opportunities in town for a person of his caliber and reputation.

Most of them carefully avoided discussing the details of his work at Clark, staying far away from potentially confidential issues. Others, when they did tread in these waters, respected his tactful dodges and did not push for more information.

Uniformly, they were interested in his strategic thinking, his quick "analysis and synthesis" skills, and whether he was an effective "organizational man" who could successfully lead engineering teams, which he had displayed at Clark.

As Dan had predicted, a second meeting often followed his first one. This would be over lunch or supper with a key subordinate, an obvious sounding board, present. There was no doubt in these executives' minds that he would be a good addition. He would also be affordable, since he was so grossly underpaid at Clark.

As he grew more confident, he entered a new realm of interrogating the executives on their strategies and the challenges to successfully executing them. His questions were incisive, and soon he could tell if he was being "fed a load of manure," as Clyde would say.

During the peak heat season in mid-August, Satish began to receive offers, some by mail and some verbally at subsequent meetings. All were for senior positions: vice president at smaller organizations, and director at larger ones. Each had a different compensation plan, with variations in stock options, bonuses, salaries, and perquisites.

When he saw the numbers, he realized how unappreciated and underpaid he had been at Clark. At first, he was angry with Tim and the rest of the management team, but then he reconciled that his inattention was equally to blame.

At first he attempted to take his assortment of job options to his Lunch Bunch, but soon all of them were unavailable. They were working on a project that Clyde had brought to them, and could not discuss it with him because of non-disclosure agreements. Monica was the only trusted partner with whom he could discuss his array of options.

He created spreadsheets—quantitative analyses of various compensation plans—to share with Monica. She liked what she saw, but felt that they were inadequate for him to make a good decision. She asked him many questions about his chemistry with each firm's executive team.

Working on Monica's germ of an idea, he added a series of aspects to his evaluation criteria. But when he drew graphs comparing scores on these two dimensions, he discovered that firms that were offering substantially higher salaries scored lower on the qualitative dimension, and vice versa. He then created numerical thresholds of acceptance on both dimensions, and found that only three of the twelve offers he had received exceeded thresholds on both counts.

Satish had learned a long time ago, the hard way, that numerical analyses in complex systems, such as in oil and gas exploration and production, could only provide a general sense of direction, like a compass. He was traversing an uncharted territory, and the engineer in him wanted more information to make an intelligent decision. That was when Tim called.

"Hey buddy! How are you doing?" Tim asked.

"Good," Satish replied. "And you?"

"Good, but it could be better. How's the job search going?"

"Good actually; better than I expected."

"By the way, if you have some time, I'd like to meet with you."

"I'd be happy to, Tim. You pick the place and the time, and I'll be there."

"How about this afternoon?"

"That's short notice, Tim. I have already scheduled a meeting for this afternoon. Are there any other slots open on your calendar?"

"I'll tell you what; let me have Liz give you a call."

"Billy's secretary?" Satish asked.

"Yeah. Actually, Billy wants to meet you. You know I'm just his gofer. I'll tell you what, set a time to visit with Billy and call me, and we'll meet at least an hour before that meeting. I'll fill you in."

"Can you tell me why he wants to meet me?"

"Can't do. I don't know the whole picture, only part of it. By the time you get here, I'll have a better idea. All I know is that Billy wants you to come back."

"Sounds good, Tim. Take care." Satish said, and hung up the phone.

He could not hide his delight. It was as if his firing had been repudiated. Monica, who heard the tone of the conversation go from mild interest to delight, was curious about the cause of this sudden transformation in her husband. He told her that Tim had just informed him that Clark wanted him back.

Monica did not share his joy, and she told him so.

"Why would you want to go back to a firm and a boss who just fired you?" she asked with rare disdain. "You need to keep your self-respect."

"I did not say that I was going to join them," he said defensively. "I just said that they wanted me back. I have no clue what it's all about."

"You should have said you are not interested. You have a dozen job offers and you would still want to go back to Clark?" she asked sternly.

"I cannot say no immediately. I have to listen to what they have to say. I cannot be emotional about it. I have to be rational. Let's do this. Take the graph that we used earlier and see what would make Clark attractive to me."

Monica was not convinced that the graph would reveal anything, but she decided to play along. Both graded Clark on its qualitative aspects and came up with different scores. He gave them higher marks that crossed his acceptance threshold, while she did not. He was disappointed with her low scores. She justified her grading with, "They exploited you for ten years, paid you less, and then laid you off. How do you expect me to see them in a better light?"

Satish stayed silent because he knew there was more coming.

"You cannot ignore the last six months. You, Seeta, and I have had a tense six months wondering if you were going to get another job. If it were not for your Lunch Bunch, you'd be still out there calling on six people a day. You can trust the Lunch Bunch but not Clark, and certainly not Tim. He was their slave master. He kept you down while all the time pretending to be your friend." She stopped abruptly.

"Are you done?" he asked.

"Yes. I am done," she said, and suddenly began weeping uncontrollably.

He rushed to her and hugged her. He asked her what had happened, and through the tears and the sobbing she mumbled, "I just realized something out of the blue. It came from nowhere: a thought that I married a blessed man, who sees no evil or bad in anyone. And thanks to your karma, when people began to hurt you, strangers came out of nowhere to help you get back on your feet. I am so sorry that I spoke out."

"Calm down, Monica. Calm down," he said as he held her and stroked her hair from the forehead back. Seeta, who was taking a nap, woke up. She saw that her mother was upset, came to her and said, "Mommy, don't cry." She shook her favorite rattle as a distraction.

Seeta followed her parents as her father sat her mother down on a sofa in the den, then sat next to her and held her while she recovered. She then climbed on to her mother's lap, stood up, and began showering her cheeks with kisses. She said, "Good, Mommy. Don't cry. Want milk?"

Monica could not help but smile when she heard her daughter ask her if she wanted some milk, a tactic she used to quiet Seeta down whenever she cried.

Slowly, she returned to normal. She kissed her daughter, gave her husband a peck on his cheek, and said, "You two are the best family any woman could ever have."

"Mommy is the best Mommy," the daughter added, and immediately asked, "Can I have a candy?"

The parents burst out laughing at this little imp's perfect timing in asking for a treat. Satish picked her up in one sweeping movement of his right hand and went to the kitchen to reward her for her contribution in calming Monica. As he gave her a piece of chocolate, he asked Monica, "Would you like to have some *chai*? I am going to make some." She uncharacteristically declined, saying that she was nauseated from tension.

Satish felt like a stranger on the campus where he had spent over ten years. Familiar security guards who a few months ago had waved him through now checked his credentials and called Billy's office to ensure that he had an appointment. Though his visitor badge said that he needed to be escorted, in his case, they made an exception.

He did not meet with Tim before his meeting with Billy, saying that he had a tight schedule. He told him that he would be happy to visit with him after his meeting. Tim offered to fill in the details on the telephone, but Satish politely declined to hear anything about it, saying he preferred to hear the details from Billy.

Tim told him that he had just snubbed his best friend at Clark.

"Never thought I'd see the day when you were so sensitive, Tim. I'll see you as soon as I finish with Billy; that is, if you want to see me," Satish replied.

Tim bit his tongue and said, "Yes. Come by as soon as you are done. I'll wait."

This time the walk down the hallway to mahogany row felt different. The carpet did not seem as plush as before. The hallway appeared dark and dingy; it needed brighter lights. The portraits of the founders had to go—they were just too grim and depressing to look at. He had been to many corporate offices, and Clark's, he mentally noted, fell in the bottom quartile.

When she saw him, Liz stood up and said, "Hello, Satish. My, you're looking good. And how is your family doing?" She guided him to Billy's office, this time to his desk rather than the conference room.

Billy rose from his high-backed leather chair behind the mahogany desk that Pete had used. He came up to him, shook his hand warmly, and led him to his personal, circular conference table.

"It's good to see you, Satish. I am glad you could make it. I hear that your calendar is pretty full," he said.

"Yes, it is, but never too full to see my old friends at Clark."

"I am glad that you see us as your friends, Satish, because we are your friends."

"Of course. So, how can I help you, Billy?" he asked, wanting to get down to business.

"First of all, let me tell you that we are very appreciative of you not meeting or visiting with any of our competitors. We heard that several of them tried to contact you and you turned them down flat. I'd like to thank you for that. It takes great courage to do that when you are looking for a job. It also reflects your principles, which, of course, we never doubted."

"Of course," Satish said. "I had no intention of working for a competitor, and there was no reason to meet anyone from the dark side," he said smiling.

"Yes, it is us versus the Empire," Billy sighed, extending the *Star Wars* analogy. "And we need your help in fighting the Empire."

With that, he stood up and started pacing. He said, "Last week I was having lunch at the Petroleum Club, where I met an old buddy of mine. We've been friends for a long time; he and I were roughnecks on the same crew. He is now president of a company, and you met him a few weeks ago. I am not going tell who it was, but he told me that he was very impressed with you, and had made you an offer that you were considering. He asked me about you, and I gave you nothing but the best reference a man could ask for. Then he said I was crazy to have let you go."

He paused and looked at the carpet for a moment. He went to his desk and brought back a cup of coffee. "Pardon my manners, but would you like a cup of coffee?" he asked.

"Yes, please."

"How do you take it?'

"Just black, thank you."

Billy stepped out of the office and asked Liz to bring him some coffee. He then continued, "First things first. I have to apologize on behalf of Clark and myself for having laid you off. We did not know that we had a diamond until others saw it. I am truly and deeply sorry for what I have put you and your family through for the last six months."

Moved by Billy's mea culpa, Satish said, "No apologies necessary, Billy. It was a good experience for me, and gave me an opportunity to improve my self-awareness."

Billy said, "My buddy at the Petroleum Club clobbered me for our bad decision. He and I are very good friends, like brothers; he takes care of me and I take care of him, and we are not afraid to call each other out when we make mistakes. There are seven of us in our band of brothers, and we visit with each other at least once a week.

"I found out that you stayed away from my brothers at our competitors, even though they repeatedly called you to meet them. You talked to only four, who were not competitors. They too clobbered me for having screwed you for all these years. Every one of them would rather have me fix things and do right by you than have you join their firms. They said I should make you an offer, rectify things. If you accepted it, they would not think any less of you."

Satish did not interrupt the older man. He listened as Liz came in and gave him coffee in the finest china, rather than a familiar disposable cup. He took a sip and waited for Billy to continue.

"So here's the deal," he said, as he read from a sheet of paper. "There are a lot of details, but here are the main points. I want you to come back as a vice president of engineering at Clark's corporate office.

"You will have a three-year contract, renewable, and if it is not renewed, you get a year's severance package. Your compensation will be the midpoint cash compensation of all vice presidents at Clark, a year's salary signing bonus, an annual performance bonus at a minimum of 15 percent, a stock option grant of a million shares, vesting over ten years with new bonus options every year depending on our performance but with immediate vesting if we get acquired. Four weeks vacation, company car, and an office two suites down from mine.

"And I know how much you like to travel to India every year, so I have included one expense-paid trip to India for you and your family per year, including business class airfare and the best room and board. Oh, by the way, all our vice presidents are automatically members of the Petroleum Club, and have a choice of a country club membership."

Satish was overwhelmed. The other offers he had received were nowhere close to this one. He sat silently, pondering how Monica would react to the offer after her recent outburst.

Billy asked, "Anything bothering you? Did we miss anything?"

"No, nothing. I am actually very pleased with it, but I have a minor problem on the home front. I would have to convince my wife that it's a good idea to come back to Clark."

"I understand, Satish. Once bitten, twice shy. If I were in your shoes, my wife would have the same problem. So why don't we do this? Why don't you and your wife join my wife and me over dinner at the club?"

Satish smiled, sipped his coffee, and said, "That's mighty generous of you, Billy, and I am sure I can convince her to join us, but she is a vegetarian. She'll just eat salad at the club."

"I'll tell you what. Why don't you recommend an Indian restaurant and give the name to Liz? She'll take care of the reservations. I've always had a hankering to taste some Indian food and curry."

A week later, the foursome had dinner at Tandoor Palace, the fanciest Indian restaurant in town, where the two men charmed each other's spouses over spicy food. It was an exotic atmosphere: soft sitar music in a faux Taj Mahal draped in colorful silks.

On their way home after dinner, Billy's wife, Frances, chided her husband for losing such a rare, principled young gentleman. Satish was tense on his ride home, until Monica conveyed to him that she liked Billy and his wife. She was surprised to see that both were in their late-sixties. She was touched when someone older than her father apologized to her personally for having "put such a beautiful young woman through so much anxiety."

The next morning, a hefty offer letter and contract was couriered to their home, and they pored over the legal document. Satish had worked on customer contracts before, but this one was different. Since he was the product being purchased, he could not be objective in his evaluation. He called Jeff, who had been his attorney and legal advisor since his first confrontation with Clark, who asked him to fax the document and come to his office immediately.

Jeff was amazed at the generosity of the terms, and he suspected the motives behind the bigheartedness. Over the years, he had taught Satish to look beyond the "stated reason" for the "real reason." But as he read the contract to appreciate the source of the magnanimity, he applied two more concepts, the "moral reason" and the "right reason." Jeff found the contract acceptable on all for four counts, and suggested a few minor changes for "legal reasons." He congratulated Satish on his good fortune.

Satish had one more stop—to check in on his Lunch Bunch. When he arrived at the outplacement center, he caught them just as they were stepping out to meet Clyde at his favorite barbecue place nearby.

All congratulated him on his offer while they stood in line for their food, which was served cafeteria style. The rustic restaurant was packed with people, so they decided to eat outside, where wooden picnic tables were set up under a covered patio in the oppressive August heat.

There was an assorted spread that would have pleased any carnivore with a penchant for spicy food. The artery-clogging, cholesterol-packed smorgasbord included barbecued beef brisket, Czech sausage, pork ribs, and chicken. Everything was smothered with a piquant and sweet barbecue sauce. Sides included thickly sliced jalapeno cheese bread, onions, jalapenos, potato salad, coleslaw, and beans. There was chilled beer to relieve the patrons from the heat of the food and the day outside.

The men focused on their food and ate silently, speaking only when they needed someone to pass some food around the table or excusing themselves for an untimely burp. As the waiters cleared the table, leaving behind only bottles of beer, Dan turned to Satish and asked, "Did you have an attorney look at the contract?"

"Yes, I did. I just came from his office. He suggested a few changes, but overall, it's fine," he responded.

Darrell asked if he could see the contract, and Satish enthusiastically gave it to him. After glancing through it and seeing the salient sections, he returned it and said, "That's a terrific offer. It's all in your favor. They want you real bad."

He nodded, and before they could ask for a celebration dinner, suggested, "Hey guys, why don't you and your families come to my place over the Labor Day weekend? We'll have some barbecue."

Clyde was the first to jump in. "Love the idea. I accept the invitation, but you know what? I'd rather have some home-cooked Indian food. I can have barbecue any time, but genuine Indian food? Now that's not something you see every day."

"Okay. Fair enough. Indian food it'll be. Bring your families. Except you, Dan. There's a limit of one family per person," he kidded.

"I might surprise you. I'll bring a date," he said. He smiled when he added, "I don't know who my date is going to be. If she has a child, that'll be my family."

Darrell and Sam said that their children were too old to hang around with their parents.

"So it's settled. Labor Day at my place. Here, let me give you my address." While Satish was busy writing directions to his home, Clyde went into the restaurant, brought back a large pecan pie, and placed it in the middle of a table.

"This is from all of us, for one helluva sweet guy. Congratulations, Satish!" he announced as he threw down forks, knives, paper plates, and napkins.

"Thank you, Clyde. Thank you all for everything. I do appreciate your help during the last six months."

"Shut up and eat. When your mouth is full, you can't talk," Clyde said as he took a gigantic mouthful.

Satish dug into the most delicious pecan pie he had ever tasted. He finished his slice and said, "I gotta run. I want to see Scott at the office and get home before traffic builds up." He excused himself from the table. "See you on Labor Day," he said. He went into the restaurant and got another pie, for his wife and daughter.

Labor Day

Come Labor Day, the Lunch Bunch and their spouses descended on Satish and Monica's home in Sugar Land.

It was a single-story, ranch home on an outsized lot. The St. Augustine grass in the front yard was manicured, and several crepe myrtles with pinkish-red flowers blossomed in the summer heat. It also had four oak trees surrounded by bushes of Mexican heather, blooming begonias, and an assortment of heat-resistant perennials, such as blue lily of the Nile and day lilies. All borders were lined with variegated monkey grass. At the entrance to the home, two large hibiscus plants displayed giant, gloriously red flowers.

The greenery outside extended into the home. Bright green potted plants adorned almost every window of this well-lit, airy home with high cathedral ceilings. Several identical pots of African violets adorned the large French windowsills of the integrated kitchen and breakfast area that overlooked the backyard.

The formal dining area, adjacent to the front door, was dominated by an antique cherry dining table surrounded by ten New England ladder chairs. They matched the table, sideboard, buffet, and china cabinet. A plant peered through the window at the far corner, where the gold-gray curtain, topped by a valance, was drawn.

Elegantly framed prints of Monet's Nympheas were neatly displayed on the walls of the formal living room, as if in a museum. The cushioned formal sofas, stationed across from them, and the curtains and valances, were understated and subdued. They complimented the colors of the pastoral paintings without overpowering them.

The Sharma's den was an informal room. Laminated Indian tourism posters, remnants from Satish's bachelor days, and colorful Indian wall hangings and sofa cushions gave it an ethnic touch. A wall unit encased a large TV and a stereo system with two large speakers, carefully positioned to create a sweet spot where he used to sit on the sofa to listen to music before Seeta was born.

The kitchen and breakfast areas, at the far end of the home, with open entrances to the dining room and den, were spotlessly clean. The white, tiled countertop displayed eight silver serving spoons neatly placed in front of eight serving bowls containing Indian dishes that a stressed-out Monica had toiled over during the weekend. *Tandoori* chicken was kept warm in the oven.

In all the rooms, ceiling fans were running violently fast, joining forces with the home's two-zone central air conditioners to cool the home and its inhabitants. They also distributed the aromas from the kitchen.

"Golly, this home sure smells like someone's been cooking," Clyde said when he and his wife, Pauline, stepped into the home. Dressed as if they were going to the rodeo—Wranglers, open-collared western shirts, and boots—they made a beeline for the kitchen. They introduced themselves to Monica, and gave her a bouquet of the finest long-stemmed roses she had seen. Clyde also brought a six-pack of beer that his host preferred.

Monica accepted the gifts graciously and said, "You shouldn't have; it wasn't necessary."

Pauline replied, "We couldn't come here empty handed, could we, darlin'?"

Clyde conceded that it was her idea to bring the roses, and his idea to bring the six-pack. "It'd look mighty strange if I brought Satish a bouquet of flowers, wouldn't it?"

Clyde looked at the array of covered serving bowls that had been set on the kitchen counter and began opening each one of them, inhaling the steamy smells. "Hot dog, Monica. Next time I participate in a chili cook-off, I want you to be my partner. You gotta tell me how you create this bouquet of aromas!"

Pauline pulled him away. "I apologize, honey. He's attracted to food like wasps to barbecue," she said. Satish smiled at an amused Monica, who was getting her first taste of an authentic Texan couple in close quarters.

Just then, the bell rang. Dan arrived with his date, Miriam, and her two-year-old daughter, Liya. Like Clyde before him, Dan and Miriam searched out Monica, gave her a gift-wrapped package, and insisted that she open it immediately. It was a mahogany plaque with a silver plated inscription in Hebrew.

Dan said that it was a house blessing and translated the inscription: "In this place there shall dwell peace. Upon this residence shall rest tranquility. Upon this abode shall dwell brotherly love. Here shall they meet with satisfaction and happiness with blessing and success. Within these beams shall sing the voice of thanks. In this residence and in this corner shall dwell the holy presence." He added that, in Hebrew, the words rhymed by stanza.

Miriam then gave another package to Liya and asked her to give it to Seeta, who did not need an invitation to open it. It was a large brown teddy bear, which she hugged immediately. She said, "Thank you. This is the best teddy bear I ever had." She hugged Liya, took her by her hand, and led her to her room to play with her toys.

"Where's the beer?" Dan asked. Satish retrieved three bottles from a large cooler filled with ice and chilled beer. He handed one each to his friends, who were gathered around the breakfast table that was laden with hors d'oeuvres. The ladies preferred chilled white wine and iced tea.

The doorbell rang again, and when Satish opened the door, he saw Darrell and Sam, both with their wives. Darrell's wife, Serena, was a tall, handsome, dark-haired woman. Satish thought she looked more Middle Eastern than Hispanic.

He was surprised to see Sam's wife, Susan, who was a stunning Oriental. Satish did not let his astonishment show as he welcomed the quartet into his home. They joined the rest of the team in the kitchen.

"You have a beautiful home, Monica," Susan said. She gave Monica a bottle of champagne, which she gave her husband. He untied its red ribbon, commented on the label and the vintage, and put it in the fridge to preserve it for a special occasion.

"Thank you, Susan," Monica said, doing little to cover her amazement that Sam's wife was of Chinese origin.

Almost simultaneously, Darrell gave Satish a large, gift-wrapped box that he politely accepted and opened. It was a foot-and-a-half tall, gold- and silver-plated mariner's constellation compass. It had four movable rings around a central compass, all encircled by two entwined dragons.

"It is beautiful. Thank you so much, Darrell and Serena," Satish said.

"You shouldn't have," Monica said.

Darrell raised the bottle of beer that Dan had just given him, turned to Satish and said, "May your True North always guide you, my friend."

The rest of the Lunch Bunch and their spouses raised their glasses, said, "Cheers!" and took quick sips of their drinks.

"Enough of this stuff. When do we eat?" asked Clyde.

"Shush, Clyde. That ain't polite, darlin'. Why don't you and the boys go outside to the purty backyard and do some men talk while we set the table," suggested Pauline.

Clyde opened the back door from the breakfast area and went outside, asking the rest of men to join him. "C'mon let's get out of their way. Satish, bring some more beer."

There were ten lawn chairs set in a circle on the covered patio. The men sat on alternative chairs, and all were cooled by the ceiling fan that created a mild breeze.

"Thank God summer's almost over and we can have an outdoor life again," Sam said, breaking the ice.

"Yup. I am looking forward to nine months of paradise on earth," Clyde conceded.

Darrell said, "You know, when I came to Houston from New England, I thought it was nothing but hot, brown, and dry, filled with tall, rough-riding, impolite Texans. But once I started visiting the place, I realized how wrong I was. Yes, it's hot, but only for three months. The rest of the year is like heaven on earth. It's green, lush, and sunny, and I can sail all year round in the gulf."

"To the best coast of the U.S.A.," Dan said, and raised his bottle.

Darrell half raised his bottle in acknowledgment and said, "Let me share something with you, Clyde, you being the only native Houstonian here. Texans are the warmest people, friendly and straight. I agree with Dan. It's the best place in America to live, work, and raise a family." He then raised his bottle to a full toast and took a gulp.

"You got that right, Darrell," Clyde concurred.

Sam, too, raised his bottle and added, "It's the diversity that makes it so livable. You can find people from all over the world here."

Dan turned to his host and said, "You've been awfully quiet. What do you think?"

Satish said, "Where could I have met such good friends? To good friends." He raised his bottle and took a swig. Noticing that his bottle was almost empty, he went to the nearby cooler, retrieved five more bottles, and took away the nearly empty bottles from his friends. As they twisted the tops off, Pauline appeared at the doorway and announced, "C'mon y'all. Lunch is served."

The men trooped in with their cold beers and sat down at the table next to their wives. Monica and Miriam told them that the children had already eaten, and had gone back to Seeta's room to play. Then a hush fell over the table till Pauline asked, "Do y'all say Grace before eating?"

When Monica nodded yes, Clyde said, "Why don't you say Grace over this food we are about to receive in your native tongue?"

Monica looked at her husband, who asked her to continue. The guests and hosts closed their eyes and bent their heads reverentially while she recited the *Brahmarpanam* in Sanskrit.

When she had finished, Miriam asked what it meant. Monica again looked at Satish, who encouraged her to translate it.

"Brahmarpanam literally means 'offering to God,' and the Sanskrit words mean:

> *The offering is God; the act of offering is God,*
> *Offered by God in the sacred fire that is God*
> *He alone attains God,*
> *Who in all his actions is fully absorbed in God.*
> *I am the all-pervading cosmic energy,*
> *Lodged in the bodies of living beings.*
> *United with their ingoing and outgoing life breaths,*
> *I consume all the various foods."*

Satish added, "Before the Brahmarpanam, what we had in front of us was food. After we say it, it becomes consecrated food."

"We don't need to say formal prayers, just a sincere prayer from our hearts, thanking God and asking God to bless the food," she said.

Pauline said, "Honey, it is so deep, it brought tears to my eyes."

"Yes," conceded Miriam, "It was beautiful."

Susan and Serena joined in to praise Monica's rendition when Clyde jumped in and asked, "When are we going to eat?"

Satish stood up and described all the dishes on the table. Monica added, "I apologize if you find it too hot and spicy."

"Don't worry, honey," Pauline said, "I'll eat anything as long as I don't have to cook!"

"Bon appetit," declared Darrell as he served Serena a spoonful of *mutter paneer* (cheese and peas).

"This smells delicious. Can you pass me some *naan* bread?" Susan asked as she served herself some chicken curry, *aloo gobi* (potatoes and cauliflower), and *raita*.

Miriam and Dan focused on the spicy vegetable *biryani* rice and the chicken curry combination

"This Tandoori chicken is delicious. Best barbecued chicken I've ever had," Clyde said, as he bit off a mouthful.

"But, I thought you were a vegetarian, Monica," Dan said.

"Yes, I am," Monica confessed. "Satish made the meat dishes. I made the vegetarian ones."

Instantly, all the wives turned on their husbands and began to reproach them for their lack of culinary skills.

For the next two hours, in an atmosphere of banter and camaraderie, these five couples sat at the table, enjoyed each other's company, and learned about how each pair had met.

"I met my wife at a honky-tonk in Pasadena," volunteered Clyde. "She was the purtiest girl on the floor. I asked her if she would dance with me, and we've been dancing together since then." He then took Pauline's hand and kissed it.

She said, "He's so romantic."

All the men in the room knew that Darrell had met Serena during one of his trips to Houston, but he had not divulged the details. The attractive spouse volunteered, "I met him on a delayed, late-night flight to Houston. He sat next to me, and during the entire three-and-a-half-hour flight, he ignored me. He had a window seat and, alternatively, he kept reading some kind of a journal and sleeping.

"When we landed, he helped me with my hand luggage. He said nothing as we both waited at the baggage claim belt, when we discovered that our luggage had been lost, and when we stood in line to fill out the airlines forms.

"He was ahead of me in the line, and after he finished filing his claim, he left. However, when I left the counter and turned around, I found him standing there. He asked me, in a most understated way, if I wanted a ride to a hotel or something.

"It was past midnight and I was not sure if it was safe to take a cab. He looked decent and respectable, so I accepted. We were staying at different hotels that were close to each other. During our half-hour ride, he said almost nothing.

"Then, when he dropped me off, he asked me if I would join him for drinks the next day. I was inclined to say no, but then something told me that there was perhaps another side to this man. I said yes. He swept me off my feet the next day, and we were married in three months."

"I had allergies and I was loaded with antihistamines," Darrel explained.

"That is such a great story, and so romantic. Somebody ought to make a movie of it," Pauline said. "Susan, how did you and Sam meet?"

"I was his student," Susan said. "He was an adjunct professor at U of H, where I had come to do my masters in accounting. He taught me during my first semester, but for a year and a half after that, he ignored me. When I was about to graduate, he came for campus interviews, to hire accountants for his firm. Instead of hiring me, he referred me to another firm, and then asked me out on a date.

"Both of us knew that we were right for each other but we vacillated for two years about whether we should get married. You know how it is; he is an African American and I am a Singaporean. We are from different worlds but we could not live without each other. So the last time he proposed to me, I accepted."

She took Sam's hand and held it. He turned to her and said, "Love you, babe."

"Who's next?" asked Serena. "Monica, Dan?"

"Let me go last," Dan requested.

Serena turned in the direction of her hosts and said, "Well?" Monica nudged her husband to tell the story and he complied.

"Ours was an arranged marriage. We got married within four days of being introduced to each other," Satish said.

There was silence at the table. They were waiting for Satish to say more. When nothing was forthcoming, Monica jumped in. "He is always so matter-of-fact," she said in the direction of Susan and Serena, who were seated across from her.

"Satish and I knew each other as children. His father and my father are friends. When we were children we met quite often, but when he became a teenager he stopped coming to our home, and I lost touch with him for more than fifteen years.

"I used to be a stewardess for a European airline. After my mother, God bless her soul, passed away, I decided to quit my job to be with my father. Satish was a passenger on my last flight.

"He was like you, Darrell—sleeping, silent, or looking out of the window most of the time. I did not recognize him at that time, even though his name was on the passenger manifest. He had a drink or two, and he hardly touched his food. He was polite, courteous, and not flirtatious. I noticed these things over a nine-hour flight. I said to myself that he was the kind of man I'd like to marry.

"I was married before. My first husband died in a motorcycle accident six months after my mother's death, and it took me a long time to get over it. Satish was the first man I saw who made me want to get married again."

She stopped, and when cajoled to continue she said, "Let my husband tell the rest of the story."

"I did not recognize her on the flight, either. She looked familiar, but then I knew her by her pet name. She was called Mona when she was a kid. I did not connect Mona and Monica.

"I was on this two-week trip to Bombay to visit my parents, and during those two weeks my parents and sister had me visit with six women, often with their families. It was very depressing. I did not feel comfortable with any of them.

"On the day of my departure, she and her father came over around lunch time and I met her again. She recognized me from the flight but I did not. Within minutes of meeting her, I knew that Mona was the one."

Monica jumped in. "Even after he talked with me for over two hours, he did not recognize me till I told him that I was the stewardess on his flight home. He then asked my father's permission to take me to a restaurant to talk some more.

"I thought he was taking me to a restaurant at a five-star hotel. Instead, he took me to an airline ticket office at the hotel. There, in front of my colleagues and friends, he asked, "Will you marry me? I will postpone my trip right now." I said yes, and we got married four days later in my home."

Pauline was weeping. She dried her tears with her napkin and sobbed when she said, "That is the purtiest story I have ever heard. Don't you think so, darlin'?" in the direction of her husband.

Clyde nodded and said softly, "Kinda gets you here," pounding his fist to his chest.

Susan reached out to her hosts, held their hands, and said, "It's wonderful when everything works out, isn't it?"

Serena lifted her glass of wine and said, "Wish you the very best in life."

Miriam raised hers and said, "That's very sweet."

While everyone raised their glasses and toasted their hosts, Dan asked, "Hey, do I get my turn or not?"

"Sure," conceded Clyde, and asked him to take center stage.

He cleared his throat and said, "But, before I start, I'd like Liya and Seeta to be here."

Monica left the table to fetch the children. As soon as the two-year-olds were seated on their mothers' laps, he said, "I met Miriam at a synagogue."

Clyde choked mockingly and said, "You, Dan, in a synagogue?"

Miriam jumped to his defense, "He is religious, Clyde. The rabbi told me that he was a regular."

Clyde apologized and Dan, unperturbed, continued.

"I met Miriam and Liya, at the synagogue I attend. She was visiting her cousins in Houston and was on a four-month holiday, visiting from Israel. Liya's father was in the army. He died more than a year ago.

"I have been seeing her and Liya since the first week she has been here, and she is returning to Jerusalem next week. But I don't want her and little Liya to go back, so I have a proposition for both of them."

With that, he pushed back his chair, got on his knees, and said, "Beloved Miriam, light of my life, will you give me the honor of being your husband, and a father to Liya?"

Tears welled up in Miriam's eyes. She held her daughter, and, trying to hold back her tears, she nodded. "Yes," she said, and placed her right hand and her daughter's right hand in Dan's extended hand. He placed his other hand on theirs and held them and said, "I promise to honor, protect, and love you for the rest of our lives."

He pulled two rings from his pocket and placed one with a large solitaire diamond on Miriam's finger. Kissing Liya on her cheek, tears in his eyes, he slid the smaller ring on the little girl's ring finger.

Pauline was bawling, the rest of the women and Clyde had tears in their eyes. All rushed to congratulate Dan, Miriam, and Liya. Seeta ran and hugged Liya and said, "Come, let's go play." Before her daughter could take off, Miriam removed the expensive ring and put it in her purse for safety.

"It's time for champagne," Satish announced, when he remembered the bottle that he had kept aside for a special occasion. When he went to get the champagne and the glasses, his guests and Monica cleared the table. She brought out a large casserole bowl with a baked dessert, and set dessert plates and forks around the table.

In moments, everyone was back in their seats with a glass of champagne in their hands. Darrell stood up and proposed a toast. "Congratulations, Miriam and Dan. To your happiness."

"To your happiness," whispered everyone.

Miriam stood up and said, "Dan always said that he did not have a family, but I can see that he is wrong. You are his family." Turning to him, she said, "Dan, you are a wonderful and strong man, and I will be very happy with you. Thank you for everything. I love you." Then she looked into his eyes and he into hers.

"This has been such a wonderful day," Pauline said to no one in particular as the dessert was passed around. She made a sign to everyone to leave. "Let's leave these love birds alone."

Everyone left the table and went to the living room, when Darrell came up to Satish and asked him if the two of them could step outside for a moment.

Once outside, he said, "As you probably have realized by now, I am a man of few words. So I am going to spit them out.

"A few weeks ago, Clyde came to us and told us that his new bank had invested a bunch in a new oilfield technology company and the company went bust. He asked me to look at it, to see if the bank should write it off or invest some more. I had a look at it, and I believe that it can be turned around and made successful.

"I have talked with Dan and Sam, and they have done their investigation. They agree with me that there is hidden value here. It is not only salvageable, but there can be a substantial reward at the end. We shared our interest with Clyde, and his bank has committed to fund the turnaround. We will be signing the papers, but we are short of someone to lead and build our engineering efforts, a vice president."

While the rest of the Lunch Bunch and the families were having an enjoyable conversation in the home, outside, under the steady drone of air conditioners working furiously to combat the afternoon heat, Dan went on to describe the opportunity. He detailed the technology, the challenges facing the company, and why he thought they could be overcome.

He concluded with, "We cannot match what Clark has offered in cash compensation. Sam and I have talked, and we can come close. We cannot do the clubs and trips to India, but we can offer you equity, the same as Sam and Dan. I would really like you to join our team."

"I am going on a road trip this week to meet investment bankers, and I would like to add your name to my presentation. I know this is sudden, so take your time, but do call me by the end of the day tomorrow."

With that, he shook Satish's hand, said "Great party," and went back inside to join the others.

When they walked in, they saw that everyone, including Seeta and Liya, was seated in the den, watching Barney the dinosaur on PBS and drinking tea.

Clyde called out to Satish and said, "This here *chai* is delicious. You'd better get a franchise going here before those coffee folks from Seattle lay their hands on it."

Pauline asked, "Hon, Monica, can I call you Mona?" When Monica acceded, Pauline continued, "Hon, Mona, I saw your prayer area, and with all the other pictures and icons there, you had a picture of our Lord, Jesus Christ, and picture of the Blessed Mother Mary and baby Jesus. Clyde always tells me not to discuss religion or politics, but I feel like you're family. Do y'all pray to Jesus Christ?"

"Pauline, my mother, God bless her soul, was a Roman Catholic. These are her icons. Satish went to a Catholic school in Bombay, and we believe that all religions are equal. We go to Hindu temples and churches, and the Hebrew house blessing you gave us, Miriam and Dan, will be on our walls too."

Upon hearing Monica, Susan spoke up and said, "In Singapore, this was exactly how we lived. I am a Buddhist, but all our friends were from different parts of the world and of different religions—Christians, Hindus, Muslims, Jews, Buddhists. Today I feel like I am back home with my friends and family, except that we are missing a Muslim here."

"I am a Muslim. I was christened Sireen." Serena said softly.

The whole room fell into a hush, and only Barney's voice on TV could be heard.

"My father was originally from Lebanon. He came to Mexico during World War II, and there he met my mother and stayed. He never went back. We grew up as Mexicans and identified more with Latin culture. Now I am a Texan and an American," she said in a pleasant, matter-of-fact tone.

"Texan first, I hope," Clyde prompted.

"Yes, I went to UT," she said. She raised her right hand, extended her pinky and index finger and waved, giving Clyde the "hook 'em horns" hand sign.

"Ah, that's okay, Sireen-ah," Clyde said, stressing on the Sireen, to her pleasure.

"Come on, Mona darlin', let me help you clear up the kitchen," Pauline said, and, as if on cue, all the women disappeared, leaving behind the men.

Sam asked Darrell, "Did you talk to him?" Darrell nodded.

"So, what do you think, Satish?" Sam asked.

"Let me think about it. I need to talk to Monica. She has no clue what we talked about, and I don't want to make a decision without discussing it with her."

"Good. I drew up a contract over the weekend, and I've brought it with me. Have a look at it, and let's talk about it tomorrow. Darrell's leaving town first thing Wednesday morning," Sam said.

A few minutes later, the women emerged from the kitchen. Susan asked Sam if they could leave, which created an avalanche of departures. Hugs, kisses and handshakes were exchanged and everyone thanked the hosts for a wonderful day. Liya begged to stay longer, while Seeta beseeched for Liya to stay.

Miriam turned to Seeta and said, "It's late now, sweetheart, and we have a long way to go. I'll tell you what. Next time, you come visit us and play with Liya's toys. OK?"

She hugged Monica and said, "You, your family, and your home will always be special to me. Thank you, so much. Lehitraot, Monica."

"Thank you for coming, Miriam. It was so nice of Dan to have picked our home to propose to you."

"You are his family, Monica," she said as she followed Liya and Dan to their car.

While Satish went with Sam to get his contract, Susan hugged Monica and asked her, "Do you speak Tamil?"

"I don't. I speak Kannada, but Satish speaks a little."

When she reached her car, she turned to Satish and said in Tamil, "You know, I grew up in Singapore. Next time I visit, I want a Tamil meal. I miss my home so much."

He replied in Tamil, "Next time, we'll have a dinner more delicious than Komala Vilas ready for you," referring to a popular Tamil restaurant on Serangoon Road.

When Sam and Susan departed, the hosts rushed back to the other cars just in time to wave them goodbye. Pauline pulled down her window and yelled, "Good bye, Mona. Thank you for everything."

Seeta, Monica, and Satish stood on the sidewalk and watched each car go down their street, take a turn, and disappear.

When they got back inside, Monica noticed the manila envelope in her husband's hand. "What's that? And what was Darrell talking with you about outside?"

"It's a little cool now. Why don't we walk down to the park, and I'll tell you everything on the way," he said.

He threw the envelope on a kitchen counter, brought out Seeta's stroller, and called out to her. After activating the house alarm, the three of them went to the park. On the way, he recounted to her the new offer he had received that afternoon.

"So, what do you think, Monica? What should I do?"

"Whatever you think is the best for us, sweetheart. We have been through a lot in the last six months."

"I have not made a decision yet. Let me think about it."

Monica sat on her usual bench in the nearby gazebo and watched the father push his screaming daughter higher and higher in the swing. She knew that he would make the right decision.

The next morning, Satish called Billy Stayton and requested a meeting. Two hours later he was in Billy's office, telling him in person that he had decided to take another offer.

Billy was disappointed and wanted to know what had tipped the balance in favor of this other firm. Was it the money, was it the options, were the perquisites not enough, or did Monica feel uncomfortable?

He assured Billy that Clark's offer was better on all fronts, and Monica would be equally happy if he came back to Clark. However, there was only one thing that tipped the balance in their favor.

"What is it, Satish? What tipped the scale?"

"I finally found my band of brothers," Satish replied.

A month later, Billy Stayton died of a heart attack. Satish was a mourner at the well-attended funeral. When he paid his deepest condolences to his widow, Frances, she whispered to him that Billy's respect and admiration for him multiplied when he heard the reason behind his decision. He was truly sorry for what happened to Satish at Clark.

He pressed her hand in appreciation, and said, "I know, Frances. Billy was a good, honest man. I will miss him very much."

A few days later, Clark's stock price collapsed. Trustmink's parent company acquired the company and fired its entire senior staff, including Tim O'Leary, whose wife divorced him soon thereafter. Satish recommended Tim to Darrell, who said, "You're too forgiving," and refused to see Tim.

The Sharma family attended Dan and Miriam's nuptials a few weeks later. Their wedding family portrait included the Lunch Bunch and their families. Satish framed that picture and as he was hanging it on the wall of his den, he admired it for a moment, and smiled. He saw that Monica was beginning to show telltale signs of her second pregnancy.

Glossary

Abhisekham: A special offering to God.

Agarbatti: Indian Incense.

Aloo Gobi: Literally, potato and cauliflower.

Appalam: Large, thin South Indian flatbread chips made from lentil, chickpea, or rice flour.

Bhel: Spicy, puffed rice mix.

Biryani: Spiced saffron rice dish made from basmati rice, spices, vegetables, and meat; served usually with raita.

Buddhu: Simpleton.

Chai: Indian tea with milk.

Chapati: Indian bread similar to a wheat tortilla.

Chutney: A crushed mixture of coconut, vegetables, peppers, and spices.

Darshan: View, sight, glimpse of a deity or a form of divinity.

Devasthanam: Hindu temple.

Dharamshala: An inn or place of rest or refuge.

Dosai: Shallow-fried pancake made from a batter of rice and lentils.

Dupatta: A long scarf that is often part of a salwar kameez ensemble.

Gayatri Mantra: Highly revered mantra in Hinduism that seeks Divine awakening of the mind and soul.

Ghee: Clarified butter.

Gulab Jamun: Fried milk balls in sweet syrup.

Guru Dakshina: Student respectfully repaying a teacher after completion of education.

Idli: Rice and lentil batter steamed and molded into patties.

Kanna: An affectionate term for a child or a baby, and infant child Krishna.

Karandi: Serving spoon.

Kooja: Portable metallic pot with a screwed on lid with a handle.

Kumkum: Auspicious red powder.

Kurta: Traditional loose shirt in India.

Lungi: Indian garment worn around the waist.

Mutter Paneer: Literally, peas and cheese.

Naan: Round flatbread made of wheat, cooked in a tandoor.

Naivedyum: Offering of flowers, fruits, food, or sweets to God.

Palloo: End of sari that is pleated and draped over the shoulder.

Pooja: Prayer in the form of a Hindu religious ritual.

Poriyal: Sauceless, stir-fried vegetables.

Prasadam: Consecrated food that is first offered to a deity and then consumed.

Raita: Yogurt with spices, and minced cucumbers and onions.

Rasam: Popular South Indian soup prepared with lentils, tamarind juice, tomatoes, and spices, eaten mixed with steamed rice, or drunk by itself.

Saambaar: Popular South Indian spicy lentil and vegetable soup usually poured over steamed rice.

Salwar Kameez: Traditional North Indian outfit; Salwar is a pajama-like loose trouser and Kameez is a long shirt or tunic.

Samadhi: Shrine created for a spiritually enlightened person's final conscious exit from the physical body at death.

Samosa: Fried pyramid shaped pastry stuffed with potatoes and vegetables.

Sari: Traditional garment worn by Indian women; a long unstitched cloth ranging from five to nine yards in length, draped in various styles.

Semya Payasam: Sweet vermicelli pudding, a staple at Indian feasts and festivals.

Supari: Dry digestif that is a mixture of Betel nut, dried fruits, spices, and sugar.

Tam Bram: Slang for Tamil Brahmin.

Tandoor: A cylindrical clay oven in which food is cooked over a hot charcoal fire.

Tandoori: Prefix or suffix to indicate that the food was cooked in a tandoor.

Teertham: Sanskrit word for water but in this context it is holy water.

Tiffin Carrier: A stack of steel or tin boxes for a lunch; each box contains a different food item.

Upma: Savory, semolina-based dish.

Vayshti: Unstitched cloth that is draped around the waist and the legs by South Indian men.

Vibhuti: Sacred ash used in religious worship; it has many symbolic meanings.

About the Author

Pradeep Anand was born in Bombay, India. He lived the first half of his life in that city before migrating to Houston, Texas, U.S.A. He is a graduate of the Indian Institute of Technology (IIT), Bombay, a prestigious engineering school in India, and has an MBA from the University of Houston.

Pradeep has lived the second half of his life in Houston, Texas, where he experienced the city's evolution from a small town to a global metropolis that gradually embraced ethnic multiplicity.

For over twenty-five years, he has lived and worked with Texans, both native and adopted sons and daughters of Texas. Moreover, he has worked for most of those years within the bulls-eye of cowboy culture in Texas, the oilfield service industry.

He is president of Seeta Resources (www.seeta.com) and lives with his family and their dog, Cookie, in a Houston suburb.

He can be reached at iicc@pradeepanand.com.

978-0-595-40790-3
0-595-40790-0

Printed in the United States
203155BV00003B/235-405/A

9 780595 407903